DON'T
LOOK
BEHIND YOU

Also by Mel Sherratt

The Girls Next Door

Somewhere to Hide
Behind a Closed Door
Fighting for Survival
Written in the Scars
Taunting the Dead
Follow the Leader
Only the Brave
Watching over You

Marcie Steele books
Stirred With Love
The Little Market Stall of Hope and Happiness
The Second Chance Shoe Shop

DON'T LOOK BEHIND YOU

MEL SHERRATT

Bookouture

Published by Bookouture
An imprint of StoryFire Ltd.
23 Sussex Road, Ickenham, UB10 8PN
United Kingdom
www.bookouture.com

ISBN: 978-1-78681-133-2
eBook ISBN: 978-1-78681-132-5

To Martina Cole and Lynda la Plante

Two strong women who inspired me
to write with true passion.

PROLOGUE

Carla Gregory left home early that morning to journey to Liverpool. Travelling from Stockleigh, she caught a connecting train from Crewe. Gazing out of the windows as the train made its fifty-minute journey, she almost wished she was moving home again as she spied the views.

It was the first week of the new year and 2017 was going to be a challenge from the get-go. She could see the water-clogged fields, the recent snowfall having melted. In the distance, white patches still covered the hills. The view brought a lump to her throat. Her daughter would have loved it.

Carla hadn't set foot in Liverpool for twelve months, yet she'd spent years of her married life there. It was the first time she'd been able to pluck up the courage to come back to the area and visit Chloe. Ryan, her husband, had just recently come out of prison, and it was the one place he knew she would be. But she couldn't *not* visit today.

She hadn't wanted to leave Liverpool – circumstances had forced her – and, even though she knew she was safer in a small city, she often wondered if she'd be better in a country village like the ones she glanced in the passing scenery. But living among lots of people versus living in isolation at the end of a country lane always won hands down. She had to blend in rather than hide away.

Once off the train, she walked the twenty minutes to her destination, slaloming through the crowds until they thinned.

She pulled in the collar of her coat – pushing her scarf further up her neck – and braced herself as an icy wind sliced through her. Keeping a watchful eye, she scanned every person walking ahead, every car going past as she marched down the pavement. Her hands were thrust in her pockets to stop them from shaking.

Up above she could see the large black wrought-iron gates, a grand entrance fit for a final resting place. It was 11.30 a.m. Several people milled around as she passed through the gates of the cemetery. A man in the distance walking his dog – too old. A woman with a pushchair sitting on a bench – no man with her. A man and a woman in their early twenties, arms around each other standing over a grave. That couldn't be him.

Even though her senses needed to be on full alert, Carla felt a calmness about her as she walked. It was peaceful in the cemetery, but still she wasn't going to hang around for any longer than necessary.

At the fifteenth row, she turned right and made her way along to the ninth plot. Even after ten years, it still pained her to see her daughter's grave. Sad thoughts that she could never watch Chloe grow up, have a career, be married, see her as a mother. Selfish thoughts that she had missed out on so much, would never have grandchildren, see her daughter flourish.

As the wind played with her long blonde hair, Carla shivered. Would she ever be rid of Ryan's ghost? She glanced around again, her eyes darting everywhere, looking behind trees, in-between the gravestones and along the pathways. She stopped and bowed her head for a moment but quickly brought her eyes up again. He could be anywhere, and she had to keep a lookout for him at all times.

'Happy birthday, my beautiful angel,' Carla said in a whisper that was taken away in the breeze. She cleared her throat, trying to remove the lump in it. 'I can't believe how grown up you are. Eighteen years old today.'

The circular framed photo of a smiling eight-year-old was on the top-right corner of the black marble headstone. She had been a beautiful baby, always being admired when she was out in her pushchair and, despite their home life, Chloe had grown into an affectionate and loving little girl. She made friends easily at school and always aimed to please everyone.

Blonde plaits hung either side of her face, red ribbons holding them together at the bottom. The eyes of her father stared back at Carla, but, while his were dark with nastiness, Chloe's were a deep sapphire blue, full of sparkly excitement. The sharp framing cheekbones and her smile belonged to Carla.

To the outside world, the smile had been there for most of Chloe's young life. Only Carla knew how it would drop almost as much as the temperature inside the house the moment her daddy came home.

She glanced around again, remembering the last thing Chloe had said to her. It had been an hour before the accident. Carla had tucked her up in bed with her favourite teddy bear and kissed her forehead, but as she stood up to leave, Chloe had reached for her hand.

'Be strong, Mummy,' Chloe had said, grasping it tightly. 'I will always be here to watch over you.'

Carla had turned away quickly so that Chloe wouldn't see her tears. What had her daughter heard or witnessed throughout the years to say that to her? How must she have felt seeing her daddy hitting her mummy and saying nasty things to her all the time? They'd tried to keep their problems hidden, but even so, no one really knew how being brought up with violence affected a child until it was too late.

Carla thought about Chloe's final words on the day her life had changed immeasurably. Would she be watching over her today? She liked to think so.

In the distance she saw a car approaching. She pressed her fingers to her lips and then placed them on the top of the gravestone.

'Goodbye, my angel,' she whispered. 'Sleep tight.'

A man got out of the driver's seat. He wore a long dark overcoat, with a black woollen hat and scarf covering most of his face and hair. But it was him, she was sure. Even after ten years, she'd recognise his stance anywhere. Carla ran to hide behind a tree.

Holding her breath as he walked down the path beside her, only a few metres away, she moved around the trunk to stay out of his vision, watching with fear as he stopped at Chloe's grave.

For a good minute, he stood in silence with his head bowed in the exact spot she had just vacated. Then he lifted it and glanced around quickly before walking away. As he passed the tree, he stopped.

'I know you're there, Carla,' he said.

Carla froze in her hiding place, glancing around for the best way to run if he came towards her. He wouldn't attack her in such a public, nor sacred, place surely? She held her breath but then he continued on his way.

Carla shrank to her knees, clutching a hand to her mouth as nausea threatened to engulf her.

Ryan wanted her to know that he had seen her.

And so it all began again.

CHAPTER ONE

Detective Sergeant Eden Berrisford wasn't sure if she was surprised or disappointed when she drove past Sally Stanton's house and spotted a familiar car outside. She pulled over, parked up and marched down the path of number twenty-seven Martin Avenue.

A bobby's hard rap found a tearful Sally answering the door, a nervousness about her that Eden had come to recognise in her when she felt distressed.

Sally hugged her thin frame. Her right eye was swelling, bruising already appearing around her cheekbone.

'What's happened?' Eden cried out in frustration. 'Did Colin do that?'

'It's nothing.' Sally pulled at her fringe, trying to hide the damage.

'Did you invite him in?'

A shake of her head.

'Is Mark still around?'

'No.'

Eden sighed. Mark was Sally's new partner. No doubt he'd had enough of looking over his shoulder all the time after he'd been assaulted too. 'Do you want me to move him on?' she asked.

'Please.' Sally's voice held a tremor, as if she was almost afraid to speak.

Eden stepped inside and went through into the living room. Colin Stanton was sitting on the settee, feet up on the coffee table, arms folded, his eyes glued to the television screen.

Eden glared at him as she tried to control her temper. Stanton was a bully of the first degree. A weasel of a man with a jaundiced tinge to his skin, his eyes were as dark as the rings underneath them, the tips of his fingers stained with nicotine and just as dirty as his fingernails. His clothes looked ready to walk away and, by the smell in the room, he'd clearly been drinking.

She'd known him from her days on the beat but over the past two years she had advised him several times about coming too close to his ex-wife and her new partner. He hadn't heeded her warning.

'Comfy there, are you?' Eden asked. 'And get your feet off the coffee table.'

'I might be.' He removed his feet regardless.

'I'm assuming you came here uninvited?'

'No. Sal invited me, didn't you, babe?'

The word 'babe' made Eden want to vomit. Coming from him, it sounded so vulgar. She glanced at Sally, who had perched on the furthest seat in the far corner of the room. The woman wouldn't meet anyone's eye.

'You need to stay away from your wife,' Eden started.

'My ex-wife.' Colin Stanton folded his arms and scowled at her.

Eden wouldn't be drawn. 'You need to keep away from Sally, and this property, otherwise I'm going to arrest you for something to get you out of here, and believe me I will take great pleasure in it.'

Eden heard a sniff and looked to see Sally wiping her nose. Her eye was getting worse by the second, colouring purple around the lid.

'She walked into a door.' Colin sniggered. 'Nothing to do with me.'

Eden raised her eyebrows. 'Is this true, Sally?'

Sally gave a curt nod, but she still wouldn't look at either of them. Eden cursed inwardly. This is what he'd done to Sally.

Turned her into someone who was afraid of her own shadow. She almost wanted to growl a warning at him.

Every time she left the property after yet another call-out, she very much hoped that Sally wouldn't give in to Colin again. After dealing with victims of domestic abuse for so long, Eden never took the hump if anyone went back to a partner. Some of the victims just couldn't cope on their own after being beaten down into thinking they were worthless by a supposed loved one. Nevertheless, she wouldn't tolerate bullies.

She prodded Colin in the shoulder. 'Sally wants you to leave now,' she told him.

Colin yawned loudly. 'I'm not going anywhere any time soon.'

'I don't think you quite understand.' Eden grabbed his arm and pulled him to his feet.

'Get off me.' Colin tried to shake off her hand. 'That's police brutality.'

Eden pushed him forward, resisting the urge to say more in front of Sally. 'Come on, chop, chop.'

Outside, as they neared the corner of the house, she reached for his arm and, dragging him out of sight, slammed him up against the wall. Holding him in place with her arm across his chest, she pushed a knee between his legs. Then she pulled out her baton.

'Resisting arrest is an offence in itself,' she said as she stood inches from his face. His breath assaulted her again but she stood her ground.

'You're mad, woman!' He tried to push her away. 'Get off me.'

But she was too strong. 'I don't like – and I won't tolerate – bullies,' she told him. 'I know of another one – Steve Wilson. Perhaps I should let it slip that you've been heard shouting your mouth off about him in the Butchers' Arms. I know he won't take that lightly.'

'I haven't said anything.'

'Oh, I know that, but I'll happily make something up so that he'll be obliged to beat seven barrels of crap out of you. You see, I think you need a bit of your own medicine every now and then. It's okay for you to get your kicks out of hitting a defenceless woman but that doesn't float my boat. It doesn't make you a man. It makes you a mouse in my eyes.' Eden lessened her grip. 'You're nothing if someone stands up to you. So what's it to be?'

'You can't threaten me,' he said.

'Watch me.' Eden stepped back. 'Now either leave Sally alone or I am coming after you. Do you understand?'

Colin stepped into her space. 'You don't tell me what to do. I'll do as I please.'

'And I'll uphold the law. So just stay on the right side of it.'

Eden saw his right hand bunch into a fist. She knew he wouldn't hurt her, but all the same she raised the baton in the air.

'Time for you to go.' She nodded her head towards the gate.

Colin leered at her before turning to leave and threw his parting shot. 'I'd watch your back if I were you.'

Eden said nothing. Empty words didn't bother her. She watched him out on the street before going back inside to Sally. She was still sitting on the settee where they had left her. The tissue she had wiped her eyes with was shredded in ribbons in her lap. Eden's heart went out to her. She couldn't begin to imagine how it must feel to be so scared in your own home. It should be a sanctuary.

'He keeps pushing his way in, no matter what I do.' Sally looked up at her. 'If I go to the shops, he follows me home. If I stay in the house, he sits on the wall opposite and watches me. I don't have a life any more.'

'Then let me help you,' said Eden. 'Let me move you to a safe place. I can see if The Willows women's refuge has a space.'

'I can't go there.' Sally shook her head. 'Besides, nowhere will be safe from him.'

'You would have safety in numbers, a roof over your head and a bed to sleep in without fear of him coming to see you again at any time of the day or night.'

'If I move he'll find me somewhere else, won't he?'

'I can't promise that he won't, but at least you'd be with others who know how you're feeling and can help you to realise that none of this is your fault and you deserve a better life. No one should live in fear.'

Sally paused for a moment but then shook her head. 'I can't.'

Eden held in her frustration, though she knew that she'd never give up trying to get Sally away from her ex-husband.

One day she might listen – or, ultimately, one day it might be too late.

CHAPTER TWO

Ella Brown tripped over her foot but somehow managed to keep upright. She giggled as the bouncer caught hold of her arm.

'Steady on, darling,' he said, laughing. 'You're not going to have a good weekend if you fall off those heels, now, are you?'

'Who put that floor there?' She smiled. Or rather she hoped it looked like a smile as he leered back at her. Jeez, he was old enough to be her father. She moved swiftly past him, heading for the exit of Sparks nightclub.

Outside, she rummaged in her handbag for her phone. It was the early hours of Saturday morning. There had been three of them at the beginning of the night, but somehow she had lost her friends, Lucy and Charlotte, after she'd slipped to the loo. She'd walked around for a while trying to spot either of them but eventually she'd given up and decided to go home.

There was a message from Lucy.

Tried to call you. Meet us at the doorway in ten minutes. If you're not there in twenty, I'll assume you're still with Dylan. I want to know ALL the details tomorrow. Lx

Ella grinned, recalling how thrilled she'd been earlier when Dylan had made a beeline for her the minute she had stepped on to the dance floor. They'd spent most of the night together and had arranged a date for next week. But when she'd gone in search of her friends, she lost sight of him as well.

Sighing, as she knew she didn't have enough money for a taxi home alone, Ella waited outside as the club emptied but still she couldn't see them. Shivering slightly, she decided to walk. It would take her about half an hour, and if she stopped off for something to eat on the way, that would cheer her up. She had enough money for that.

Twenty minutes later, a cone of chips but a distant memory, Ella was almost home. She walked along the high street that would take her past The Cavendales and on to where she lived, just a few streets further on. Squinting as she passed the first of the large houses inside the walled estate, she dreamt of one day living in something so grand. Being eighteen and in her last year of a two-year A-level course at sixth form, she had a long way to go.

When she came to the cut-through that would take her to where she lived, she paused. She hated walking that way but she had done it for years, and it would take a good ten minutes longer to walk around. Taking a deep breath, she started the quick march to the other side.

Without warning, she was pushed in the back. Landing on all fours, someone from behind grabbed a fistful of her hair, dragging her along the pavement.

'Hey!' Ella cried as her knees scraped along the tarmac. In desperation, she tried to hit out at the hand that still had a firm grip on her hair as she scrambled to her feet again.

A few steps into the walkway, she was pushed up against the wall. She turned quickly to see a man. He was slightly taller than her and wore a black woollen scarf covering his mouth and nose, and a black hat. All she could see were his eyes, blue and menacing.

His hand squeezed her breast roughly.

Knowing he could overpower her in seconds, she put up a fight, pushing him in the chest.

'Get off me!' she cried.

But he came back at her, and she gasped as his gloved hand found her neck. She slapped at his face, his head, grabbed for his hat. Taking both of her wrists, he tried to force her to the floor.

'No!'

If he got her to the ground, it would all be over. Her fist caught him on the side of his face, the next one on his cheek. As he tried to grapple to catch her arms, she cried out as loud as she could.

'Help me!'

He struck her in the face. It felt like minutes passed, like everything was going in slow motion as she began to lose control. But in reality it had only been seconds. Ella groaned as pain engulfed her, her legs giving way.

He pushed her to the ground and straddled her. It was a few moments before she realised what he was doing next, a few more before she knew she was powerless to do anything about it. When one last bout of resistance brought another punch to her face, she went inside herself. The pain in her head intensified, yet she was almost thankful for it. It stopped her from thinking about what else he was doing to her.

CHAPTER THREE

Eden pulled up alongside a black Range Rover to see a woman inside having a go at the children in the back of the car. She caught Eden looking, and the woman rolled her eyes. Eden smiled at her, thankful that her days of the school run were over. She was still a taxi service during the evenings and weekends for her sixteen-year-old daughter, Casey, but at least she didn't have to sit in traffic each morning and join the yummy mummies in the playground.

When the lights changed, she pressed on the throttle and the Lambretta shot forward. A puff of blue smoke came from the exhaust, its tinny engine way behind that of the Range Rover, which had already turned a corner before she'd got across the road.

Eden's car had gone in for a service. She could have asked for a lift to the station, but that wouldn't have been half as much fun. It was definitely not scooter weather, but at least it was dry and there was no ice on the roads. In winter, she never got much time to enjoy the feel of the wind rushing past her. It was certainly a wake-up call.

She pulled in to the station car park to jeers from a group of uniformed officers who had congregated around the back door.

'Morning, Twiggy. You been out on an all-nighter?' said one, sniggering at his own joke.

'Yeah, yeah,' she said, pulling off her helmet. 'At least I get some action all night.' She looked him up and down. 'How old are you? Fifteen?'

'Old enough, Sarge,' he shouted amidst laughter as she made her way inside. 'Old enough.'

Eden threw him the finger over her shoulder but she was smiling. She didn't give a stuff who took the mickey out of her. She loved her Lambretta.

A few minutes later, she was at her desk and waiting to go in to see her boss. Detective Inspector Sean Whittaker was responsible for overlooking the Major Crimes Team, as well as Eden's team, and split his time between the two accordingly.

The Community Intelligence Team had been set up six months earlier, on a twelve-month trial, and Eden had been asked to put in for the position of detective sergeant to head it up. She had two detective constables to manage, and if Eden could have chosen who to have in her team they would both have been top of her list.

Twenty-nine-year-old Jordan Ashcroft had been with the police for eight years, and had transferred from Manchester two years before to be a detective constable. His sunny disposition served him well as an officer, enabling him to deal with all types of people and situations.

His colleague, Amy Nicholls, was three years younger and had served just over six years at Stockleigh Police Station as a police constable before her recent promotion. When Eden had first met her, she'd thought Amy all sweetness and light but had been pleased to see she came into her own when pushed. Then she seemed to have wisdom beyond her years.

With Sean at their head, they were a good team, working well to gather intelligence about the residents of Stockleigh. Together they had helped to solve a few cases in the department's five months of operation. Already Eden was dreading the end of the trial year. She had never loved getting her teeth into her work so much as she had these past few months.

'So, what exciting things have you two been up to over the weekend?' Eden asked as she logged on to the police computer network while Amy collected mugs for drinks.

'Please tell Amy not to mention the "W" word.' Jordan put his head in his hands. 'I really can't cope with another fancy or a guest list or order of service thingumajig. It's way too early.'

'Oi!' Amy hit him on the arm as she walked past. 'My wedding happens to be the most important thing in my life right now. And I don't care what you think or say. I'm going to bore you all for the next five months, three weeks and five days.'

Jordan groaned. 'Can't you sack her for gross negligence, for putting her colleague's mental health at risk? Or something. Anything!'

Eden grinned. 'Oh, I don't know. I'm all for a good knees-up as long as I can wear my Doc Martens under my dress.'

'Can't wait to see that.' Jordan pointed to the computer. 'Anything come in for us over the weekend?'

'An assault we need to follow up on. Oh, and Colin Stanton causing the usual trouble.'

Jordan rolled his eyes. 'Nothing new there then.'

Amy came back with the drinks. She plonked their cups down and handed two to Eden. 'For the boss. He's ready for you.'

Eden went through to Sean's office. 'Morning, Sean. You wanted to see me?'

Eden and Sean Whittaker had worked together since they had joined the police force, in one role or another. He was in his early forties, blond hair cut short due to the fact it was receding rapidly, with intense brown eyes that could stare some people into submission. He removed the glasses he used reluctantly for close-up work.

'Morning. First things first,' Sean replied, glancing up and then back to his computer screen.

Eden slid a mug of coffee across the desk to him and sat down opposite.

'Right then. Ella Brown.'

'She was raped on Friday night,' said Eden, getting out her notebook. 'Well, it was the early hours of Saturday morning. I'm cross-referencing it with an attack that happened a couple of weeks ago. The case has been passed to us to investigate, to see if they're linked.'

'Is that looking possible?'

'I'm not sure. According to Ella's statement, she usually got a taxi home with her friends, but, after losing them in Sparks nightclub and not having enough money for the fare, she walked home. Unless someone was walking behind her on the off-chance that she would lose those friends, she would have been home in a taxi with them. The other girl had been at Sparks nightclub too.'

'Okay, do your stuff and look into it. And Colin Stanton?'

'Don't believe everything you hear, sir.' Eden dropped her eyes for a second, her skin burning up. Although she stood by what she had said and done to the creep, she had been angry with herself when she'd overreacted. 'The guy is totally deluded when he's been drinking,' she added.

'It was half past nine in the morning.'

'He was drunk from the night before. Anyway, I just hope it means that he stays away from Sally for a while, because she's too scared to tell him to leave. I've tried to get her into working with SWAP or going into one of the self-defence classes at The Workshop but nothing has got her out of the house so far. Can't say I blame her though.'

The Workshop was an enterprise centre in the middle of the Mitchell Estate, one of two large housing estates notorious for trouble in Stockleigh. It had been opened in 2012 for people to rent out rooms at a lower-than-normal price, with business start-ups in mind. Due to a lack of interest from the residents, it had turned into a place for lots of evening classes and social gatherings. Stockleigh Women Achieving Potential (SWAP), a support group run by some of the mums from the estate, had pooled their resources and come up with courses for adults, teenagers and young children that had been second to none.

'I think she will always see herself as a victim,' said Eden. 'I don't mean that in an unkind way. I just think the idiot ground her down so low that she might never get back up again unless he leaves her life completely. Which he won't do. Even if he gets sent to prison, he'll be out in a few months and up to his old tricks again, no doubt.' She paused. 'Maybe we should have another word with Josie.' Josie Mellor was a housing officer for Mitchell Housing Association. 'Perhaps there's some money left in the pot to sort out some security on her property that would make her feel safe. Sally was doing okay with her new partner too until Stanton whacked him around the head with a golf club.'

'When's he due in court for that?' asked Sean.

'Next month. The sixteenth, and not a day too soon.'

Sean nodded in agreement. 'I wanted to see you, by the way, because we have a sick-note coming back this morning. Phil Sillitoe. Do you know him?'

'Vaguely.' Eden hadn't worked with him before, only knew him on the beat some years ago. If she remembered rightly, he'd been a bit of pain back then.

'I have to place him for a few hours each day over four weeks until he can get back to working full-time in CID. He can't re-join his own team to do active duties yet.' He rolled his eyes.

The look on Eden's face was comical as she realised she'd been lumbered with him. 'There's nowhere else he can go?' she asked, putting her hands together as if in prayer. 'I'll beg if I have to. I'll even pay for the next round of drinks – and curry too!'

Sean smirked. 'He's okay in small doses.'

Eden enjoyed working with Sean. Their jesting was light. Most of their chats ended with jokes, except when they were dealing with higher-level cases that needed to be passed over. The Community Intelligence Team couldn't cover everything they needed to. Which was a shame. Because they were about to get their most intense case yet.

CHAPTER FOUR

Eden went back to her desk and was just about to sit down when she heard someone shout her name. Jordan walked towards her, a man following behind him.

'Someone to see you, Sarge.' Jordan jerked a thumb over his shoulder. 'Phil Sillitoe.'

She looked from one man to the other. There couldn't have been a more opposite pair. Whereas Jordan was young, tall and incredibly suave but without the attitude, Phil was middle-aged with a large belly bursting from his shirt and wearing a jacket that was a size too small. The knot in his tie was crooked, his annoyed face ruddy and what little hair he had was a mess.

'Hi, Phil.' She smiled, pushing aside all her prejudice. 'Good to have you back. I'll just get a couple of things off my desk and then I'll be with you.'

Phil's smile didn't reach his eyes. Eden wondered if it was because she was a woman or if it was because, at thirty-nine, she was nearly ten years his junior – or if he was just nervous about coming back to work after a long break away. Whatever it was, he didn't look pleased at the prospect of being placed with them. She kept smiling at him nonetheless.

'You know Jordan and Amy, I think?'

'I've probably been working on the force more years than the two of them put together.' Phil gave each a curt nod before sitting down.

Amy rolled her eyes at Eden, who shook her head quickly. She wasn't sure if Amy was joking or if she was being serious. She hoped their lovely little team wasn't going to become a battlefield.

Eden decided to take Phil out with her and checked out a pool car. She wanted to speak to the young woman who had been attacked two weeks earlier.

Becky Fielding was twenty-two and worked in Sunnyside Café. It was a greasy spoon but without the grease. Eden often called in on her rounds as they made the best bacon butties. They had takeaway from there too. But even though it was inevitable, she was still a little shocked when she realised she knew the victim after reading the case notes. She'd served her many times, always with a smile. She was bubbly, with curly blonde hair, brown eyes and red lipstick, and there was always a laugh and joke to be had with her. She seemed a valuable part of the business.

'You've worked in here for a while now, haven't you?' Eden said as Becky brought over tea and toast and sat down with them.

'Yes, I started as a Saturday girl, then stayed on when I was at college and uni. I've become part of the furniture since, because I can't decide what to do with my life. Trouble is, this place doesn't pay much, but I'm a people person and love a gossip.'

Eden smiled. 'I wanted to talk to you about the attack you reported on January seventh.'

'Oh, right. Well there isn't much I can tell you that I didn't put in my statement.'

'I thought perhaps you might have remembered some more about it. Often when people are attacked things come back to them later.'

'Well, I was in Stockleigh. I'd just come out of Sparks. It was freezing and there were no taxis so I decided to walk down from the high street.'

'Were you on your own?' asked Eden.

'No, I was with my friend, Sasha Lamont.'

'Do you often walk home?' Eden watched as Phil added three sugars to his tea and then stirred the spoon in the cup noisily. She glared at him when it became annoying.

'Yes, we usually leave about 1 a.m. Sometimes there are no cars and it's just as quick to walk as it is to wait for one to come back.'

'And, of course, you spend your money on drink,' Phil said, 'which means you think you're infallible when you're out late at night.' He clanked the spoon one more time on his mug before putting it down on the table.

Becky opened her mouth to speak but thought better of it. She turned back to Eden. 'I've lived in Stockleigh all my life. It's as safe as houses. You'll always get the odd nutter who wants to have a go.' She looked at Phil. 'But no one will tell me that this city is dangerous.'

Eden laughed under her breath. She liked the girl's attitude. 'So you walked home?' She moved them all along.

Becky nodded, checking her watch when a group of mums came in, prams and toddlers in tow. 'I only have a few more minutes,' she said. 'I live the furthest away so I said goodbye to Sasha and carried on walking.'

'This would be where?'

'Towards Coventry Street. You know it?'

Eden nodded. There had been a block of forty new builds erected last year. The locals had been up in arms over it because the land being used was a playing field. But it had been to no avail. The houses had gone up and the builder had erected a playground in the middle of it to pacify everyone. So far it hadn't become a hotspot for rowdy teenagers to hang around.

'I was walking along, minding my own business, when this guy came up behind me and punched me in the side of the head.' She laughed snidely. 'I think it was his intention to daze me, but

I'm made of stronger stuff than that. Then I thought he might be after my bag so I clouted him with it. He grabbed my arms and tried to drag me into the bushes. That's when I started to scream. He kept on pulling at my wrists so that I would go down but I was too strong for him.'

'Did he say anything to you?' asked Eden, trying not to be put off by Phil munching his toast, butter dripping down his finger.

'No, I called him a fair few things though. When he realised he couldn't get at me, he ran off.'

'Did you see where he went?'

'I bloody didn't! I ran as quickly as I could until I was home. When I got up the next morning and told my mum, she said I should report it. I thought it would be a waste of time but she talked me into it. Said she would never forgive herself if he attacked someone else's daughter. Just because I can look after myself, she said, wasn't reason not to say anything.'

'Your mum was right,' said Eden. 'You never know what might have happened, and what might happen if he tries anything again in the future.'

'And has he?'

'Has he what?' Eden knew what she was getting at.

'Tried again? That's what you're here for, isn't it? I mean, I reported this about two weeks ago, gave a statement and I've heard nothing.'

'We're looking into something,' Eden told her. 'But there is nothing connecting the two incidences so far. I just thought we would come have a chat.'

'Becky, need your help over here,' a man's voice boomed across the room.

Becky stood up and took her notepad from her apron. 'I do hope you get him. I can look after myself, but you never know what he might do next.'

As Becky headed over to serve the young mums, Eden stood up too. She was due at The Willows women's refuge in half an hour. Phil picked up the remainder of his toast and took it with him.

'Don't any of them think not to go around on their own late at night?' said Phil as they got back to the car.

'What do you mean?' Eden turned to him after buckling up the seat belt.

'Well if these young girls didn't walk around in clothes that were so short you can see everything, then half of these attacks would never happen.'

Eden's mouth dropped open. She expected Phil to have a grin on his weather-worn face, even though it would have been a pathetic attempt at humour. But no, he seemed deadly serious.

'With an attitude like that, I assume you think that men can get away with anything,' she replied, an edge in her voice that she had hoped to keep out.

'It would make our jobs a lot easier, don't you think?' He glanced at her through narrowed eyes. 'If all these women stopped leading men on.'

Eden stayed open-mouthed for all of a few seconds before she started up the engine and pulled away from the kerb. He was winding her up, she was certain. No one had such a screwed-up moral compass nowadays, surely?

CHAPTER FIVE

After taking Phil back to the station, Eden drove out to Harold Street for her fortnightly drop-in session at The Willows. The property was at the far end of the street and had previously been two three-bedroom semi-detached houses, but after a large family needed more space, it had been converted into one big home with six bedrooms. The family had lasted all of eight months before they'd caused enough trouble and moved on, leaving thousands of pounds of damage and a thankful street of residents who had suffered their antisocial behaviour for way too long.

The property had then stood empty for a few months until it had a change of use. Josie Mellor had earmarked it for a refuge and, with the help of a government grant, had set up The Willows. It wasn't designed to be a safe house as it wasn't secure enough, but it was a place where a woman could stay: a bolthole for a few lucky victims of domestic violence to get a breather, maybe a handle on moving on for good.

Although the residents on Harold Street had been outraged at first, Josie had won them over, and even an unruly partner turning up every now and again was better than living near to the 'Addams Family'. It had taken a few months for everyone to settle and now it was working a treat.

At The Willows, Eden was trusted by the women and gathered lots of intelligence from them about the people of Stockleigh that she needed to keep an eye on. It was good that some women felt they could talk to her, and her drop-in sessions had proved very useful on several occasions. She'd been pleased to be able to keep them as a responsibility of her new team and was hoping to pass the role on to Amy soon. She would fit in well and be a great asset here too.

She pressed a button on the intercom. A buzzer went off, and she pushed on the heavy reinforced door. Some of the women inside complained that it kept them locked in as much as it kept their partners out, but it was there for their own protection.

She stepped into a small but bright hallway. The flooring was old, wooden and hard on the feet, and it didn't have a long mirror, a coat rack or a welcome mat. This one had nothing close by that could be used as a weapon.

At the head of the hallway, at the side of a flight of stairs, a woman stood waiting at an open door. Lisa Johnson was in her late thirties. Her face was free of make-up, her dark brown hair cut short and her clothes were tidy yet classic, with not an ounce of fashion.

Eden had always prided herself in looking good and would have fitted in well in the sixties era that she loved so much, with her blonde elfin haircut, long legs and striking resemblance to Twiggy. She didn't care if she stood out from the crowd, whereas the woman standing in front of her seemed to feel the need to blend into the background. Eden had seen this so often in her previous role working as a detective constable on the Domestic Violence Team.

Nothing surprised her much nowadays. Only last year she'd had a case where a man had attacked a woman several times over a number of months, and yet when he'd put a knife into her leg, she still said it was her fault, that she had goaded him. Eden had persuaded her to move out but a week later she was back with him.

'Blustery out there, isn't it?' Lisa came towards her.

'I can't believe the chill in the air.' Eden shivered as she unwound her scarf from around her neck. 'Anyone would think it was winter or something.' She grinned. 'Oh wait. . .'

'How about a coffee to warm you up?' Lisa asked with a smile that lit up her face.

'You say the nicest things.' Eden nodded in gratitude. She followed Lisa into a large kitchen, where a table that could seat up to ten people stood in the centre of the room. The units were a pale beech Shaker style, recently refurbished by Mitchell Housing Association. Winter sunlight blasted in through the window – dust bunnies dancing in the air – and bounced off the yellow painted walls, but still it didn't make the place feel warm and homely.

'Another day to be thankful for,' said Lisa. 'Although I can't wait for the bitter winter we're having this year to recede.'

Eden nodded in agreement. While Lisa made drinks, she read a poster to her right advertising a self-defence class every Tuesday and another session on self-assertiveness starting the next month. Taking back control was the easy part, she mused. It was sticking with it afterwards that was the problem.

Lisa was a live-in manager and a qualified social worker. She had been at the refuge since it had opened two years earlier. She and Eden had seen a few of the residents through some of the worst atrocities, seen them come and then leave with their violent partners because they weren't able to cope without them, or were bullied into going back home. Emotional blackmail was a huge part of the control cycle and one that was hard to break free from. Eden couldn't blame the women, though she found it very frustrating. Lisa understood, because she had been through it all too. Thankfully she had got away. As had others. Some women who left The Willows never came back. They were the fortunate ones.

Eden found out lots of information when she was at the refuge. She liked to know as much as she could about who was on their patch, what trouble they were likely to cause in the near future. This last month, the refuge had been quiet. Just the way she liked it.

'How're things?' she asked as she pulled out a chair and sat down at the table. 'Anything I need to know before I start my session?'

Lisa handed her a mug and sat down across from her. 'One regular back again,' she said. 'Tanya White.'

Eden sighed. 'How long do we give her this time – two weeks max?'

It wasn't an unkind remark, or a dig at Tanya herself, but she had a habit of turning up at the refuge and then leaving a few days later. Recently, she'd had a reprieve when her husband, Vic, had been sent to prison for a year, but as Eden recalled, he had got out recently.

Even though The Willows housed women from out of the area, Tanya had used its facilities several times already. Lisa wouldn't turn anyone away, even when it brought trouble to the door. Eden had also tried to help several times over the past few years.

She hadn't expected Tanya to be back so soon. In itself it was a sure sign that everything would escalate for her again. The woman didn't cry wolf, clearly apparent by the bruises she would turn up with, but often, before the bruising had faded, she would be back living with her husband.

'So he's up to his old tricks again?' Eden asked. 'How long has she been here?'

'Two days. Luckily we have room. We're quite full just now.'

'Ah. That's what I wanted to talk to you about.' Eden explained the situation with Sally and Colin Stanton.

'If you can persuade her to come, I'll find room for her,' said Lisa. 'If she's desperate, I'll sleep on the sofa until you can move her to somewhere else.'

Eden reached across the table and gave Lisa's hand a quick squeeze. 'Where would I be without people like you?'

'In a lot of trouble, I'd imagine.' Lisa laughed then became serious almost as quickly. 'Something else bothering you?'

Eden explained what had happened to Ella Brown and Becky Fielding. She took a sip of her welcome warm drink before speaking again.

'I won't get to see all the women, so could you have a chat to them? I'm concerned this guy might go on to attack more women before we catch him.'

Lisa nodded. 'You know me – I'm vigilant anyway so I'll keep my eyes peeled. You're certain he'll attack again?'

Eden shook her head. 'Not yet, no. I just need all women to be extra careful at the moment. The story is being covered in the local press but I'm concerned it might not be enough. Will you pass that message on for me please? Just to make the women aware and, hopefully, not to scare them.'

'Carla has a session this afternoon. I'll mention it to her.'

Carla Gregory was a counsellor at the refuge, in her early forties, with a tragic past that she hid behind a bubbly persona. Eden had known her for a year now, since she had started to work there. She had sat in many sessions with her and heard her talk at several SWAP meetings too.

Carla gave presentations on self-defence, self-assertiveness, anything to do with self-help really. Yet Eden saw a distinct change in her as soon as she came off the stage or her talk finished. On stage, Carla was captivating and funny. Off stage, she was less willing to engage with people, keeping herself to herself.

It helped a lot of the women at the centre to talk to her. She had an air of 'I know what you've been through but I'm not going to tell you my story. I want to know yours.'.

'Thanks.' Eden gave Lisa a half-smile. 'Although, I guess, for the best part, they're always looking over their shoulders for some evil bastard to do something to them.' She sighed loudly. 'Sadly, most of them will be doing that for the rest of their lives.'

CHAPTER SIX

When Carla Gregory finished at The Willows, she called at the supermarket for a few groceries and then headed home. She had worked for five hours today, but only three of them would be paid. After the 2 p.m. session, she'd started chatting to Marsha Ward, who had gone to pieces when Carla had questioned her gently.

When it had come to the end of the session, it hadn't seemed right to leave her in such a state. Carla sensed that the woman needed to talk, felt that she wanted someone to listen. She loved that about her role. She hadn't been listened to during her earlier life, only talked at and down to constantly. So it was fine for her to be there, even if it went over her working hours. She didn't mind so much as she had nothing to rush back to nowadays.

Home for Carla was a small two-up, two-down terraced house on the edge of Harrington, an area in the north of the city. She didn't need any more than that now she was on her own, and even having a spare bedroom reminded her that Chloe was missing from her life. She could just imagine how it might have been if she were still alive, full of make-up and clothes and shoes, music playing. Perhaps Chloe would be working, or maybe even at university and only coming back at weekends when she could.

Carla had rented this property fully furnished so that she was ready to go, with just two suitcases to fill. She had moved several times over the past few years from her home in Northumber-land – as well as Liverpool, she had stayed in Birmingham and Manchester – and had been living in Stockleigh for two years now. She liked it here. It was a small city, more of a town really, and most of its residents were friendly. Of course, she read tales in the local newspaper of the two large estates notorious for trouble, but there were more areas full of people who prided themselves in looking after their homes and raising families to be proud of.

Settling in Granger Street permanently was a lovely option but one that she would probably have to put on the back-burner. Most likely she'd have to move on soon now that Ryan was out of prison. Like the Marsha Wards of this world, she had excess baggage to contend with in the shape of a man who was too handy with his fists.

Once inside, she checked that the house was secure, going into every room, checking locks on windows, bolts on doors. Satisfied that everything was in order, she went into the kitchen and set about putting away her groceries. These days she never switched on the radio or the television for background noise. She preferred to listen to the silence.

She opened the larder unit and put away the tins. A bang made her jump and she looked up at the window. But it was only Thomas, who was prowling up and down on the sill. She opened the window enough for him to crawl through and then picked him up.

'What have you been up to, you dirty old man?' she asked, stroking his head and being rewarded with the loudest of purrs.

Thomas was a tabby cat. Carla hadn't seen him for three days but only ever worried about him after a week had gone past. He wasn't her cat officially. Thomas belonged to Granger Street. Everyone knew him, and wherever he laid his paws was his home. He was good company though. Carla couldn't have a pet in case she had to leave anywhere quickly, and some of the places she could rent at short notice didn't allow pets, so that would never do. She had to be ready to run at the drop of a hat. Be one step ahead as long as she could.

Or as long as she wanted to. Because it was getting quite tedious to live her life like this. She'd love to settle down, be safe in her own home without the threat of Ryan finding her, attacking her viciously again like the last time. While he was in prison, she could sleep well, even though she had still moved on with each letter that arrived. She wasn't sure how he found her, just that he did. And every time he'd made contact, she had moved cities. It was a game he was playing, a deadly game of cat and mouse. She just wished she wasn't the mouse.

The feeling of being watched never left her, both here and at the refuge. Yet just lately, for a couple of weeks, she'd sensed it more; although she couldn't help but hope it was her imagination playing tricks on her now that Ryan had been released from prison. After all, she had been on the lookout for years, always thinking that someone was glancing her way. Often, she'd turn round, scared of her own shadow, and then laugh to herself with nervous relief when there was no one there. She wondered if she'd ever be rid of that fear. Then she doubted it immediately.

Coffee in hand, she went through to the tiny living room. It was all white plastered walls that she couldn't decorate, furniture that wasn't to her taste, but it was better that she couldn't leave her mark anywhere. She would hate to leave a place that she had sunk her heart into.

A lone photograph of Chloe stood on the fireplace, taken just before she died. It went everywhere with her, and it was the only one of Chloe she had in her possession. The rest of them were in a safe-deposit box at a bank in Stockleigh. Ryan would never get his hands on those. She knew without a doubt that he would destroy them. He wouldn't want to keep them because his daughter was dead. He would want to cause her the maximum pain by ruining them.

It was sad that she had no possessions to call her own, but at least she still had her life.

TWENTY-ONE YEARS AGO

I was completely bowled over when I first met Ryan. Back then I was a shy nineteen-year-old living in Newcastle and working as a receptionist in a local garage and showroom. I loved the job, mostly because the mechanics used to tease me all the time.

I lived at home with my parents. I had been to college for two years to train as a counsellor, but I couldn't find work after I qualified because I had no experience. I took the job at the garage to tide me over. It didn't pay much but it was great fun, and the women I worked with were good company.

I remember clearly the first time I saw him. His eyes were the first thing I noticed, deep blue and, yes, there was a twinkle there as he smiled and chatted to me while I booked his car in for a service. His hair was dark, cut short and fashionable for the nineties. Boot-cut jeans and thick-soled boots went well with his Barbour jacket and checked shirt, making him stylish with the minimum of effort.

His large hands were clean, no signs of manual work. He caught me glancing at him as he filled out a form. And then when he'd handed me the keys to a Porsche 911, well, I'd been blown away. Ryan worked as an insurance sales rep. He told me he had a company car but that this one was his own pride and joy.

Behind me, I could feel the eyes of Steph and Kerry almost burning a hole in the back of my head as we chatted. I tried desperately not to blush but failed dismally. He laughed at my discomfort, but along with me, not at me. His smile was contagious. I felt myself blush even more.

He took me to dinner one night the following week, and I think I fell in love on the spot. It's a cliché, love at first sight, but if you believe in that kind of thing, that's what happened.

Ryan was my first serious boyfriend. I'd recently broken up with David who had lasted just over two months. He'd told me he was staying over at his nan's house because she was poorly and undergoing chemotherapy. His nan turned out to be an eighteen-year-old woman he'd met at the pub one weekend. I soon gave him the push when I found out the truth. I was quite assertive in my younger days.

Which is why, so many years on, I suppose – in a way – I can understand why I fell for Ryan. He was seven years older than me and felt so mature compared to David. I guess Ryan must have seen something in me that I hadn't known existed until he'd come on the scene; *vulnerability*. I was too nice.

And to men like Ryan, being nice was a weakness to exploit.

CHAPTER SEVEN

Eden arrived home early on Wednesday evening. After working a couple of late ones on the trot, she'd managed to finish at six. Often she was at work until past eight at night trying to catch up on paperwork. When a case came in that warranted she work on it with the Major Crimes Team, or CID, then she would work around the clock with them too. Luckily she had her sister, or Joe, to keep an eye on Casey if it was too late.

Joe was out with his friends that evening. They'd been together for nearly a year now and, after asking her several times if she wanted to live with him, he'd given up. Although she was used to seeing him most evenings, just lately he'd taken to having a few nights out without her. Eden wasn't sure if this was deliberate so that she would miss him when he wasn't there, because she *did* miss him, or whether it was because he was tired of her non-committal attitude to their relationship. Either way, they had been together for a long time and yet she still had never fallen head over heels in love with him.

It was all to do with the ghost of her husband still haunting her. If they had got round to divorcing, Danny Berrisford would have been her ex, but she hadn't heard from him in over two years, not since he'd walked out on her and Casey. She still couldn't believe he hadn't been in contact, despite a few attempts on her part to get in touch with him.

After the trauma she'd been through when her niece, Jess, had been kidnapped last year, Eden had wanted to see if Danny was okay. It always piqued her curiosity as to where he was. But Danny had never replied to the text messages she'd sent. He clearly hadn't been interested in her, or his daughter.

It had been hard at first. He'd cleared their bank accounts, leaving her broke and also saddled with some of his debts. It was only then she'd found out the true nature of his gambling habit. Even now, though, it was hard to say good riddance when they had unfinished business. As well as her heart taking a beating, Danny had stolen information from her that could lead to her losing her job if anyone on the force ever found out.

So when loving, dependable Joe came along, Eden was concerned she was settling for someone just because – and that spoke volumes to her. It wasn't the commitment she was afraid of. It was committing herself to the right man after being with Danny for so long. Joe was stable, reliable, a kind of boy-next-door who she knew would look after her. Eden didn't want a nice boy though. Her marriage had been fine until the point of Danny's walkout. They'd had their volatile moments – they were both hot-headed at times and could give each other the silent treatment for days – but they were good together in a way that she and Joe could never be. She hadn't worked out yet if that was a positive or negative point.

Casey was in the kitchen, sitting at the breakfast bar.

Eden smiled. 'Hi there, mini-me.' It pained and excited her in equal measures to see them looking so alike. In one way, she was grateful that Casey was growing up into a strong, well-rounded and well-liked individual with her own personality, yet at other times it reminded her of her own passing youth. Casey looked so much like Eden had when she was the same age.

Casey looked up from her school books and smiled. 'Hi, Mum. Good day?'

'I've had better.' Eden leaned over to squeeze her daughter's hand as she walked past. 'Have you eaten?'

'Made myself a chip butty.'

Eden frowned. 'You'll be getting spots again if you eat too much fatty food.'

Casey pointed to a cluster on her chin. 'I already have them! So I might as well treat myself.'

Eden couldn't help but smile at her logic.

'Is Daphne in?' Daphne was their cat, a two-year-old blue Persian.

Casey shook her head. 'She has been. I gave her something to eat and she went out again. Must have a hot date or something.'

Eden laughed just as her phone rang. It was her sister moaning about her niece misbehaving again. 'Would you like me to have a word with her?' she said after she had listened for a few minutes. She knew this was what Laura was getting round to.

'I'm not sure it will make a difference. She's just a bloody nightmare, to be honest.'

'I'll see if I can collar her this weekend. We're still okay for Sunday lunch?'

'Yes. Looking forward to it. Is Joe coming too?'

Eden paused. 'It'll just be me and Casey.'

'Oh?'

'Joe wants to watch the football on TV and you know how much he hates it when we start gabbing over it.'

'That's not a good enough excuse to turn down roast beef and Yorkshire pudding in my eyes. What's going on, Eden?'

Eden sighed. Her sister never missed a beat.

'We're just having a few issues, that's all.'

'He's got fed up of you, hasn't he?'

'You make me sound like the catch of the day!'

'You know what I mean. He's a really nice guy, he thinks a lot of you and now that he and Casey are getting on, I thought—'

'Ever listened to that George Michael song?' Eden snapped. 'When he says he can't make you love him? Well I can't make myself love Joe enough and that's not his fault. So it's not fair that I string him along.'

'Said after being with him for a year.'

'He knows the score!'

'So he's finally getting the message and cooling off?'

Eden pinched the bridge of her nose. 'Possibly. I don't know for sure.'

'And are you worried?'

The million-dollar question. Would she be upset if Joe handed back his front door key and said it was over? Eden very much doubted it. But she didn't want to get into the same old argument again.

'Are we having apple pie?'

'That's avoiding the question.'

'I don't know *how* to answer,' said Eden, 'because I don't really know if I would be bothered or not. And that's something I need to work out, rather than leading him on.'

'But you told me you loved him.'

'I do! In my own way, but that might not be good enough.'

'You need to be saying this to him, not telling me.'

'You're supposed to listen and not give advice.' Eden was referring to Laura's job. She worked at CrisisChat, a chatline for teenagers.

'That's for teenagers, not grown-ups.'

Eden sniggered. 'Yes, Mum.'

'I'll see you at the weekend. Text me if you need me.'

Eden disconnected the phone with a sigh. She switched on the grill and got out two slices of bread and a pack of cheese. Right now, all she wanted to do was eat and not think about anything more taxing than that.,

CHAPTER EIGHT

Tanya White sat down on the single bed with a thump. She looked around in despair at the room that she would have to stay in for the foreseeable future. She was sick and tired of this routine every time Vic came out of prison.

She'd thought she'd never end up back at The Willows when he'd promised not to hit her after the last time. Yet he'd only been out for two days and already she was here.

The room was clean to the point of being clinical, with its cream walls and dark brown carpet. But at least she could lock her door every night and feel safe, and that was the main thing. No one to have a go at her, no one to threaten her if she didn't do as she was told, or stepped out of line for a second.

She'd slept in this room the last time she had fled here. Then it had been for three weeks, and she'd gone back when Vic promised to change. She wondered who had stayed here after her, and if they were happy now that they had moved on. Some of the women she'd met had gone on to live good lives without their violent partners but most, like her, had a tendency to go back to them because they didn't really see any other solution. She wondered if they all hated that they were weak too.

Tanya glanced at herself in the small wardrobe mirror as she made her way over to the window. Her clothes hung where they should have shown curves. She had never been into taking drugs as much as Vic, but her teeth and skin had paid the price regardless and she looked ten years older than thirty-seven. Her hair needed a good wash; once she had done that she would be respectable again. Make-up would cover the bruising if necessary, if she could be bothered. Having bruising here was a sign of belonging, she reckoned.

At least she would sleep easy in her bed tonight. Vic couldn't get to her. She was safe here and, once she had come to do what she had set out to do, she would make friends and move on.

She unpacked what little belongings she had brought with her from a Morrisons shopping bag. Two pairs of jeans, some knickers and a bra, socks, a few T-shirts, leggings and a jumper. She had come in a coat, and apart from the long cardigan that she was wearing now that was it. A few personal items scrambled together and she was on her way. Getting the bruising had been the last straw. He didn't have to be so mean.

Once what little belongings she had were in their place, she locked the bedroom door behind her and went in search of a cup of tea. If she kept herself to herself, then maybe the ordeal would be over before she knew it, and she could get out of here and on with her life.

CHAPTER NINE

He stood across the road, watching from the shadows. There was no point in causing a commotion. It wasn't worth risking someone calling the police. Besides, he didn't want her to know he was there just yet.

It was the sense of excitement he had missed since he'd arrived in Stockleigh. The chase, the thrill, call it what you may. It never left him.

She was here, right in front of him. He would bide his time before letting her know he was here. It was fun watching her. She was his obsession, yet he could take her down any time he liked, and that was far more rewarding.

He didn't really need to stand back in the shadows. Even though he wore dark clothes, he was sure she wouldn't have noticed him anyway. He'd been following her for several days, yet she hadn't suspected a thing. Which was pathetic, really, given the circumstances.

He'd been standing there for some time when a light went on upstairs. He saw her walk to the window before quickly drawing the curtains. Was she thinking of him? Was she wondering when he would catch up with her?

Did she realise how much trouble she would be in once he got his hands on her?

Did she even know he was coming after her yet?

Headlights shone bright in the distance, and he ducked behind a van. It wouldn't do to be seen hanging around.

The vehicle went past and he resumed his position. He smirked. Boy, was he going to have some fun and games. It wouldn't be fun for her though. She was going to get what was coming to her.

Checking it was all quiet again, he took the hefty brick from the pocket of his coat and walked stealthily across the road. As he reached the refuge, he pulled up his scarf to hide his face. Then he threw the brick at the large front window with all his power behind him.

It hurtled through the air and smashed into the pane, causing an almighty bang. There wasn't time to relish in the screams because he didn't stop until he was halfway down the street and away.

CHAPTER TEN

Eden was at her desk trying to persuade Ella Brown's mum to let her see her daughter, but she was having no luck. Mrs Brown said Ella was too traumatised to go through it all again. Eden couldn't blame Ella, even though she knew they could be missing out on vital evidence if the attacks were linked, she knew how protective she would be if it had been Casey. Relenting a little, she finished by asking Mrs Brown to get in touch if Ella remembered anything else.

There was a voicemail on her mobile. It was Lisa from the women's refuge telling her that a brick had gone through the downstairs window the night before. Eden had a meeting to attend nearby so she made arrangements to pop in afterwards.

At The Willows, Lisa buzzed her in.

'It took the council hours to come out last night, and all they've done for now is board it up until it can be repaired.' Lisa rolled her eyes. 'That's all well and good for anyone if it's a random act of vandalism, but the women here are terrified that it was done so that someone could come back this evening, force the boarding off and get into the refuge.'

'I'm sure it'll be glazed again soon,' Eden soothed. 'Although it will have to be made to measure, I guess. You know where we are if you need us.'

'Fat lot of use that will be in the middle of the night. It'll be too late.'

Most of the time, the two women saw eye to eye but often Lisa became so passionate about her role that she could become confrontational. Eden knew it was because Lisa had had a violent partner. Her husband had attacked her for years, and she'd put up with all kinds of abuse, until one night she'd plucked up the courage to leave.

Josie Mellor had found a room for her in a hostel and from there she'd been given a flat. The position of live-in refuge manager had been perfect for her when it had come along six months later. Eden had been certain that Lisa would do a good job because she knew the fear that drove these women to come to the refuge. She had felt it for years, put up with it for years. It gave Lisa a sense of purpose, people to look after, and she'd become popular in the team of workers who provided care at The Willows.

Tanya White popped her head round the kitchen door. She was the last person Eden had expected to see. She wondered if she wanted to speak to her or Lisa.

'Hi, Tanya, how are things?' she asked, pointing to a chair in the hope that she might come and join them.

Tanya hovered in the doorway. Her hair hung loose, and she wore leggings and an oversized jumper. The borrowed slippers on her feet were worn, their fronts scuffed of pink fur.

'I know what you're thinking,' she said.

'What about?' Eden cocked her head to one side.

'About me being back here again.'

'She doesn't think anything, Tanya,' Lisa came to Eden's defence. 'We're both here for support if you need it.'

Tanya folded her arms and stared at Eden. 'I'm doing okay.'

'That's great to hear.' Eden smiled. 'Have you spoken to Carla yet?'

'I've made an appointment. I'm hoping not to be here too long though. I'm going to make a go of it this time and find myself a flat or something.'

'One step at a time,' said Eden. 'We need to keep you out of Vic's way first.'

'Well what else do you expect me to do? I'm doing my best here.'

'We're just saying,' said Lisa, 'please be careful.'

'Yes,' Eden reiterated. 'We both know it took an awful lot of courage for you to come back here again. Like Lisa says, we're here for you whenever you need us.'

'Like anyone has ever been there for me,' Tanya snorted. 'And the brick through the window? That had nothing to do with me either, so don't go blaming me behind my back.'

Eden opened her mouth to speak again but Tanya was already gone. She frowned. She would have thought it better not to mention it if she was involved. Just the fact that Tanya had brought up the vandalism made her wonder if she had seen who had done it but was too afraid to say.

CHAPTER ELEVEN

Alice Clough slid herself along the back seat of the taxi, turned and put her feet on to the pavement. A rush of air hit her and she wished she hadn't drunk so much on the train home. She'd had a fabulous day in London but was already dreading the hangover she knew she'd have in the morning.

'I feel sick,' she muttered.

Having climbed out of the taxi first, her friend Lacey grabbed for her hand and pulled Alice to her feet. She closed the car door and banged on the side. 'Thanks, mate,' she shouted after the car as it moved away.

'What a great day,' Alice said, gaining her colour back again as she stood. 'That's much better. A bit of fresh air is what I needed. I'm probably a bit travel sick after two hours on a train.'

'More like a bit too tipsy after we knocked back so much wine!' Lacey grinned. 'You're right though. It was a great day. We must do it again soon. I haven't laughed so much in a good while. It felt good.'

Alice gave her friend a hug. The trip to London had been her idea after Lacey and her long-time partner had split up. They had been together for five years, and Lacey had thought they were due to be married and start a family. It had come as a huge shock to everyone when Sebastian had just upped and left when an opportunity to work in America had come up.

'I'm sure your heart will mend soon,' Alice sympathised. 'I'm so sorry you have to go through this, but you will come out stronger.

I'm certain of it. And if he can just leave after five years, then he's not worth bothering with anyway. He was an idiot. Couldn't see what was right underneath his nose. My beautiful Lacey.' She broke away. 'You're too good for him.'

They hugged again, then went their separate ways. They both lived off the main road in streets next to each other. It would only take Alice a few minutes to get home. She pulled the collar of her coat nearer as the icy cold began to get at her.

Epsom Street was in darkness as she went down it. It was just past midnight as she opened her gate and closed it quietly behind her. She tiptoed up the path to stop the heels on her boots from making too much noise. At the door, she popped down her shopping bags and zipped open her handbag. She hummed to herself as she rummaged around inside for her keys.

A sound made her freeze, but she didn't have time to look round before someone grabbed her from behind. A hand covered her mouth and she was dragged backwards down the path. Her grip on her handbag slipped and it clattered to the flagstones, her arms flying out as she resisted. All she could do was hit out with her fists, kick out with her feet.

She was pushed to the side, almost twirling in mid-air before falling heavily to her knees on the grass. As she tried to scramble away, her attacker was on her in seconds. She could see it was a man just before a punch to the face dazed her. Still she tried to fight. He straddled her, his eyes dark with anger. It was all she could see of his features.

In front of her was her parents' bedroom window, in darkness. Her mum and dad were in there, and if she could just alert them. . .

'Dad!' she screamed.

But he covered her mouth.

Then he hit her again.

She stopped screaming when she passed out on the third punch.

CHAPTER TWELVE

The next morning, Eden knocked on the open door to Sean's office. 'There's been another attack, sir,' she said. 'Alice Clough, twenty years old. The first statement says she was badly beaten outside her home in Epsom Street.'

'Sexual assault?'

'I don't think so.'

Sean cocked his head to one side. 'Wanna take Phil with you and go over her statement? Get him out of the office?'

Eden paused. Was it best to take him or leave him at his desk? She thought back to their last conversation when she'd wanted to snap at him over his prejudiced remarks, but it was his first week back. She decided for now not to mention anything to Sean.

She rolled her eyes in a playful manner. 'If I must.'

Alice Clough lived in the north of the city with her parents. Epsom Street was wide and had a semi-rural feel to it, overlooking a large tree-lined green. The private housing estate had been built around a lake, and Eden could just make it out in the background.

A young woman opened the door, sporting bruising to most of her face and neck. She held on to her stomach as they showed their warrant cards.

'Hi, Alice?' Eden introduced herself and Phil. 'Might we come in and have a few words with you?'

Alice showed them into the living room.

'Are you alone?' Eden wondered if her parents would be coming to join them.

'I insisted my mum and dad went to work. I needed some space.'

Once Alice had lowered herself down on to the settee, Eden sat next to her and opened her notebook. 'Are you able to go through it all again for me?' she asked. 'I know it's painful but maybe something might come back to you that you haven't realised yet.'

'Painful is the broken rib he left me with,' Alice snipped before nodding. She looked down at her hands in her lap.

Eden watched Phil move to stand in the window. On the dresser, behind a large vase of flowers, she noticed a framed photo. Alice was in the middle of two other women, their smiles wide as she took the selfie. In front of her now was someone who seemed merely a shadow of that young woman. Someone who had been traumatised by her experience. She hoped in time that Alice would be able to move on and not let the creep who had done this ruin her life.

'I hope you don't mind us calling,' Eden started, 'but it's often useful for us to talk to victims so that we can cross-reference things. Can you go through what happened last night, please?'

'I'd just come back from London,' said Alice.

Eden smiled her encouragement.

'Me and a few friends had gone down early in the morning and caught the train back. We'd been on a shopping trip, followed by a few drinks in a wine bar. We were slightly loud, I admit, but nothing too much. No one was complaining.'

Eden smiled supportively at her again when she stopped.

'The trip to London had been my idea. My friend, Lacey, has split up with her boyfriend so I wanted to cheer her up.'

'How many of you were there?'

'Four. There was Manda Bridlington and Summer Maddison too.'

'Do you know if the rest of the girls got home okay?'

'Yes, they've all been sending me messages today.'

Eden saw the bitterness that flashed across Alice's face as she realised it could have been any of them but she was the unlucky one.

'So you got back to the station. . .' she said.

'Manda and Summer were picked up by Manda's dad and me and Lacey got a taxi.'

'Which firm did you use?'

'I'm not sure. We just got into one on the taxi rank outside.'

'What time would this be?' asked Eden, checking over the statement that she'd chased up with uniform.

'About half past eleven. Lacey lives on Riley Street, two streets back, so we got out on the main road. We chatted for about ten minutes and then we said good night. When I got home, my parents had gone to bed and I couldn't find my key. That's when he – he ran up behind me, grabbed my hair and, before I had a chance to turn around, threw me to the ground.'

'In your front garden?' Eden couldn't help sounding shocked. Surely he knew the risks he was taking so close to home? Anyone could have come out of the surrounding houses to help if they had heard anything. It didn't make sense.

'Did you scream out, Alice? It doesn't matter if you froze. I know a lot of people do that.'

'No, I screamed. I tried to fight for a while until he punched me.' Alice looked up at her. 'I realised he was too strong for me when he punched me again. Sorry, I can't remember anything after that,' she said through her tears.

Eden gave her an apologetic smile as she continued. 'Did he have a local accent?'

Alice shrugged. 'He never said a word.'

'Did you recognise anything about him? Something that you'd seen on someone else? Or a tattoo maybe? Any distinguishing marks?'

'There was nothing. It was too dark to see much.'

Eden could see that she wasn't going to get anything else from her. Bringing it all up again was painful enough. She closed her notebook and stood up.

'You will catch him soon, won't you?' Alice looked up through swollen lids.

'The case has been passed to my team, and I work with a good bunch of detectives.' Eden stared at Phil but he didn't even look at her. So much for giving him another chance – he hadn't said a word! She smiled warmly at Alice. 'As soon as I know more, I'll let you know. Thanks for speaking to us again today. You've been so brave.'

Outside the house, Eden breathed in lungfuls of air. It was all so bloody futile at times, but they would keep at it. If they caught him, it would let Alice sleep well in her bed. That had to be a bonus.

'You were very quiet in there,' she said to Phil, once they were in the car.

'Not much to say, if I can't speak my mind.'

'Well you could have asked some questions. I would have—'

'Don't tell me what to do. I've been on this job for more years than you.'

'I don't know how,' Eden muttered.

'You have to tolerate certain things in this world. I'm not here to make friends, and working with a team that I only have to be part of for four weeks before I go back to my own job isn't my idea of fun.'

Eden had been brought up to respect her elders but it took all her strength not to bite back.

'I'll go out on my own tomorrow,' said Phil.

'I don't think—'

'I'm sure I'm capable of more than sitting next to you.'

'We'll see.' Eden started up the car and drove back to the station in silence. Four weeks, Sean had said. Well it seemed both she and Phil were counting down the days already.

CHAPTER THIRTEEN

Carla had a meeting with Tanya White booked in for that morning. Tanya hadn't been to the refuge since Carla had taken up her role so they hadn't met yet. Usually, anyone new was asked if they would like to have a chat with her. Already she was wondering if Tanya would turn up. She seemed a bit shy, keeping away from the women for most of the time, but then again she had been here several times. Maybe she felt like she shouldn't be back – or that she shouldn't have left the refuge before. Carla wouldn't judge anyone for that.

In the small room off the lounge, she caught up on a few notes as she waited for Tanya to arrive. The room was where one-to-one meetings were held with social workers, case workers or the police. It wasn't an ideal place to chat, but it was the only one available, as all other rooms were needed for women to sleep in.

At the moment, the refuge only had one spare bedroom. One lucky woman could have a roof over her head if she was brave enough to walk out on her violent partner. Although it wasn't ideal that woman had to suffer abuse to get a space at the refuge, Carla always preferred to have a vacancy than hear that the refuge was full.

A knock at the door and she looked up to see Tanya. They had met earlier when Tanya had first arrived. Mondays at the hostel were always the busiest. Lots of couples had more time to spend arguing over a weekend when the alcohol flowed, as was often the case. Sometimes a woman plucked up the courage to leave first thing Monday morning after a particularly disastrous weekend. Carla hoped to find out more about Tanya during this one-to-one, see if she could help her in any way, or if not perhaps signpost her to someone who could.

She hated the saying 'people like' but her gut feeling was that people like Tanya were desperate to get out of their downward spiral of destruction. Tanya's clothes were clean but seemed two sizes too big. Her long hair, definitely her greatest asset, was tied back from her face in a ponytail that she was twisting around her finger. Green eyes sliced around the room before landing on her, and she tried not to squirm under their scrutiny.

'Hi, Tanya.' She smiled and pointed to a chair. When Tanya stayed in the doorway, she beckoned her in again. 'I don't bite, and this is voluntary. You don't have to tell me anything if you so wish, but at least come and have a cup of coffee.'

Tanya gave her a wary smile and walked slowly across the room.

Carla watched her. She had the typical stance of wanting to be invisible, as if she wasn't worthy of gaining any attention. She felt sad that someone had made her feel that way. Hated that she had let it happen to herself too all those years ago.

She got up to make a drink, pointing to a small machine at her side. 'What would you like? Espresso? Cappuccino? Hot chocolate?'

'What are you having?' Tanya asked, her head swivelling around like a child's in a sweet shop.

'Always cappuccino for me.'

'I'll have that too. Thanks.'

Carla had bought the coffee machine herself. It had proved a great hit and also meant that a drink was on hand so that she didn't have to interrupt any session for too long, or leave a client when it was necessary for her to stay nearby. The room was locked when it wasn't in use, or else she knew it had the chance of going walkabout. But when she moved on, it would stay behind.

The whole process took less than a couple of minutes and soon she was sitting across from Tanya.

'I have notes on a file here,' she pressed a hand to a brown folder, 'but I'd prefer if you told me about yourself.'

Tanya took a sip from her drink, wincing as it was way too hot. 'Not much to tell that you haven't already heard a thousand times in this place, I guess.'

'Humour me.'

'I'm a recovering drug addict. I've been to prison several times for shoplifting in my late teens – nothing lengthier than a six-month reduced to three for good behaviour stretch.'

'Do you have any family that support you?'

Tanya shook her head. 'I got pregnant when I was eighteen but after having my first child, who is nineteen now, I went off the rails and destroyed myself completely with heroin.'

Carla said nothing, just nodded as she talked to encourage her to continue.

'Lee – he's my eldest – was taken into care when he was six months old. The same thing happened when Latisha and Lenny were born. They're seventeen and sixteen.'

'Do you have contact with any of them?'

Tanya shook her head, her ponytail swishing around. She began to play with it again. 'I wasn't capable of looking after myself back then, never mind my kids. They were better off without me.'

'And now?'

Tanya looked away for a moment, then back at Carla. 'Do you have children?'

A part of Carla hidden deep inside her made her stomach lurch as she thought about Chloe. Her life had to stay a secret. She shook her head in reply, but as much to rid herself of the pain that would no doubt follow. 'How long have you been with your current partner?'

'Have you never wanted kids?'

Carla ignored her. She wouldn't be swayed to reply. Aiming questions at her was often a diversionary tactic yet, if she wasn't careful, it could lead to her showing Tanya that talking about her past was incredibly painful too.

The room dropped into silence. A door slammed outside in the corridor, making them both jump. They smiled at each other. Another layer seemed to be removed as Tanya opened up again.

'I've been with Vic for twenty years. I met him when I was seventeen. He's the father of all my kids, the love of my life and the evil bastard that got me hooked on drugs, dependent on him and then ruled the house with his fists. I don't know why I love him, but I do.'

Carla nodded. 'Does he know that you're here?'

Tanya's shoulders rose up and down again. 'This is the fifth time I've done a runner so he'll come looking for me soon. He always does. Only the once, mind. He'll kick up a fuss and then he'll leave me alone.'

'Is that a good sign?'

Tanya shook her head and sighed loudly. 'Because then I miss him and he gets under my skin again. And I'll leave here, go back to him thinking everything will be hunky-dory, and it will be for the first couple of weeks.'

'And then?' Carla probed as Tanya stopped.

'Slowly everything will start going back to how it was before. The beatings, the late nights out drinking with his mates, the lack of money and food, the drugs to take to block it all out.' Tanya twirled her ponytail round her finger at an alarming rate. 'It's a vicious circle, isn't it? Like circling the drain forever.'

Carla's heart went out to the woman. She wanted to tell her that she knew exactly how she felt, that she had been in the same position once. But how could she give Tanya hope after what Ryan had done to her before he left? She wasn't brave like the Tanyas of this world.

'Look, I can't help you to stay away from Vic,' she said. 'That needs to come from you. But maybe we can work on helping you to feel strong enough to cope without him. So that you won't go back to him. There's no sugar-coating I can offer you, but we can help if you'll let us.'

They chatted a bit more before the session ended, and Carla was pleased when Tanya agreed to see her again the following week. As they stood up, she hid her surprise when the woman gave her a hug.

'I hope that, one day, I won't go to bed so scared that I don't want to wake up in the morning.'

'I hope so too.' Carla hugged her back, holding in her tears at the thought that someone else had lived a life similar to hers.

'I bet you've never been that terrified.' Tanya stared at her for a moment too long. It made Carla uncomfortable until she gave a sad smile.

Tanya's words hung in the room long after she had gone. Of course, Carla hadn't replied. But she had wanted to say, yes, she had been that terrified. She *had* been lucky to come out with her life. And now Carla was thankful for every day she got to spend before Ryan found her again.

CHAPTER FOURTEEN

Christina Spencer searched for her car keys in her handbag. She'd just finished an eight-hour shift at the petrol station she worked at.

'You in tomorrow?' her friend, Sam, asked as she popped an overall over her head before getting up on to the stool behind the till.

'Yes, I'm a glutton for punishment.' Christina rolled her eyes. 'I can't believe I'm working all weekend again. I'll miss my Sunday dinner.'

'Well, I'll see you tomorrow, as I'm in too.'

Christina held the door open for a man as she came out on to the garage forecourt. Her car was parked in the multi-storey car park next to it. She'd managed to squeeze it into a space on the second floor today. Much better than the sixth and having to use the lift. She hated lifts with a passion, often taking the stairs when she was on the higher floors.

Market Street was busy as she crossed over to the car park. It was Saturday evening and lots of people were heading into Stockleigh for a night out before she had even finished for the day. She remembered being one of them a few years back, when she was young and carefree. Now she was married and planning a family, there was no extra money, as they were spending every penny on their new home.

She took the stairs to the second floor. In the distance, she could hear the noise of the traffic, but in the stairwell it was quiet. Christina relished the silence after the noise of the petrol station.

On the second floor, she pushed the door and walked towards her car. Her keys jangled in her hand as she hummed a tune she'd heard not long ago on the radio.

From behind, an arm came around her neck. As she cried out, her hands shot up to protect herself and the keys were forced from her grip. Someone pressed the key fob, covering her mouth with their free hand. A few metres away, the lights flashed on her white Ford Fiesta. They shuffled towards it. The door was opened and she was pushed down on to the back seat.

The man wore a scarf covering most of his face, and she clawed at it, hoping to reveal his identity.

'Let go of me, you bastard!' she screamed as she slapped at his hands.

He punched her in the side of her head, but still she fought back. He punched her again, this time dazing her. Quickly, he slipped a hand up inside her skirt and pulled at her knickers. She tried to kick out but he was too strong, almost ripping off her underwear.

There was a peal of laughter behind them as the lift doors opened. The man clamped a hand to her mouth again, his body pressing down on hers as an elderly couple came walking out on to their level.

They walked in the opposite direction to her vehicle, still laughing. He kept a hand over her mouth. Christina knew he was trying to silence her until they were alone again. It was her only chance.

She kicked at his shin and then let out an ear-piercing scream.

The couple stopped and turned to look.

Christina screamed again.

He turned away to look behind him. Then he groaned and punched her in the face again before pushing himself off.

Watching him running away, Christina quickly scrambled out of the back seat and into the front. Putting down the locks, she sobbed hysterically. The guy was going to rape her. Thank God someone had come to their car at the right moment. Another five minutes and. . . she tried to catch her breath, trying not to think of what might have happened.

'Are you okay?' A knock came on the window. It was the elderly couple. 'We heard you shout.'

Christina nodded. She could barely see for crying.

'Are you sure?' the man shouted, as if she hadn't heard him the first time.

She sat with her hands shaking, trying to gain her composure enough to drive away. They wanted to help, but there was no way she was getting out of her car again. She nodded once more and wiped at her tears.

Finally they moved off. She started the engine and drove out of the car park, not stopping until she arrived at Stockleigh Police Station.

CHAPTER FIFTEEN

Eden had thought that Joe would change his mind and join them at her sister's on Sunday. Which is why Laura was annoyed that he had decided to spend his lunch at the pub with his friends, watching the football.

Laura sighed as she cut up a joint of beef that had been sitting for ten minutes. 'It isn't even a big game.'

'He has a life too, you know.' Eden wouldn't be drawn into another discussion of her and Joe's tepid relationship. 'No Sarah this week?' Sarah was Laura's older daughter.

'No, she's working.'

'So how has Jess been?' she asked, hoping to change the subject.

'Okay, I guess.' Laura sighed. 'She's broken up with Cayden again.'

'Ah.'

When Jess had been kidnapped the previous year, several teenagers had been assaulted and Eden had found out more than she had bargained for about Jess and her boyfriend, Cayden – they'd been stealing mobile phones and getting paid for them. Eden was still looking into that case but the leads so far had come to nothing. Jess and Cayden had also been sharing photos online that they shouldn't have. Both she and Laura were hoping that the relationship between them would peter out. It had and then it hadn't, several times over the past few months.

'I wish I could say this time will be the last, but I'm not too hopeful,' Laura continued. 'I heard Jess crying in her room this morning. I didn't have the heart to go in, as I know I'd make things worse by saying something insensitive, like there are more fish in the sea. She doesn't want to hear that, even if it's true.'

'Who did the finishing this time?' Eden wanted to know.

'He did. Said she was smothering him and he needed more space.'

'And how long were they apart during their last break-up?'

'Three days.' Laura couldn't help but grin. 'The longest yet.' She sighed again. 'I know they won't last more than a few months in total, but I wish she could see what we see right now. They aren't meant for each other.'

'Who are we to think that?' Eden mused. 'I certainly can't with my track record.'

'You make it sound like you had tons of relationships! Or lots of one-night stands anyway.'

'I wish!' Eden grinned and popped a small piece of roast potato into her mouth.

'Stop thieving!' Laura reached over and smacked her hand playfully.

'What are you two up to?' said Jess as she came into the room. Her long blonde hair was freshly washed and straightened, make-up plastered to her face the way some teens loved to wear it – black kohl-lined eyes, lashings of mascara beneath smoky grey lids and deep red lipstick.

Eden knew she'd look back at photos in years to come, as she and Laura often did, and say, 'What was I thinking?' But then again, she could remember thinking she was the bee's knees during her teen years.

'Hi, Jess.' She stepped towards her niece and embraced her. 'How have you been this week?'

'Fine.' Jess hugged her back. 'But cut the crap. I heard Mum telling you that Cayden had ditched me.'

'Poor you.' Eden squeezed her again. 'You know I think it's for your own good though.'

Casey came in then, rolled her eyes when she saw them hugging and left the room. Eden frowned then turned to Laura and rolled her eyes at her sister. What was up with her now? Kids!

'Can you start dishing the food out on to the plates, Jess?' asked Laura. 'Keep everything as hot as we can.'

'Won't be a moment,' said Eden. She popped back into the living room. Casey was sitting on the settee, legs outstretched, arms folded, and a scowl on her pretty face.

Eden flopped beside her and draped an arm around her shoulders. Casey rebuffed it and moved away from her.

'What's up?' Eden was hurt.

'Whenever we come around here, it's all Jess, Jess, Jess,' she said. 'I'm here too.'

'I know, but I see you every day. Besides, Laura wants me to have a word with Jess.'

'What about?'

'Just to see if she's coping.'

'You see?' Casey raised a hand in the air before dropping it. 'Laura never wants to talk to *me*, ask *me* if anything is wrong.'

'Is there anything wrong?' Eden posed the question. Had she not noticed something going on right underneath her nose?

'No.' Casey folded her arms again.

Eden tried not to smile as she put an arm around her daughter's shoulders and pulled her close again. This time there was no resistance.

'Oh, Casey, my angel. *You're* special because I don't need to worry about you. You'll always be special because of that.'

Casey looked at her mother from underneath the same blonde block fringe that her cousin had. The two of them were so alike in looks, if not temperament.

Eden gave her a squeeze. 'I'd like a good Sunday, with no bickering. Joe isn't here to wind anyone up either. Can we have at least one afternoon without an argument between you and Jess?'

Casey shrugged. 'She always starts it.'

'Well, let's make sure *she* has no ammunition today then.'

'Grub's up!' Laura shouted through.

Eden reached for Casey's hand and pulled her to her feet. 'Come on, you.'

After they'd eaten the main course, Eden and Laura started sharing tales of their teens. Both Jess and Casey were always enthralled to hear what their mothers had got up to in their youth.

'Do you remember when I was sixteen and you were eighteen,' Eden pointed at Laura, 'and I fancied the pants off your boyfriend? God, what was his name now?' She wracked her brain but she couldn't think of it.

'Barry Braindead!'

'Oh yes.'

'Seriously?' Jess gasped, then put a hand over her mouth as she realised they had made it up.

'Barry Braindead was the nickname we gave him because he was so stupid,' said Laura. 'He tried to play us off against each other.'

'He thought you wouldn't find out about him arranging to meet me,' said Eden, 'but Mum wouldn't allow me to stay out late so Laura had to be my chaperone.'

'To a date with my own boyfriend!'

Jess and Casey laughed.

'I can still remember his face when we rolled up together,' said Laura, 'and he had to pretend to you that it was a joke.'

'While you looked insulted and outraged that he would trick you so much.' Eden laughed too.

'I got him in the end, though, didn't I?'

'Yes, I ditched him there and then. You dated him for a further week and then ditched him too. I wonder who he moved on to next?'

'Some unlucky sod!' Laura grinned. 'Can you remember the time when we went to the fair and met two lads on their bikes?'

'Bikes?' said Casey, pouting. 'You'd never let me out to meet anyone who had a motorbike.'

'She might if it was a scooter.' Jess laughed, nudging her cousin.

'Pushbikes!' Eden and Laura said in unison.

'I can still remember when I had a date with Mike and I had to have you tagging along with me. I can still recall your face when I went off with him and left you alone all night,' said Laura. 'When I came back to you, all loved-up after a good snogging session, you ignored me and left me to walk home twenty yards behind you. You were livid.'

'I was in love with him too!'

'You never told me you wanted to go out with him!' Laura protested.

'She was cruel to me when we were younger,' Eden told Casey and Jess, who were still laughing. She reached across the table and gave Laura's hand a squeeze. It was good to share memories with their daughters. They might not have their parents now, and their partners were gone – Laura's husband, Neil, had been killed in 2009 in a hit-and-run accident – but they had each other. Something they were both grateful for every day. As well as family Sunday lunches.

Eden's phone beeped and she reached for it. It was Sean.

Another attack – might be linked so I've sent the details over to your team. Have a look at it first thing, will you? Thanks.

Eden groaned.

'Bad news?' asked Laura.

'There's been another woman attacked last night.' She looked up at them. 'I don't mean to scare anyone but you three, and Sarah, need to be careful at the moment. No going anywhere on your own after dark. Please be extra vigilant until he's caught.'

TWENTY-ONE YEARS AGO

Our first weekend away was perfect. Ryan took me to York, and we had the most wonderful time. I absolutely adored him and we became inseparable soon after. I was completely and utterly besotted with him because he was a true gentleman.

He was always buying me gifts – flowers would arrive at the office, a teddy bear, chocolates. He'd take me out on a date and surprise me with champagne at a restaurant, just because. He made me feel like a million dollars.

Pretty soon I was seeing him most nights he wasn't working. He introduced me to his acquaintances, but most of the time we would stay in together or go out for a romantic meal. I lost a few friends because he wanted me all to himself, but I wasn't too bothered at the time. Everyone falls in love and loses some friends, don't they? He was so good to me that I didn't feel like I was losing out. He was so attentive. I felt so lucky to be with him.

Yet , it was all about luring me in, giving me a false sense of security. Getting me to wear clothes he thought were flattering when they were dowdy and boring rather than colourful and fashionable as I was used to. Getting me to spend the evening with him rather than out with my friends because he didn't want to be apart from me. Getting me to listen to his classical music rather than my upbeat songs. I never saw it coming. I was just a girl in love.

Even now I can't begin to understand how much he tricked me. How he could be so loving for so long without showing me an ounce of the aggression to come. If only I had seen the signs.

I resigned from my job shortly after meeting Ryan. A position had opened up where he worked, and he said I'd be far better suited to it than working in a greasy garage with a load of men leering at me. I said it wasn't like that, but he wouldn't listen. Besides, he said, he'd be able to see more of me then. I missed working with the girls, and I missed the banter of the men in the garage, but this was a promotion and I was so pleased he was looking out for me.

Ryan often stayed overnight in some of the places he visited during the week. That was okay though because he'd call me several times each evening, just to chat. I thought it was such an attentive thing to do and showed how much he cared about me. How much he missed me.

I had the most fabulous two years. Then he asked me to marry him. That blew me away too. More fool me for saying yes. He played me well. Two years he had waited, watched and schemed, getting under my skin, loving me, making me feel protected.

I don't know why I didn't spot his potential for violence earlier. I know now that it was all a game to him. To see how long he could control me with the verbal abuse before the violence started. And boy did he win. Every time.

He was too strong for me. From the outside, Ryan was smart, successful, caring, friendly. But from the minute he came home, it was as if a switch had flicked and he turned into a control freak – a manipulating, vicious bully. It was as if he needed something to overpower. Someone who wouldn't answer back, who would give him the emotional need and support he craved. Then he'd go out into the world the next day, leaving me behind with my bruised ego, my sense of fear, my failure.

I couldn't begin to tell you when it went wrong. He was like a disease that crept under my skin and I couldn't help getting contaminated. Ryan was like a drug, an intoxication, something that I had to have. Before that I had been happy in my life; when I met him I was ecstatic. Or so I thought. Funny how love can cloud your judgement.

CHAPTER SIXTEEN

'There's been another attack, boss.' Jordan looked up from his screen when Eden came into the office the next morning. 'A young woman in a car park. Christina Spencer.'

'Yes, Sean sent me a message yesterday.'

'Coincidence or linked, do you think?'

'If there's a link, we'll find it.' Eden gnawed on her bottom lip. 'But why pick such a crowded place?'

'It was 8 p.m. The multi-storey car park gives me the creeps at midday, never mind late at night,' said Amy, coming to the desk. 'There are so many hiding places.'

Eden glanced at Phil, who was sitting in his chair, going from side to side with his legs out straight. He was looking down the corridor as if he couldn't wait to escape.

'Phil, can you re-interview a witness please? An elderly couple think they were there when the attack happened. I'd like the details on my desk as soon as possible please.'

Eden had thought that he'd be pleased to get out of the office but a curt nod of the head was all she got. She watched as he hurled his cumbersome frame up out of his chair and held in a sigh. Talk about hard work.

Thirty minutes later, Eden knocked on the door at the address Jordan had given her from the call log. A woman answered and introduced herself as Christina's mum. Mrs Spencer showed her into the living room where a younger version of herself was sitting in an armchair, the television on.

'Hi, Christina,' Eden said. 'May I talk to you?'

Christina nodded. 'I don't think I have anything else to say though.' She looked up at Eden. 'I told the officer who interviewed me after it happened. I was attacked and, luckily, the bastard was disturbed before he did me any real harm.' She pointed to the bruising on her face. 'A small reminder, but I was very fortunate.'

Eden admired her attitude. She hoped it wasn't a front and that Christina wouldn't crumble after she'd left. She'd hate her to be looking over her shoulder all the time or be trapped in the house for fear of going out.

'I know you've already made a statement so I don't want to go through the attack with you again,' said Eden. 'I have everything I need in here. What I wonder is if you've remembered anything else since Saturday night? I often ask people to go through as many of the five senses as they can. So, for instance, can you remember anything else that you heard or smelt, or even felt?'

Christina looked blank for a moment and then seemed to understand what Eden meant.

'I could smell his aftershave. I can still smell it in my car. It has a woody tang but I don't have a clue what it is. I could smell leather too – from his gloves as they covered my mouth.'

'Well done,' Eden encouraged. 'Did he say anything to you?'

Christina shook her head.

'Did you notice anything unusual about him?'

'I don't think so. He was mostly covered up.'

'What about facial scars? The colour of his eyes?'

She shook her head. 'I'm sorry.'

Eden reached across for Christina's hand and gave it a quick squeeze. 'You're doing great. Sometimes this exercise makes you focus more on things that were around you rather than the attack itself.' She stood up and put her notebook in her pocket.

Mrs Spencer, who had been sitting quietly until then, burst into tears. Christina went across to her immediately.

'Don't cry, Mum.' She put an arm round her shoulder. 'You're supposed to be looking after me, not the other way around. And you know us Spencer women are a strong breed. I won't let it get to me.'

Eden left the women to it. It made her all the more determined to get the man who had attacked Christina, and possibly the other women, off the streets of Stockleigh.

CHAPTER SEVENTEEN

Phil sat in the living room of Mr and Mrs Reynolds' bungalow. It was a pleasant room with a large bay window but it was crammed with bric-a-brac. All around him were ornaments and pictures in frames and collections of, well, stuff. He perched uncomfortably in a rocking chair, the only chair that was clear of anything on its cushion.

He tried not to look bored as he listened to the couple he'd gone to re-interview.

'I haven't been able to get the scream out of my head since I heard it,' said Stanley Reynolds, a man in his late seventies, with bushy eyebrows and a large belly. Stanley's wife was about the same age, with short grey hair, her face subtly made-up, complimenting her maturity. Phil guessed they had made a handsome couple when they were younger, especially when his eyes flew over some of the many photos.

'We'd just been out for coffee and cake – that's me and my wife, Marian – to celebrate a friend's seventieth birthday,' he continued. 'We don't get out much nowadays, what with my arthritis, and Marian's sciatica playing up all the time, but on special occasions we always try to make an effort.'

Phil coughed, hoping the old man would hurry up. It was nearing lunchtime, and he was only working until 1 p.m. There was no way he was running over if he could help it.

'It took us ages to find a parking space as near to the ground floor as possible, driving round and round until a spot came up.

Finally, we were lucky to nab one on the second floor. My eyesight isn't the best nowadays either but I can still manage to squeeze the car into the tightest of spaces.' His voice was full of pride as he puffed out his chest.

'He doesn't want to hear every detail, Stanley,' said Marian as she rolled her eyes.

Phil smiled his gratitude while silently thanking her, his mind already on the 1.30 p.m. horse race he was aiming to bet on.

'Anyway,' Stanley sat forward a little to continue his tale, 'we were walking back to the car, chatting about what a great night we'd had, when we heard a scream, didn't we, Marian?' He turned to look at his wife.

'That's right.' Marian took over the story. 'At first we assumed it was someone messing about, and we thought nothing of it, but when we heard it again, Stanley and I walked back to see what was going on.'

'A man ran past us,' said Stanley, 'and when we got nearer to where we thought the scream had come from, we saw a woman get out of the back of her car and scramble into the driver's seat. She was crying quite loudly. I knocked on the window and asked her if she wanted help, but she shook her head. And then she just drove off.'

Marian looked at Phil, teary eyed. His gaze tried not to stray to the deluge of photos framed on the wall by his side. If it did, he knew he'd never get out. He had a feeling these two would want to tell him everything about each family occasion.

'Were we there when it happened?' she asked.

Phil nodded and got out his notebook. 'Did you see what the attacker looked like? Can you describe him at all?'

'He was quite small, I thought,' said Stanley. 'What would you say, Marian?'

'I'd say he was quite tall, really, Stan. We're both smaller than we used to be and he was taller than us.'

'I suppose so. And he had a black woollen hat on, so we couldn't see his hair, and a scarf covering his mouth.'

'What else was he wearing? Any distinctive clothing or colours you remember?'

Stanley paused before shaking his head. 'Not that I can recall.'

Marian shook her head. 'I can't remember anything either. All I can see is dark. A dark jacket and trousers, dark boots and hat. We're not being any use whatsoever, are we?' she asked dejectedly.

'Anything might help us, Mrs Reynolds. Did you see where he went? Did he get into another car or was he on foot?'

'Well, we only saw him fleetingly before he got into a taxi.'

Phil looked up. 'I thought you were on the second floor.'

'We were, but you can see down between the barriers. He got into a taxi and it drove off.'

Phil looked up. He'd seen this in the statement and thought the Reynolds' had been confused. 'You're sure it was a taxi?'

'I'm certain.'

'Did you see which firm it was?'

'Yes, EveryDay Taxis. We use them quite a lot. They aren't the best for tidiness but they are cheap for fares.'

Phil noted it down. It was over in the north of Stockleigh, in Harrington, over by the bypass.

'I still can't get that scream out of my head,' said Mr Reynolds. 'Was the woman hurt badly?'

'Please don't feel too bad about it.' Phil's hard demeanour dropped a little. 'It's looking likely that he panicked when he saw you two. I think you saved that girl from a much worse attack.'

The smiles lit up their faces.

As Phil got up to leave, he was smiling too. He'd got the first lead on the case. Someone must have picked up the attacker and driven him somewhere. But first the 1.30 p.m. race was beckoning him. If he was quick, he would just about make it.

CHAPTER EIGHTEEN

Late that same afternoon, Tanya walked to the shops on Vincent Square. The cold wind was welcoming – she needed some fresh air. The refuge always made her feel claustrophobic, with all its rules and regulations, its self-help happy-clappy nonsense. And that woman, Marsha, was doing her head in. She hadn't stopped crying since she'd got there. Tanya was through with giving her sympathy now.

On her way back, she turned into Harold Street and a shadow crossed her, making her jump.

'Vic!'

He took her by the hand and they stopped, hidden by the back of the bus shelter.

'What are you doing!' she cried.

'I don't want to be seen with you beforehand, do I?' He grinned as he pressed his body to hers. 'Have you missed me?'

Tanya gazed at the man she had loved for most of her life. He'd changed so much since they had first met in their teens. Their lifestyle had taken its toll: his face was drawn, his skin had a greyish tint and there were dark rings underneath his brown eyes, but still she found him irresistible because she could see past that. She remembered how he used to be.

He was taller than her by a good few inches, protective of her when they were out. Always an arm around her shoulders, or his hand in hers, squeezing her fingers hard if she so much as glanced at another man. They belonged to each other, despite not being good for each other at all. Vic had a hold on her that she despised, yet she ached for him when he wasn't around.

As his lips found hers, Tanya tried to resist but found herself melting into his embrace. She couldn't help it. She *had* missed him. She ran her fingers through his hair and pulled him as close as she could. Then she stopped.

'You shouldn't be here,' she told him.

'I just wanted to see you. There's no law against that, is there?' He went to kiss her again but she stepped away.

'I have to go.'

But Vic followed. She could almost feel him behind her, ready to put his hands on her. Scared of what he would do, she scurried along.

At the door to the refuge, she stopped and looked behind her again. He was a few feet away. But as soon as she had gained access by pressing buttons on the lock, he flew at her and pushed her inside the property. She landed on the floor in the hallway. He pulled her up by her hair and slammed her into the wall.

'Leave me alone,' she screamed, hoping to alert someone.

Lisa came through from the kitchen. She gasped as she saw Vic with his hands around Tanya's neck.

'Get off her,' she cried, stepping nearer to the alarm.

'Piss off,' Vic said without taking his eyes off Tanya.

'Ow! You're hurting me!'

Three women from the lounge came rushing out to see what was going on. They stood rooted in the doorway.

'I want you to leave.' Lisa gingerly took another step forward. 'You have no right to be in here.'

'Oh, I'm going all right, but she's coming with me.' Vic turned his face to her sharply before looking back at Tanya.

'She doesn't belong to you,' said Andrea, one of the women still standing in the doorway. 'She isn't a piece of property.'

'Mind your own fucking business.' Vic released Tanya, pushed her to the floor and bent down to whisper something in her ear before walking off.

As soon as he was outside, Lisa closed the door and then knelt down beside Tanya. Her face was red, marks already appearing on her neck where Vic had dug his fingers in.

'Did you let him in?' Lisa's tone was accusatory.

'No! I didn't know he was there. I – I was coming back from the shops, and as soon as I opened the door, he ran up the path and pushed his way in.' Tanya put her own hand where Vic's had been at her neck and gasped for air again. 'I thought he was going to kill me. I'm sorry,' she said, bursting into tears.

Lisa shook her head in disbelief. 'I thought he might come after you, but I didn't think he'd get in.'

Andrea spoke again. 'I thought this was supposed to be a safe house.' She moved into the hall now that the danger had passed. 'I gave up everything to come here. If my Derek finds me and can get in that easily, then I'll probably be a goner before you can get help.'

'Can someone really get in that easy?' Theresa, the latest resident, seemed to pale at the thought.

Lisa held up a hand. 'Look, ladies, we do everything we can to keep this a safe space but there is always a danger that one of you will be followed back and everyone needs to be mindful of that.'

'Well, that's not gonna help us if my old man comes in here with a knife.' Andrea drew up her sleeve to reveal a deep scar, several inches in length. 'He did that in the blink of an eye.'

'Please try not to panic. These things happen occasionally, but one thing we have here is we look after one another.' Lisa looked around at the sea of anxious faces. 'I think tea would be a good idea? Shirley?' She looked at one of the long-term volunteers for help.

Shirley came towards them and took Tanya's arm. 'Sure thing. Come on, love.'

Carla came rushing in. 'Is everyone okay?' she addressed the room. 'Sorry, I didn't hear anything. Maria came in to tell me. Did someone get in?'

'Tanya's fella,' said Andrea, folding her arms and tutting loudly. 'I hope no one else gets—'

'No one else *will* get in,' said Lisa.

'How sure of that can you be?'

Tanya saw the look between Carla and Lisa. No one could say that anyone was safe, could they? Which meant Vic could just as easily get in again.

A smile played on her lips. Perfect.

CHAPTER NINETEEN

After taking a call from Phil, Eden drove over to EveryDay Taxis. Despite him being all pleased with himself that he had found a lead, she wasn't hanging around waiting for him to have time to visit. Besides, with Sean overseeing Phil's return to work, she was conscious that he'd been sent to her to do mostly desk duties until he was back to full-time hours again.

The taxi base was on an industrial estate and it took her a few minutes to find it due to it being pushed into the smallest of spaces at the end of a long road of offices and storage facilities. If she had to bet on it, she would guess it was the office that had the lowest rent.

She pushed heavily on a stiff door to open it and entered a dark reception area where a woman sat behind a desk surrounded by piles of paperwork. It was so untidy that Eden wondered if the receptionist could ever know what was where. A coffee machine sat on a small table to her right, along with a well-fingered magazine and a bin full of wrappers and plastic cups. Dirty spoons sat in a saucer.

'Morning, are you the owner?' Eden held up her warrant card.

'No, I only work here part-time and I'll be retiring soon thankfully. That will be Mr Minton. Ray?' the woman shouted over her shoulder.

'What's up now, Doreen?' a voice shouted back.

'The police are here to see you.'

Eden heard a chair scraping across the floor, and a middle-aged man with thick-rimmed glasses appeared in the doorway of a room at the back.

'Come on through, love.' He beckoned to her with his hand.

Eden held her tongue as Doreen lifted up the counter and she walked across the office. In the room, the man was now sitting behind a desk. Well at least she thought it was a desk. It could have been a kitchen table. There were piles of paperwork on here too: tickets, invoices and black box files dated 2007 onwards were stacked precariously on the corner.

'What can I do for you, love?' he asked.

'Well you can stop calling me *love* for starters. Detective Sergeant will do.' She smiled at him sarcastically. 'I need to know which of your drivers picked up a fare from the multi-storey car park at twenty past eight last night.'

'Let me see.' He pressed the mouse to wake up his computer and clicked a few times. 'Here we are, a list of last night's jobs. Twenty past eight, you say? That would be Scott Daniels.'

'Is he here yet? Can I have a word?'

Ray glanced at the clock on the wall. 'He's due on shift in the next ten minutes, which means you might catch him in the canteen. What's he been up to?'

Eden told him what she could about the assault the night before. 'A witness saw a man getting into one of your taxis,' she told him.

Ray pointed through a window. 'There's a Portakabin out the back. You'll find him in there.'

Eden crossed the yard, slaloming through several cars, and pushed on the door to the Portakabin. Inside were four men and a woman, sitting on two old battered settees. A coffee table in the middle was littered with plastic containers, dirty mugs and a few car magazines. The air was musty; she wasn't sure if it was from the room or its occupants. She sniggered when she thought of Ray describing it as a canteen.

'Which one of you is Scott Daniels?' Eden flashed her warrant card as she stepped into the centre of the cabin, watching where she put her feet as her toe made contact with a rogue mug.

'That will be me, officer.' A man stood up to his full height. His dark hair was stylishly messy, kinking up at the neck of his shirt, which was covered by a thick-knitted jumper and a ribbed gilet. He thrust his hands into its pockets and smiled, blue eyes twinkling at her. 'What can I do for you?'

'A word, please?' Eden smiled before nodding in the direction of the door.

'You been a naughty boy already, Scott?' Another of the men slapped his backside as he passed. There were a few jeers as they went outside.

An articulated lorry thundered past them, and Eden waited for it to move away a little before she began to speak. 'Your boss says you picked up a fare at twenty past eight from outside the multi-storey on Market Street last night?' She raised her voice to be heard as she looked up at him.

Scott nodded. 'I picked up a lot of fares last night. Can you give me anything else?'

'It would have been a male, dressed in dark clothing. He must have flagged you down?'

'Ah, yes, the small dude with the beady eyes. He only wanted to go round the corner, back to the high street. I told him I'd charge a minimum fare, and he didn't seem bothered by it.'

'Where exactly did you drop him off?' Eden took out her notepad and jotted down the details.

'What's this to do with?' Scott asked.

'A woman was attacked last night.'

His eyes widened. 'And you think he was your man?'

'I need to rule him out regardless. The attack happened just before you picked him up. Can you remember what he looked like?'

'I didn't really take that much notice of him, sorry. I pick up so many people, and they're mostly sitting behind me.'

'And where did you say you dropped him off?' Eden tipped her ear towards him as another lorry went past.

'At The Snooker Club, halfway down the high street. You know it?'

She nodded. 'Did you see him go inside the building?'

'No. Like I said, I was on to my next call by then.' Scott raised his hands up to his sides and then dropped them again in resignation. 'Sorry, I feel useless but I didn't think anything of the fare at the time. People like that aren't very memorable. It's the ones that are abusive or throw up on the back seat or do a runner that I remember the most.'

Eden could empathise. It sounded very similar to her job at times. She handed the driver her card. 'If you do recall anything else, can you let me know, please?'

'Sure thing.'

Eden left the offices of EveryDay Taxis after making a note to ask one of her team to search out the CCTV footage that showed their attacker and where he'd gone once he'd been dropped off. The Snooker Club was less than a minute's walk if you cut through the side of the multi-storey car park. Flagging down a passing taxi meant someone wanted to make a quick getaway.

CHAPTER TWENTY

After the attack on Tanya, it had taken a while for the women in the refuge to settle. Once things were reasonably normal again, Carla found herself in the kitchen with Lisa.

'It brings back bad memories, doesn't it?' said Lisa. 'When something like that happens. Makes you feel vulnerable again.'

Carla nodded. She and Lisa had confided in each other as their work relationship had grown into friendship. Both women knew each other's background but each recognised that not everything had been shared. Some things were too painful to talk about, and others were too private to share.

'I hope this isn't the start of attacks on the refuge,' Lisa added. 'Once a man finds a woman here, sometimes he can cause a disturbance for several nights – often several weeks.'

Carla shuddered. 'Perhaps it will die down now he's realised he can't get in to her so easily.'

'He did get in easily!' Lisa retorted.

'You know what I mean. Maybe now he's seen her, he might give up. I hate to say this as we've both been through similar things, but sometimes it's the chase, isn't it?'

'I suppose.' Lisa sighed. 'Having seen Vic White here several times now, I wondered if this was the time he would give up.'

'But it seems he's going to try and inflict maximum pain to ensure Tanya never disobeys him again.'

'It's all mind control with them, the cowards.' Lisa couldn't keep the sharp tone from her voice. 'Most of the time, the front door and the alarm system are a good deterrent. But sometimes it isn't enough. Just before you started to work here last year, I had a man stab his partner on the steps outside.'

'What?' Carla looked at her in horror then reached for Lisa's hand.

'The woman – Shelley – died the following day. It had a big impact on the women in the house. The residents on the street, who were always trying to get the refuge closed down anyway, took a long time to stop complaining about us. Even more, it had a massive effect on me. I should have saved her.'

'You can't save everyone! Not from something like that.'

Lisa held up a hand. 'I know. Eden mentioned that on average people get attacked fifty times before they report their first incidence of domestic abuse. I went through a down patch but I got out of it with the help of some very kind souls. People like Eden and Josie, and some of the mothers from SWAP got me through.'

Carla went to speak, then changed her mind. But Lisa had noticed.

'What is it?' she asked.

'Do you ever wonder if your husband will find you again?'

Lisa nodded. 'All the time. I know he moved out of the area, but I never stop looking over my shoulder for him when I'm out and about. It's like living with a ghost, isn't it?'

Carla nodded. 'Does he know you're here?'

'Yes, I think so. But he seems to have moved on now. I know some other unfortunate woman might be at his beck and call. I just hope he met his match and someone gave him what I couldn't. In the form of a backhander.'

Carla smiled, but it didn't reach her eyes. She knew what it was like to want to retaliate but thinking better of it because the punishment afterwards would be too much to bear.

'How about you?' asked Lisa. 'I can tell you're worried about something. You haven't been yourself for a few weeks.'

Carla wondered whether to share her concerns, despite her preference for secrecy. But while Lisa was a work colleague, she was also a friend, and someone who could understand her fear.

'Ryan's recently got out of prison. I'm afraid he'll come after me.'

Lisa pressed a hand to her mouth. 'Does he know you're here?'

Carla thought back to the day in the cemetery when the sound of his voice had sent chills through her body. 'I'm not sure, but I do know wherever I've moved to during these last nine years he's found me. I'm on tenterhooks he'll come creeping out of somewhere, but what else can I do but live my life?'

'Maybe he won't find you again. It might have been a game he played to scare you while he was in prison. Now he's out, he might go straight.'

Carla raised her eyebrows. 'You really think that?'

'Just trying to make you feel better.' Lisa reached across and squeezed Carla's hand. 'You know any time you feel in danger, there's a room for you here. I don't care if I spend months on the sofa, I'm not sure what I would do if he got to you and I could have done something to prevent it.'

'He said he would always find me, no matter where I went. And then he told me he would beat me to a pulp, take me to the nearest quarry and bury me so that no one would ever find me.'

'Oh, Carla. What a bastard.'

No, what a bastard he was to do what he did to Chloe. That was what she wanted to say. But she had said that once and look at the trouble it had landed her in. She changed the subject. Lisa didn't have to know everything.

'Will Tanya be okay?' she asked.

'I hope so.' Lisa glanced at her watch and got to her feet, sweeping both mugs up in one go. 'I'll always find room for her too. I can't let anyone down, no matter how many times they leave and come back. She's a nice woman, underneath, I think, if only she could escape his clutches.'

As she sat with her thoughts, Carla hoped nothing would happen to Tanya, but she knew even if she did get free of her husband, it wouldn't stop the memories flooding back – again and again. Every time she heard a story on the news or in real life about domestic abuse, things that Ryan had done to her came back into her mind. No matter how hard she pushed them away.

What would happen if Ryan turned up here and came after her? She would hate to have it on her conscience if he attacked any of the women to get to her. And she didn't think she'd be strong enough to continue working at the refuge. It would be too painful.

More importantly, he'd threatened to kill her when he did catch up with her. Vic getting into the refuge today had shown her just how vulnerable she was too.

CHAPTER TWENTY-ONE

Eden was preparing that evening's food while going over everything that had happened during the day. Apart from the teenage girls who'd been set upon last year before the trial of sixteen-year-old Deanna Barker, she had never dealt with a case where three women were attacked in one week. Was it the same person? The cases were different in one sense – one woman raped, one badly beaten and one attacked – but did it all equal the same thing? If the attacker hadn't been interrupted, or had been given the opportunity, would he have gone on to sexually assault Alice Clough and Christina Spencer as well? And was Becky Fielding's attack a fortnight ago his first attempt? Were there four victims in total?

There had to be some link they were missing. Hopefully, as evidence came in and forensics were processed, they could find something overlapping. At the moment, all they had to go on was that all the victims were young females out alone at night.

Eden had also been told about Vic White turning up at The Willows refuge. She couldn't believe that he'd do that – well she could, but didn't want to. He was such a bully. All the women in the refuge would be worried now, and she couldn't blame them. She hoped Tanya had listened to her advice before running back to him like she usually did.

Now it was just after 6 p.m. Joe was coming over straight from work and Casey was due in any moment after having netball practice after school. All their family had been good at games, with their long legs and thin statures. Casey was talented at most sports, but Jess wasn't interested in anything sporty, which surprised Eden. Her niece had that competitive streak about her, and it was a pity that she couldn't use it to let off some steam. Laura was always worrying about her, unlike with Sarah. Her eldest niece was a darling.

Eden was halfway through cooking the mince when she heard the front door open. Casey came into the kitchen like a whirlwind, seeming to make as much noise as she could. She pulled her earplugs out as she got to Eden.

'Hi, Mum,' she said. 'What's for tea?'

'Spag bol. That okay for you?' Eden knew it would be. Over the last few months, Casey had turned into a fussy eater but pasta was her favourite food.

'Perfect. Is Joe coming over?'

'Yes, about seven.'

'So we're all eating at seven, or can I have mine before?'

'You can have yours before.' Eden gave the mince another stir. 'It'll be ready in about half an hour.'

'Great! That will give you and Joe time to be *alone*.'

The emphasis on that last word made Eden smile. Casey never missed a trick.

'What's that supposed to mean?' she asked.

'He doesn't seem to be coming round as much lately. And it's not like him to miss out on Sunday lunch at Laura's, is it?'

'You'd make a great copper with this,' she said, putting a finger on the end of Casey's nose. 'When you get to my age, you'll realise that sometimes love isn't as straightforward as you'd like it to be.'

'But if you tried harder—'

'Since when did you give me advice on my love life?' Eden cried. 'It should be the other way around.'

'Oh please.' A raised palm. 'I'm only sixteen. I'm not interested in boys yet.'

Eden almost snorted at the comment.

'Just kidding!'

Eden gave her a quick hug. 'As long as you find someone to love you when you're old and grey, that's the most important thing.'

There was a pause. 'Did you ever think that you and Dad wouldn't be married when you were old and grey, Mum?'

'No one really knows if forever means forever, darling.'

'But you miss him, right?'

Eden turned the question around so that she didn't have to answer it. 'Do you?'

'Yes, but I also think he's a bastard for walking out on us.'

'Language, Casey!'

'Sorry.' Casey blushed a little. 'I just wish I could see him and tell him how much I hate him.'

'No, you don't.'

Casey raised her eyebrows, showing Eden a flicker of anger that she knew people had seen in her own eyes many times. 'Do you want to bet?'

Eden changed the subject. 'Do you want to get out some garlic bread for me? I think there might be a couple of slices of that cheap but gorgeous gooey stuff.'

Hearing a car pull up outside, Eden's stomach lurched. Joe waved as he let himself in the front door.

'Hi.' He came through to the kitchen, waggling a bottle of wine about in his hand. 'Thought you might like this if we're in need of a chat.'

'Oooh.' Casey was suddenly all ears. 'On second thoughts, I might be able to join you for something to eat after all.'

'Never you mind, lady,' said Eden. 'Up you go and get changed.'

Once Casey had left them alone together, they smiled at each other then stood looking at one another, each unsure of the other and what to do next. Finally, Joe took off his coat and went to hang it up in the hallway, and Eden opened the wine.

Try as she might to smile and laugh and joke and chat with him, to Eden it all seemed so false. She could tell by his demeanour that he felt the same way but, in the end, she left it up to him to start the conversation.

'Everything okay?' Joe asked as he watched her playing with the spaghetti.

Eden looked up and smiled. 'Yes, fine thanks. It's just this case at work, that's all.'

'If it isn't this case, it's the one before or the one after.' He put down his fork. 'People told me being in a relationship with a copper would mean I'd always come second. I should have listened.'

'Meaning what exactly?' Eden's tone was sharper than she had intended.

'Your mind is always on the job, the case you're working on, regardless of whether it is or not. It's just an excuse, isn't it?'

'Oh, so that's what this is all about.' Eden put down her fork and slid her plate away from her. She hadn't been hungry when she came in, and now she had lost her appetite completely. 'Me and you time.'

'Well we hardly get any now, do we?' Joe sulked.

Eden sighed. It was about the fifth time Joe had brought her job into the equation, saying that she put it before him. The truth was he was probably right. But then again, she and Danny might not have lasted as long if that were the case. Danny had hardly ever complained that she was out of the house for long hours, just accepted it was part of the job.

'I don't want to have this conversation again,' she told him.

'Neither do I,' said Joe. 'But it's been playing on my mind for weeks now and, well, maybe we should take a break. Cool off for a while and see what happens.'

'You think time away will improve anything?' Eden gave him a weak smile, not wanting to hurt his feelings by saying that it was probably for the best.

Joe shrugged. 'Yes. No. I don't know. But I do know that I can't keep doing this. You. . . you're still in love with him, aren't you?'

Eden looked at him sharply. 'No, I don't think I am,' she replied.

Joe huffed. 'Even the way you reacted shows me that you are.' He reached across the table for her hand. 'It's okay, I get that you haven't had closure. But I need you to move on, and if you won't commit to me after nearly a year, then I'm not sure you'll ever commit to me.'

Eden opened her mouth to speak but he urged her to stay quiet as he continued.

'It's heartbreaking because I love you so much. But I won't play second fiddle to anyone, least of all someone who walked out on you and Casey.'

Eden could feel her skin heating up. Joe was right about some things but not everything. For a moment, she sat in the silence that had dropped. Then she looked from behind her fringe at the face she'd woken up to on a regular basis for the past twelve months.

'Do you want to cool off for a while?' she asked him.

He pushed the question back to her. 'Do you?'

She couldn't answer because she wasn't sure how to reply. But to Joe, saying nothing spoke volumes. He stood up and reached for his coat.

'I can't do this any more,' he said as he pushed his arms through the sleeves. 'It's hurting you and it's hurting me but for very different reasons.'

'Wait, Joe!' He was almost at the front door before she caught up with him. 'Don't go. Let's sort this out.'

She'd surprised herself the minute she had said it. Was her heart telling her that she did want to make things work with Joe, or did she feel sorry for the pain she was causing him?

Either way, it wasn't enough to stop him leaving.

'I'll call you,' he told her. 'Perhaps in a week or so. See how you're doing.'

He couldn't look at her as he left the house. She wondered if he was crying. She was sure she'd seen his eyes watering.

Eden ran a hand through her hair before bursting into tears. A break from Joe might not be a bad thing, to see if she could put her feelings into perspective. Because right at that moment, she couldn't decide. Was it him? Or could she really still be in love with Danny?

CHAPTER TWENTY-TWO

Carla parked the car and switched off the engine. She had just made it in time to her doctor's surgery. She'd had a recent flare-up of eczema that she hadn't been able to control so needed a prescription for her usual cream. The traffic had been terrible – trust her to make an appointment during the morning rush hour.

She got out of the car and ran across the road, dashing into the reception with a minute to spare.

The waiting room was full, the smell of damp coats and hair filling the room, but there were two chairs free. She sat down next to a woman who had a young girl sitting on her knee. The girl wore her school uniform underneath her coat, her cheeks red and blotchy. Her worried mum was trying to console her.

'We'll be going through in a minute,' she soothed, wiping a hand over her forehead. 'You're very hot.'

Carla threw her a sympathetic look, a lump forming in her throat. Memories of Chloe came rushing forward so fast that she felt breathless. She recalled when she had sat with Chloe in a waiting room when her daughter had been running a fever. It had turned out to be chickenpox. Ryan had gone mad, at first blaming her for taking Chloe to school. At the time, chickenpox had been doing the rounds in Chloe's class. Carla had thought that Chloe had missed that bout, but still, she couldn't keep her from attending school.

Chloe had come down with flu-like symptoms so it was hard to see what was really wrong with her until the morning she awoke covered in blisters. It had been dreadful to see her itch her way through it. The scabs had been everywhere.

Carla looked at the little girl beside her. She would give anything to be able to turn back the clock. She missed Chloe more and more each year.

'Carla Gregory?' someone called.

Ten minutes later, she was out with a prescription. She fastened up her coat against the elements and left the surgery. It was pouring down outside so she dashed across to her car. By the time she'd got inside, she was soaking. Her hair hung down, her fringe dripping. She groaned as she caught her bedraggled reflection in the mirror.

She switched on the engine. As the wiper came on automatically and cleared the windscreen, a man walked past her car. His head was tucked in against the rain, his black coat buttoned up.

It was Ryan.

Carla let out a sob and slid down further into her seat, flipping the lock on the door. It wasn't until he was fully out of view of her side mirror that she realised it hadn't been him. Her imagination was playing tricks with her.

She let go of the breath she was holding and gave a huge sigh. But tears fell anyway. In that split second, all her fear had come back. Damn Vic White for unsettling her. She could never stop looking over her shoulder because she knew Ryan was out there and could get to her whenever he wanted.

She wondered what was the better option. Waiting for him to find her, to show himself, or getting it over and done with. She felt trapped. Moving around hadn't worked, and in that moment she wondered if there was any point in trying again.

NINETEEN YEARS AGO

Over the years, once we were married, Ryan became so controlling. He'd lose his temper constantly, shouting and complaining at the slightest thing. Once he'd calmed down, he'd be so loving, and I'd be lured back into a false sense of security before it happened again.

He gave me money every week, which I had to manage and account for. It wasn't so much the control; I could cope with that. It was the verbal abuse that ground me down. Being told you're useless at everything you do, well, eventually you start believing it. I burn the toast slightly – I'm a useless cook. Being told I looked at someone the wrong way when he took me out – I'm a slag. Being found drinking a cup of coffee and reading a magazine – I was a slob. Being told this by someone who was seething with rage and standing an inch from my face at the time, I didn't really know what to do.

You see, people like Ryan, they get under your skin. You don't see it coming. They manipulate you, they smother you with love and affection, making out you're the only thing that matters in their lives, and by the time you realise who they really are, it's too late.

They have you.

They have taken your life, your friends and your support system are gone. They grind you down until you have no self-esteem, nothing to get back up from. And the worst feeling of all is that you let them do it.

And that's when the acceptance sets in. The feeling that you have to put up with it because you are worthless. Ryan kept on saying that no one else would want me. My friends were few and far between as I didn't get to see them much, if at all. I hardly ever saw my parents, as Ryan would cause a fuss if I arranged it without checking with him first or cry off sick so that I would stay home with him. I lost count of how many times he said I was a useless piece of shit.

And when you start believing that – because if you are ever in this position, eventually you *will* believe it – then he has you. It's a vicious cycle. It doesn't have to be about violence. It can be about power, taking away your emotional well-being, your financial freedom, your independence.

The control was one thing and it crept in slowly, even though I could feel it there in the background, tensing myself up for the onslaught that was inevitable. Brick by brick, the wall went up around us – and I couldn't penetrate it to knock it down again.

It wasn't long into the honeymoon that the cracks started to appear: the moment I told him I was unwell and I didn't think it was because we'd had some dodgy food in the Caribbean. The stomach bug turned out to be morning sickness. And that's when all my troubles really began. Because Ryan always wanted to be the centre of attention.

For me, it was too late. I was already under his spell. No one knew what was going on behind closed doors. To the outside world, I was just a person who got on with life and enjoyed it. Inside those four walls I was a totally different me. I was trapped. The minute the ring went on my finger, there was no looking back. But getting married wasn't the defining thing for me in our relationship. That would be the first punch.

CHAPTER TWENTY-THREE

Eden scrunched up the wrapper from a chocolate biscuit and wiped her hands of crumbs. She glanced at her team, who were all sitting at the desks around her. 'Okay, so far what do we have on the attacks?'

Jordan and Amy automatically looked up, eager to get going with things. Phil busied himself popping a mint into his mouth. He'd only come in a few minutes ago and looked as if he'd got up less than ten minutes earlier and not had a shower or taken an iron to his clothes. There was a stain on his tie and last night's stubble on his chin, which was only attractive on someone who looked after himself. Eden noticed his eyes were a little bloodshot when he finally gave her his attention.

'Phil, are you with us?' she asked him.

'Oh, yeah, sorry.' He nodded, arms folded, now sitting back in his chair.

'How far have you got with checking CCTV footage, Amy?'

'I've checked all through when the taxi driver says he dropped off our attacker on the high street but I can't find him anywhere.'

'You mean he didn't go into The Snooker Club?' Eden looked puzzled. 'I thought that was where he was heading. I wonder if that was a decoy?'

'No.' Amy shook her head. 'I mean, I can't find sight of his taxi dropping off anyone in the street at that time. I've looked through everything half an hour each side of the time and there's nothing.'

Eden frowned. 'Where does he drop him off then?'

'Well that's the thing. The next time that particular taxi is seen in the street pulling up at the rank is forty minutes later.'

'Okay, Phil, can you take over from Amy and check the camera footage from the multi-storey car park please? We need to go back to where the attacker was picked up from.'

Phil's sigh could be heard all through the office. 'I thought I'd be coming out with you this morning,' he said.

'Not today. I need someone to go through the footage.'

'Amy can do it.'

'Right. Because I haven't got a gazillion other things to be dealing with.' Amy slammed her pen on the desk. 'There is no "I" in team, Phil.'

'Are you saying that I'm not a team player?' Phil snapped.

Amy raised her eyebrows and was just about to reply when Eden shook her head as she caught her eye.

'Of course Amy *can* do it,' said Eden, 'but I have something else for her to do this morning. Besides, I'm asking you to do it. You know how soul-destroying looking through footage hour after hour can be. It's a mental and physical challenge. One I'm sure you're up to though.' She looked at him until he dropped his eyes. Another loud sigh followed.

Eden continued with the meeting. Only two and a half more weeks.

'Phil whiffs a bit, doesn't he?' Jordan said as they got into the pool car to drive over to EveryDay Taxis.

'You've noticed too?' Eden wrinkled up her nose. 'At least he's not with us for much longer.'

'I suppose, if it wasn't for the chip on his shoulder, he'd be quite a nice bloke.'

Eden smiled. Jordan was one of the most upbeat people she had ever come across. If something was getting him down, you might not notice. He always saw the positive in everything, which was a great outlook to have as a police officer.

'Considering he's getting on,' Jordan added, 'he makes a mean dash to the bookies when he leaves the office.'

'Ah. That's why he's so keen to leave dead on one o'clock.' Eden indicated to pull out of the yard. 'He won't be with us forever. And, love him or loathe him, everyone needs a second chance.'

'Oh, you and your second chances. Not everyone deserves one.'

Eden glanced at Jordan to see him smiling. What he said was true, but Eden was a firm believer in the philosophy that people can change. Not many of them did in her line of work, admittedly, but she was always ready to give someone a second chance. Only the once though. She might be nice and smiley most of the time, but she wouldn't allow people to take advantage of her good nature.

In the reception area of EveryDay Taxis, the same woman was sitting at the front desk. Eden wondered how she found it working predominately with men all day, every day, and possibly through the night. Did she have a laugh and a joke at their inevitable banter, or did they, like her team, look up to her as a senior figure, someone who would care for them, someone they could turn to for help? She seemed to be in her late fifties, although, with hard life written all over her face, she might have been younger.

She smiled at Eden. 'You want the boss again?' she asked, jerking a thumb over her shoulder. 'He's just arrived. Do you want a cuppa? I'm making him one.'

'No, thanks, Doreen,' said Eden. 'DC Ashcroft, my colleague, would like to have a chat with any of the drivers here. Is that okay?'

Doreen nodded and pointed to a door. 'Through there, first Portakabin on the left. It's rush hour for us so there might not be too many of them around.'

As Jordan went outside, Eden followed Doreen through the tiny reception area.

'Police again, Ray,' said Doreen, knocking on the door of his office to get his attention.

Eden hid a smirk as she watched him scowl before he put on a plastic smile.

'What can I do for you again, Sergeant?' he asked. 'Have your lot not heard of picking up the phone or emailing?'

'Email?' Eden scoffed. 'I'm surprised you have a system that will allow that. Your computers are so old.'

Eden noticed that this time there was no chair pointed at. It was clear that her visiting twice in such a short space of time was a nuisance for him.

'Scott Daniels. How long has he worked for you?'

'Only a few weeks, why?'

'You know anything about his background?'

Ray shifted in his seat, skin reddening slightly. 'Not yet – should I?'

'How irresponsible.' Eden shook her head. 'Are you registered with the city council?'

'Yes, I'm all legal, if that's what you're asking.'

'And is he?'

Ray leaned back in his chair. 'Drivers, they come and go so frequently. I can't always keep on top of them.'

'So in the meantime you let anyone drive your taxis? That's a real smooth operation you have here.' Eden couldn't hide her distaste any longer. 'Do you have GPS in your cars? Or provide the drivers with phones with it installed?'

'No, but drivers are booted out if the Disclosure and Barring check comes back and I don't like it,' he insisted. 'All drivers need clean ones. I'm waiting for him to bring his in.'

'That would be reassuring to hear if you weren't allowing him to work while you waited on it.' Eden sat down across from him. 'In the meantime, your taxi drivers could be on the Sex Offenders Register and picking children up from schools. Your drivers could be thieves casing up properties to rob when they drop clients off at their homes. Your drivers could be—'

'Okay, okay.' Ray held up his hand for her to stop. 'I get the picture.'

'I don't think you do.' Eden leaned forward, resting an elbow on the desk and her chin in her hands. 'Because if I do checks and find out this firm is dodgy, I'll see to it that you're investigated – and closed down if necessary.'

'Wait – there's no need—'

'People are in enough danger each day without the risk of taking an unsafe car home.' She stared at him, enjoying his blush. 'So, Scott Daniels. What do you know about him?'

Ray glanced at her sheepishly before reaching among a pile of brown files. He pulled one out and opened it. 'Not much, I have to admit. I was a driver short as Charlie Dixon's done his back in so I took him on temporary to see what he was like.'

'Where does he live?'

Ray flicked through the paperwork. 'Sudbury Avenue, Warbury. Number forty-eight.'

Eden could see an upside-down image of Scott Daniels. She leaned over and tapped her finger on it. It was a photocopy of his driving licence.

'Can you do me a copy of this please?'

Ray gave the paper to her. 'Take this one. I won't be using him again if he's this much trouble.'

Back in her car, as she waited for Jordan to finish, Eden studied the image on the photocopy. Scott Daniels was just a regular-looking man, but there was something edgy about him – he obviously had some kind of charisma. It was a shame that the women who had been attacked hadn't seen the face of their assailant.

She started the engine as she saw Jordan walking towards her.

'Nothing doing out there, Sarge,' Jordan told her as he buckled up. 'Only two drivers in and neither has worked with Daniels for more than one shift. Neither of them had much to say about him. One of them said he felt he didn't trust him but that's only gut instinct and could be because I'm talking to him.'

'Well either way it will get them thinking about him when they do see him next. And that can't be a bad thing.' Eden gave the paper with Daniels' photo on it to Jordan.

'He looks familiar,' the DC said.

'Oh? Let's go see if he's at home.'

CHAPTER TWENTY-FOUR

Sudbury Avenue was a narrow road consisting mainly of terraced properties. The bins were out today, and Eden absent-mindedly wondered how the wagon would get down the narrow street to empty them all. After squeezing the Mini into a row of parked cars, they got out and she knocked at number forty-eight.

Scott Daniels frowned when he opened the door and saw them standing there.

'Hello again.' Eden flashed her warrant card. Jordan did the same behind her.

The door opened straight into a large open-plan room, a flight of stairs on a diagonal across its middle. The front of the room was empty bar a small dining table; the back of the room lived-in with a large three-seater settee, widescreen television and a coffee table with a mug on top.

'Do you live here alone, Scott?' she asked.

'This is my brother's house. He's working away so I'm staying here until I can get a place of my own. He's just split from his wife. She took most of the furniture, so I'm paying him rent. I guess it will come in handy.'

Eden nodded. 'We've discovered some discrepancies in the information you gave us the last time we spoke. I asked if you had picked up a fare at twenty past eight on Saturday just gone, and you told me a man had flagged you down and you'd taken him to The Snooker Club on Stockleigh High Street. Is that correct?'

Scott picked up the remote control and muted the sound on the television. 'Yes, but I was mistaken.'

'Sorry?'

'It wasn't me who picked him up. I was nowhere near the multi-storey car park. I collected someone from the car park outside the Old Sally pub on Butler Street, further up the road.'

'And why haven't you contacted us to let us know?'

'I was just about to. You beat me to it.'

Given her conversation with Ray Minton, Eden didn't believe him for a minute. 'Where did you drop off that fare?'

'He went to the train station, Station Road.'

'So you didn't drop anyone off by The Snooker Club?' Jordan checked.

'Yeah, I did but it was about an hour later.' He looked at him. 'Really sorry, I got my times mixed up. I'm new to the job.'

'I gathered,' said Eden. 'Ray, from EveryDay Taxis, said you'd only been working there for a few weeks?'

A dark look passed over Scott's face, recognition dawning that they had been to see his boss. Eden watched as he composed himself quickly and smiled.

'Yes, that's right. It's temporary, but I'm hoping to get taken on permanently soon.'

'Are you enjoying the job?' Eden queried, knowing full well that he wouldn't be going back to work at EveryDay Taxis.

Another smile and a nod. 'Too early to tell,' he said.

'And you're new to the area? What did you do before you came to Stockleigh?'

'Oh, I'm not new here. I was born and raised in Warbury.' He glanced at her briefly before looking at Jordan again. 'Your man here knows me from Manchester. You used to work there, didn't you?'

Jordan nodded. 'You used to work on MacDonald's building site.'

'Yeah, we were always getting our tools pinched. I remember seeing you a few times. Nothing came of it though.'

Eden saw Jordan pause and wondered what was going through his mind.

'So you've been working in Manchester for a few years now,' she said. 'Any particular reason you've come back to Stockleigh?'

'The build had finished so I decided to come home for a while.' Scott shrugged. 'Driving is something I'm doing until I can get fixed up with another building job.'

After a few more questions, they went on their way. Once in the car, Eden turned to Jordan.

'I left him thinking we were satisfied he was telling the truth about the night in question, but he wasn't, was he? For starters, the taxi log said it was him who picked up the fare.'

Jordan shook his head. 'His name is Aiden Daniels, not Scott.'

Eden frowned as he continued.

'He's assaulted a couple of ex-girlfriends over the years. If I remember rightly, though, only one was willing to file a domestic-abuse charge against him, which she later withdrew. A bit different from now with the CPS. At least if the woman changes her mind now we can still prosecute as long as we have evidence to back it up.'

'But why the different name?'

'I'm not sure. I didn't have any dealings with him, but he seemed extremely vicious by all accounts. I think he's been in Manchester for about five years.'

'Makes sense why we don't know him then. He's only been in Stockleigh for about a month.' Eden started the engine. 'Can you check him out once we get back to the station? I don't want to jump the gun but he knows more than he's letting on.'

CHAPTER TWENTY-FIVE

'Get anything more from Salford?' Eden asked Jordan later.

Jordan shook his head. 'The guy I need isn't in. I left a message for him to get back to me. But I did find out about a victim closer to home.' He pointed to his screen. 'Sylvia Latimer. According to our records, she's still in Stockleigh. Daniels assaulted her a few times but she wouldn't press charges. I believe one of her brothers put the boot in after his final attack on Sylvia.'

Eden raised her eyebrows. 'I do love it when someone gets a taste of their own medicine. Can you pass me her address? Maybe she can give us some idea of what we're dealing with.'

Jordan wrote down the details, tore the sheet off the notepad and handed it to her. He pressed a few keys on his keyboard and brought up a file. 'I also remembered why I know his name. Some women in an office near to the site he was working on complained he was leering at them through the windows. He was on scaffolding two floors up so could look over at them. He was all but touching himself apparently.'

'Ugh, what a creep.' Amy, who had her head down, shuddered.

'Thanks,' Eden said to Jordan. 'Can you check if we have any more cases connected in any way?'

'Sure will.'

Eden patted him on the shoulder as she passed him. The door was open to Sean's office so she went in. 'You busy?'

'There's a murder just come in. A teenager's been stabbed. He was in surgery but we've just heard he didn't make it.'

'Oh no. Anyone I know?'

'Paul Thistle. Lives on The Cavendales. I think he was mistaken for someone else, someone from the Hopwood Estate.'

'Ouch.'

'He wasn't a member of the family in question so at least there might not be any repercussions. Just a bloody big headache for us. What's up?'

'Well I was going to chat to you about work and say that Phil is a bit of a weirdo, but I guess now isn't the time.' She rolled her eyes anyway.

'He'll be out from under your feet soon.'

'I was always taught to respect my elders, but even I have to keep biting my tongue when I'm around him. I just want to tell him to do something.'

Sean smirked. 'Was there anything else?' Sean's eyes flitted to his computer screen and then back to her.

'I just wanted to keep you up to speed with what was happening on the case of the assaults and Scott Daniels. Also known as Aiden Daniels.' Eden told him what they had found out so far.

'So he has form?' Sean gnawed at his lip. 'Maybe that explains some of the attacks.'

'Usually men who are violent in relationships don't carry out attacks on other people.'

'Who knows what someone capable of that is thinking.'

'Well I'm going to see Sylvia Latimer, and I'm also going to pop in to see Josie Mellor to see if she knows of him. The fact that he's now denying picking up the alleged attacker is bugging me. Phil is checking out the CCTV footage.'

'Any connection between the women attacked so far?'

'Apart from all being around the same age?' She shook her head.

'What about the press? They playing nicely with you?'

'Yes. I'm not sure we can say too much yet as we have no evidence the attacks are linked. It's just a gut instinct.'

'That's always good to follow.'

Eden nodded. It had proved very useful for her in the past.

CHAPTER TWENTY-SIX

While Jordan continued to search out intel, Eden and Amy went to see Josie Mellor. The Mitchell Housing Association office was on the outskirts of the Mitchell Estate. Almost half of the properties were owner-occupied or belonged to the city council, and the rest were rented out by the association. These were the ones most likely to cause Eden and her team a fair amount of grief. Like any urban area, there was good and bad in every street behind closed doors.

The office itself was a single-storey building that had once been a small primary school. They were shown through to the back room where, after catching up with the staff for several minutes, Eden stopped at a desk.

Josie Mellor was talking to someone on the phone, her hands flapping around as she gave directions. 'No, you can't drive down Derek Avenue now – you have to go up! The times I've nearly been run over by a bus because I've looked the opposite way. I'm not sure I'll ever get used to it. Yes, we're still here and open until five. Yes, see you then. Bye.' She put down the phone and smiled, pushing her glasses up her nose and her hair behind her ears. 'Eden! Good to see you.' She pointed to a desk by her side. 'Pull those chairs over while I make coffee. Your usual?'

Eden smiled. 'You're a good one.'

While Josie was away, she sat looking around the office, twirling round in the chair. Amy was with one of the housing officers. Eden grinned, knowing she would be gleaning some good information if she was still talking to him.

On Josie's desk, she noticed a photo and picked it up, drew it near. It was of Josie and her partner, James. Eden felt a tug on her heartstrings. They looked so happy, so in love. Memories of her and Joe tried to come forward in her mind, but she pushed them back, their argument the night before still raw.

'How're things going in the Community Intelligence Team?' Josie asked when she came back.

'Great. Too good to last,' Eden replied with a sigh. 'I love this job, but if something is working, the powers that be always find a way to sabotage it.'

'It's a travesty.' Josie passed her a mug. 'If you ask me, they should be setting up a team like yours in all towns and cities. It seems to be working incredibly well.'

'It is. Something to get my teeth into and learn all the local gossip at the same time. The font of all knowledge, as they say. And if they do decide to end the team once my secondment has finished, then I'm hoping to get into the Major Crimes Team.'

'There's nothing like a good mur-dar.' Josie smiled. 'Anyway, what can I do for you?'

'I wanted to know if you've ever had dealings with a guy called Scott Daniels. Or Aiden Daniels as he's known to us as well.'

'Is this the man you emailed me about? Is he the one who's attacking these women?'

Eden sipped at her drink. 'It's a strong possibility.'

'I'll have a look online, but I don't recognise the name. Is it a recent thing we're talking about?'

'He's known on our system from years ago – domestic violence against a former partner. He wasn't charged with anything as complaints were withdrawn and then he moved to Manchester. Jordan's looking into him, as that was his neck of the woods before he came to Stockleigh, and we're going to see the victim. I just wondered if you had anything.'

Josie's eyes flitted around her computer screen as she checked her records. She shook her head after a moment. 'I've done a search for both of those names but nothing has come up.'

'What about Sylvia Latimer?'

Josie clicked a few more buttons and shook her head. 'But this system is only five years old.'

Eden sighed.

'I can check with the local housing office if you like? See if they have any records of him on their database? It might take a couple of hours if there isn't anyone who knows off the top of their head. Shall I get back to you when I'm done?'

'Saves me doing it, thanks.' Eden stood up to leave. 'How are you and James by the way? Still loved-up?'

Josie's smile told her everything.

'And you?' asked Josie. 'Things still good with Joe?'

Eden nodded, not wanting anyone to know they'd fallen out.

'Looks like we're *all* loved up,' said Amy, catching the last of the conversation as she came over to join them.

'Don't encourage her.' Eden threw a thumb at Amy. 'It's wedding central at the station at the moment.'

'Ooh, yes, I remember.' Josie smiled at Amy. 'How long until the big day now?'

'Five months, two weeks and one day.'

Josie raised her eyebrows. 'That's precise.'

'My mother-in-law tells me every time she sees me.' Amy grimaced.

Eden was just about to say more when Josie's phone rang. Instead, she pointed to the door. 'Catch up later?'

CHAPTER TWENTY-SEVEN

Sylvia Latimer lived in Morrison Avenue on the Hopwood Estate in a block of six flats, on the first floor. Eden followed Amy into a small hallway and they took the stairs.

'I wonder if she'll talk to us or clam up?' Eden said as Amy knocked on the door with a firm rat-a-tat-tat. She nudged her arm. 'Not the bobby's knock – she'll never come to the door.'

Amy grinned. 'She's expecting us.'

They heard several locks being unbolted. The door opened the fraction of an inch the chain across it allowed.

'Ms Latimer?' Eden smiled warmly, holding up her warrant card. 'I'm Detective Sergeant Eden Berrisford, and this is my colleague Detective Constable Amy Nicholls. I spoke to you on the phone earlier.'

Sylvia Latimer released the chain on the door and let them in. It saddened Eden to go into homes where victims of domestic abuse lived. They were so similar to show homes – nothing out of place, curtains straight, cushions plumped, not a crumb on the carpet or a magazine lying around.

But then again, most of the places she visited in these circumstances were not homes but houses. Somewhere a victim could sleep but never rest, lay down their head but never leave their fears behind. Lock every window and door, go to bed with the phone and maybe a piece of wood in the room to use as a weapon.

She'd seen it so many times in her job. Hated it every time, yet never being in the situation herself, she could only empathise. But she would never blame. She'd seen first-hand the damage a man, or a woman, could do to a so-called loved one. Luckily, she hadn't experienced the jerk of a head as a closed fist flew into the side of it, the sting of a cheek as a hand lashed out, the break of a rib as a kick was aimed, the split of the skin, the colouring of a bruise.

'Is he doing it again?' Sylvia asked.

Eden's shoulders dropped. From the corner of her eyes, she saw Amy's do the same.

'We're not entirely sure yet.' Eden couldn't lie to her.

The woman hugged herself. 'He'll find me.'

Eden bit her lip. She wished she could tell Sylvia she was safe but she couldn't lie. There was always a chance he would. Instead, she let Sylvia compose herself, waiting until she'd raised her head before continuing.

'Are you able to talk about what happened?' she asked.

Sylvia looked at them both, then away momentarily. 'It was such a long time ago, but it still feels like yesterday. I haven't been able to work since the last attack. Depression, suicidal thoughts, fear of going out. I think I see him everywhere when I do. It's much easier to stay indoors, or go out with Gary.'

'Gary's your . . .?'

'My partner. I found myself a good one this time. He's such a lovely man.'

Eden smiled back at her, hoping that he was. So often women in Sylvia's position went on to swap one abusive partner for another.

'How did you meet Aiden. . . did you know him as Aiden or Scott?' she asked.

'It's Aiden. His brother is named Scott.'

'Oh. That's interesting.' Eden looked at Amy then back to Sylvia. 'Sorry, go on.'

'I was on a night out with friends. We got chatting, he asked me out and we started dating. A few months later, he moved in with me and that was when everything changed.'

Eden fumed inwardly. It happened a lot – get the victim onside being all loving and romantic, lure them into a false sense of security and then once they were in your grasp, go for the jugular.

'I was renting from the council then. I tried to talk to the housing staff. They were very understanding when I asked to be moved but there were no properties available, so I went to stay with my sister. He followed me there, but she told him to leave. He left me alone for a week and I went home, changed the locks, kept everyone on alert but he broke in and got to me. I nearly lost the sight in my eye that time.'

'Yet you still wouldn't press charges?'

'He told me he would kill me if I went to the police again. I believed him. He also decided to move on from that point – after I told my brothers and they sent him on his way. I've never seen him since.'

'Does Gary know everything that happened?'

Sylvia nodded. 'Everything. The times I was raped. The times I was battered to within an inch of my life. The knife he held against my throat. I couldn't stop him, no matter what people think.'

'We don't think that,' said Eden. 'But we do need your help, maybe to put him away if we can.'

Sylvia shook her head. 'I can't.'

'Not even to help get him behind bars?'

'Sorry. It's a part of my life I want to forget.'

Eden nodded. There was no point in pushing her: she had made up her mind. Mostly Eden didn't blame her, but the police officer in her selfishly wanted Sylvia to help.

Eden looked at Amy, who had been busy writing the interview down, and stood up. 'We won't keep you any longer, Ms Latimer. Thank you for your time. I know that couldn't have been easy.'

'*Has* he attacked someone else?' Sylvia asked again, looking at them both.

'Like I mentioned, we're following enquiries at the moment,' was all Eden would confirm.

'If he has, and you can get him in a cell, give him a good firm kick in the bollocks from me, several times. I would take great satisfaction in knowing that you had.'

Eden smiled, admiring her for finding a little bit of spirit. 'I can't do that, but I'll have so much fun thinking about it.'

As they left the property and got into the car, Eden turned to Amy. 'Evil bastard, isn't he, Daniels?'

'Yes. How can anyone do that to another person?'

'I don't know, but it's our job to stop them. And to find out why he's masquerading as his brother.'

EIGHTEEN YEARS AGO

Giving birth to Chloe was the best and the worst thing that happened to me. She was my world, the light in some very dark days. What I couldn't believe was how much Ryan changed because of her.

When Chloe was born, she was a good baby and didn't cry too much. She was fun to be around and I adored her. Yet the minute we got home from the hospital, Ryan became like a man obsessed. He wanted to be with me every spare minute, no matter his other commitments. His work began to suffer as he wasn't attending meetings, bringing in any new business or going to see clients who needed his expertise.

I still can't understand why he wouldn't leave me alone with her. At first I thought it was because he didn't trust me. Perhaps he thought I had post-natal depression or something. I was a new mum with no friends or family to help me out and, yes, it was tough because of that, but I coped well.

Ryan wanted our family unit to be the three of us, but he smothered me. That's when he started to drink heavily. Come to think of it, maybe he had been a heavy drinker and I just hadn't realised until then. All those work lunches and after dinner drinks. . . By the time Chloe was one, he had started to drink every evening.

The first time he hit me came without warning. I had taken Chloe to see my parents. Ryan didn't know we were still in contact as I kept our visits secret. It was much easier to do that than have him make so much of a fuss that I usually ended up not going, just to keep the peace. It had been a lovely day. Chloe had taken her first steps the night before – two proud parents watching her, marvelling at her, encouraging her before she fell on her bottom again.

After visiting my parents, as the summer weather treated us to a bright and sunny afternoon, we stopped off at the local park. We sat down on the grass, away from the noise of the older children in the play areas. I took Chloe out of her pushchair, as I wanted to see her walk again. She took a few steps and collapsed in a heap of giggles. I held her hands and she walked with me behind her, one delicate step in front of the other.

'Mummy's clever girl,' I said to her the last time she did it. And that was when I saw Ryan marching towards us. I picked up Chloe and pointed at him.

'Look, here comes Daddy,' I said, delighted in the smile that lit up her face as she spotted him, legs flapping, arms waving in excitement.

But Ryan ignored her. He grabbed my arm, gripping it so tightly that I could already imagine the bruise imprints of his fingers.

'Where the hell have you been?' he seethed as he took Chloe from me and put her into the pushchair.

'What do you mean?'

'I come home and you're not there.'

'It was a nice day and I thought we'd come to the park.'

'You have no right to take her out without asking me first.' He pointed up at the blue cloudless sky. 'In this heat, it's irresponsible.'

'Of course it isn't,' I cried. 'She's fine, and I'm not stupid. I've covered her up and any bits on show have factor fifty suntan cream on them. It's specially for babies.'

Annoyance crossed his face as he stood by my side with clenched fists. I'm sure he would have struck me then if there weren't people around.

We marched back, Ryan holding on to the pushchair. I tried to keep up with him, but he was too fast, tried to call him back, but he kept on going. I could hear Chloe getting upset because she couldn't see me.

As soon as the door to the house closed, he slammed me up against the wall.

'Don't you ever put our child in danger like that again,' he seethed. His eyes darted back and forth as he glared at me, nostrils flaring, chest moving in and out rapidly.

'She wasn't in danger,' I sobbed. 'I was with her all the time. I was looking after her. I'm quite capable of that.'

His fist caught my chin, the force of it knocking me backwards. Confused, I held on to it as he came at me again.

I had never seen him in such a rage. This wasn't normal behaviour for him. Usually he would just be sullen. Often he'd administer a slap or squeeze my arm until it bruised. But this time it was as if something exploded, as if he couldn't control his temper a moment longer.

I flopped to the floor. 'Stop,' I croaked as a fist went into my stomach again. 'I can't breathe.'

He grabbed my hair and pulled me to Chloe's pram. My poor baby was screaming by this time, her bottom lip trembling as tears poured down her face.

'Get her out and look after her properly,' he said, almost pushing me into the pram with her. 'Or you'll have me to answer to.'

He went upstairs, leaving me a shrivelling wreck and wondering what the hell had gone wrong. I found out two weeks later that he had lost his job. He told me he'd been laid off, but I learned years later that he'd been sacked due to bad timekeeping, poor sales and being drunk on several occasions.

I realise now that he was becoming paranoid too. Instead of the control freak who wanted his woman to act as if he owned her, he was taking out his rage by saying I couldn't look after his daughter, that I wasn't a fit mother.

As I plotted my escape, I prayed he wouldn't use it in the future, building up a case so he could get custody of Chloe. To the outside world, he was very convincing. He'd end up getting his own way – even it was just to spite me. And I couldn't lose Chloe. I just couldn't.

CHAPTER TWENTY-EIGHT

'How can a man inflict such pain on a woman?' asked Amy, as Eden drove them back to the station. 'It's beyond me.'

'Whatever kick they get out of it is too,' said Eden. 'Yet so many women get stuck in the trap and they can't get out.'

Eden was glad that Sylvia Latimer had a new partner. The look on her face when she spoke about him was lovely to see. She seemed happy now, although Eden was sure she would never stop looking over her shoulder.

Eden's phone signalled an incoming message just as she was parking up in the compound. She reached in her pocket, nearly dropping it in shock when she saw who it was from.

Danny.

I have to see you.

'It's Joe,' she fibbed to Amy. 'I'll come in to you after I've rung him.'

Once Amy was out of the car, Eden's hand shook as she stared at the message again. After all this time, he wanted to see her? She typed out her reply.

Why now?

Her finger hovered over the send button. There was so much that had been unsaid, so many questions unanswered that had left her unable to move on. Anyone in their right mind would want to know why their partner had run and where to, instead of facing the consequences of their actions – why they hadn't manned up. Wouldn't they? Danny had left her to take the rap for what he'd done. And he'd left her to explain to Casey why he had gone.

Did she want to meet him? She had to do it. She pressed send.

She was about to get out of the car when her phone beeped again. Goosebumps erupted all over her body as she saw he had replied immediately.

She picked it up, her finger once more hovering over the open button. What the hell was opening this text message going to do?

She couldn't open it.

She couldn't *not* open it.

Her finger pressed on the screen.

I need to speak to you.

Eden stared at the message, angry tears forming in her eyes. One dripped down her cheek and she wiped it away quickly.

What about?
Can we meet?

Eden went cold. What would it be like to see him after two years? She might finally get some answers about why he'd left – and somehow that was just as terrifying as never knowing.

Another message came in.

Can I ring you?
No.

She'd sent it before she had thought about it. She couldn't speak to him over the phone.

Does that mean you don't want to meet?

A pause as a patrol car pulled up beside her. She waited as an officer got out of it. He didn't notice her in the car and walked off. She looked down at her phone again.

It means I don't want to talk to you on the phone.
Can we meet then? Tomorrow night maybe?
Working.

She'd lied, but he wouldn't know that. She wanted the meeting to be on her terms. Somewhere in public – somewhere she could walk away and blend in with a crowd if she panicked at the last minute. Somewhere she could say what she wanted and then leave if necessary. She quickly typed back a message.

Meet me at Starbucks on Stockleigh High Street. 8.30 a.m.
Tomorrow morning. You can make that?
Yes. See you then.

Two police constables came out of the building, laughing and joking. Eden put away her phone and glanced at herself in the rear-view mirror. A ghoulish face stared back at her. She reached in her bag, slicked a layer of lipstick over her lips and pinched her cheeks a few times to improve her complexion.

She'd have the whole station asking if she was all right if she went in without doing that.

CHAPTER TWENTY-NINE

'How have you been since seeing Vic on Monday?' Carla asked Tanya during their one-to-one session. 'Has he left you alone?'

Tanya sighed loudly. 'Yes, apart from he's been hassling me on my phone. I've been switching it off, but you can't always do that, can you? I mean, what's the point in having a phone if you can't use it?'

'I might have a spare one you could use,' Carla said, remembering several pay-as-you-go phones she'd bought for herself throughout the years. 'It won't be a smartphone, but if you can get a SIM card, it might give you a bit of peace.'

Tanya shook her head. 'Thanks for the offer, but if I did that and he couldn't get hold of me, he would do his nut when he bumped into me again.' She raised her hands to mimic inverted commas when she said the word 'bumped'.

'But I thought the whole idea of moving here was to get away from him?' Carla's tone was sharper than she had expected. 'I mean, you do want to be here?'

'No, I don't want to be here,' snapped Tanya, her ponytail swishing around in her fingers. 'I want to go home, but I don't have a place to call home, unless he's there.'

Carla stayed quiet for a moment, hoping to gain control of the meeting. She was supposed to be there to listen and give advice, not to preach.

'I miss my kids,' Tanya said all of a sudden.

'Did you ever think of getting in touch with them?' she asked. 'I mean, now they're older?'

'It wouldn't be right. They're settled into their own lives now.' Tanya's eyes filled with tears. 'I can only remember Lee when he was a baby, before he was taken from me. He had a white teddy bear with a blue collar with his name embroidered on it. He took that with him, and I wish I'd kept it.'

Carla knocked her notepad to the floor as she pictured that teddy bear. Ryan had bought Chloe one with a pink collar. They had been all the rage at the time.

She composed herself and picked up the notepad. 'So you haven't seen any of your children since they were adopted?'

'No.'

'Would you like to? I could help to set it up for you.'

Tanya stood up. 'What's wrong with you people? I don't want to see any of my kids again. Do you think I want them to know how their mum and dad turned out? How their mother gets beaten by their father and is afraid of her own shadow? That they both take drugs to get off their faces because life is too hard for them? That they've both been in and out of prison? What kind of an example is that?'

'People change,' said Carla, trying not to react to her outburst. 'I think you'd be surprised how much they might want to see you.'

'Don't even think about it. My children aren't precious to me. I gave up rights to be their mother a long time ago. They're better off not knowing. Children should be sacred, don't you think?'

Carla looked up to see Tanya staring at her purposely. 'I. . . I guess they should,' she said.

'Well then, they'll be better off without me and Vic butting into their lives.'

Tanya turned on her heel and left Carla mulling over her words. Tanya was hurting, but so was she. If Tanya hadn't brought up the memory of the teddy bear, she might have handled the situation a bit better. She still had that teddy bear, locked away in the safe-deposit box with all her other mementoes. Despite Ryan insisting it was to be buried with Chloe, it had been the one time she had continued to say no.

Carla cursed herself inwardly for being sharp. Tanya wasn't to know what memories her story would evoke. She'd have to learn from this meeting to keep her feelings to herself as much as she could in the future. Especially where Tanya and her children were concerned.

CHAPTER THIRTY

Eden took a shower as soon as she got home from work that night, letting the hot water wash away her tears. Despite her work, she hadn't been able to stop thinking about Danny since they had shared that text conversation. Because she'd thought they were okay until he'd upped and left, and that's what stung the most.

She realised soon after why he had gone, which made it a little more bearable, but it still didn't mean she could hate him. Time should be a healer, but it felt like no more than a second had passed when someone contacted you again, turned your world around and made your heart beat faster.

Things cooling with Joe had been her fault. But now, with this happening, she realised she did care for him, though not in the same sense she cared for Danny. Even though he had abandoned her and Casey, she had to see Danny to discuss what he wanted to talk about.

Maybe he wanted to come home. Was that even a possibility now? Could they turn the clock back two years and start again? Was she even willing to do that, or was seeing him all she needed? Getting him to explain why he'd left could be enough to heal her wounds and make her realise that she'd be better off without him. Or maybe she was still smarting from Joe suggesting they take a break. They'd both known it would be more permanent than that.

But, regardless of whether or not things worked out with Joe, he deserved to be treated better than she was capable of. Then again, if she saw Danny and he categorically didn't want to come back, then maybe she *would* be able to settle down with Joe. Maybe they should give it a try.

There was so much that could go right – and wrong – in the morning, depending on whether certain questions were answered to her approval. There was a lot she needed to hear – and a lot she needed to say.

Mostly she wondered how she would react when she saw Danny again. From the very first night they'd met at a Soul Night in Stafford in their late teens, he'd taken her breath away. She had been on the dance floor when he'd danced past her. She'd always been a bit of a tomboy – her sister Laura would vouch for that – and yet she'd gone to pieces when he spoke to her. At first he'd been dancing around her, and then with her, and then he'd asked her if she wanted to stop for a drink.

When she'd found out he lived in Stockleigh too, she had to stop herself from beaming. He was right up her street. They'd married three years later and then Casey had come along.

She groaned loudly. Danny had never bothered with the fact that she'd gone into the police force. His work as a garage mechanic was a manual job, but he'd enjoyed it, and it had brought in great money when he'd become known as the best in the area to do a full car respray. It was only when he lost his job that things began to unravel for him. Had she realised that before he left, Eden might have been able to help rather than have him take advantage of her position.

But whatever he wanted to tell her, the main thing she needed to know was why he had left – and why he hadn't contacted her, or Casey, for so long.

She went downstairs and sat in the living room. A few minutes later, Casey came in.

'What's up, Mum?' She flopped down beside her. 'You look sad.'

'Oh, I'm fine really.' Eden put an arm around her and drew her near. She smiled when Casey cuddled up to her, the warmth of her daughter soothing her. 'I've just had a bad day at the office. Nasty stuff, you know.'

Daphne came sidling in and jumped up on to Casey's lap. They both stroked the cat at the same time, her purrs becoming so loud that they smiled at each other.

'How's everything with you?' Eden asked her.

'Okay. What are you watching?'

'Nothing in particular. Why?'

'Do you fancy watching a girlie movie with me?'

Eden nodded. 'Sure. There's some ice cream in the freezer. I won't tell if you won't.'

'You're supposed to set a good example, not encourage me!' Casey was trying to sound convincing but Eden noticed she was already up on her feet.

'How about *Dirty Dancing*?' she asked.

'Really? Again?' Casey shook her head. 'How about *Bridesmaids*?'

Eden nodded, trying to muster up enough enthusiasm. 'That's great.'

No matter what she watched tonight, nothing would take her mind off meeting Danny the next morning.

CHAPTER THIRTY-ONE

Carla sat on the settee, legs up, a mug of coffee at her side. There was nothing she wanted to watch on the television so she was reading a book. Thomas was curled up in her lap. Peace at last.

After the day she'd had at The Willows, she was grateful to be able to come home and switch off. It seemed an age since she had been the woman in Tanya's position, yet Vic turning up at the refuge earlier in the week had upset her just as much. Some of the women had been scared too. So for the next few evenings, if there were any police available to drive past sporadically, they would be up and down Harold Street keeping an eye out.

Carla was worried about the attacks across the city too. Even though it was all over the news, Eden had rung Lisa to say that there had been another one in a car park in Stockleigh city centre. This one had been stopped before it went too far, luckily, but Eden said the attacks might become more frequent so they were all on alert.

She heard a noise and looked up to see out of the window that a car had arrived next door. A couple in their early twenties got out: she holding a bottle of wine, him laughing as he locked the car door. It was quiet again moments later.

Carla had been lucky with Granger Street. It had a reputation for having a friendly neighbourhood feel to it. People would watch out for each other but not be on each other's doorstep all the time. A sense of independence but always having someone there. So with that, and the emergency alarm system that Josie

Mellor had put into the property for her and that sent an alert through to a control room if she had need to press it, she felt as safe as she could.

She went to the window again and looked outside, both ways, up and down the street in the dark. There was no one around. It was just her mind playing tricks with her. She closed the curtains and settled down again.

Despite going early to bed, just after midnight, Carla sat up, her senses on full alert. She'd been woken by something. It couldn't have been Thomas, as she'd put him out before she'd come to bed. She listened but there was nothing.

She stayed sitting upright. Memories from years ago flooded back, of waiting and hoping that Ryan wouldn't come into the room and take his temper out on her – alcohol-fuelled attacks that filled the air with his putrid fumes before he would collapse next to her, spent, in a stupor. Often she had slept on the floor so as not to wake him up.

She heard another noise. Her eyes were trained on the bedroom door. There was no one there, but there was someone outside, because it sounded as if the back door handle had just gone down.

She heard it again. There *was* someone outside. She flicked the bedside lamp on – her pale face in the wardrobe mirror making her jump – hoping to scare away any opportune thief that was trying his luck.

She grabbed the rounders bat that she kept by the side of her bed, although she wasn't sure if she would have the courage to use it. Then again, she wasn't the woman she had been all those years ago.

Even though she knew she had checked them over before coming to bed, she needed to see if all the windows and doors were secure. If they were, then it didn't matter who was outside as long as they couldn't get in.

She got up, took hold of the bat and crept downstairs. Shaky fingers checked the front door to find it still locked, and it hadn't been tampered with. In the kitchen, she found the back door intact. She pulled the blind to one side at the window to check the handles were locked securely. A shadow made her jump. There was a figure dressed in a black jacket, a woollen hat covering their head and a black scarf around the bottom of their face. Eyes stared at her for a moment before the person ran away.

Carla took a step backwards and screamed. The bat in her hand clattered to the floor, and she dropped down beneath the sink unit so that she couldn't be seen. Covering her mouth, she tried not to hyperventilate. Tingles came up her fingers and she reached up to the cutlery drawer behind her.

The first thing she grasped was a brown paper bag that she needed to breathe into, to stop her from having a full-blown panic attack. The second was a kitchen knife. If anyone came into the property right now, she would use it.

Fifteen minutes later, there had been no more noise – no one forcing their way into the property to grab her hair and drag her outside. There was nothing. When she plucked up the courage to look again, there was no one there. For a split second, she wondered if she'd imagined it.

The other part of her knew she hadn't. There had been someone outside her window. She scrambled across the hallway. Praying that a figure wouldn't walk past the front door, she ran upstairs.

Tears tore down her cheeks as she threw herself on to the bed. Could it be the man who was attacking women? Was he looking to break in somewhere? Or could it have been Ryan? Had he found her? She'd have to move again. She didn't want to keep running, but despite her bravery about staying where she was, she just couldn't.

Carla shivered. If it was Ryan, then he was playing with her. He was letting her know that not only had he found her, he was coming to get her for what she'd done.

CHAPTER THIRTY-TWO

Eden pushed open the door to Starbucks the next morning. Her heart thumped away inside her chest so loudly she thought everyone might turn round to see where the noise was coming from. She wiped sweaty palms on her trousers as she stepped inside the building.

How could her emotions be playing tricks on her like this? She'd hardly slept a wink last night. She'd thought she would be fine seeing Danny again, but even now, upset after her recent fall out with Joe, she still wasn't prepared for the rush of anxiety. Her stomach flipped over almost as if they were meeting for a first date.

She was worried that she wouldn't spot him, but as she looked past the queue waiting to be served, past the tables at the front of the shop and out to the back, she saw a hand go up. And there he was.

It was as if she'd stepped back in time. Two years ago, they had regularly come here for coffee and Eden wondered if she should have thought of somewhere else to meet.

Pushing her reservations to one side, she walked towards him, squeezing past a couple in their teens who were hell-bent on eating each other's tonsils as they waited for their order.

With every step closer, she noticed something different about him and it stung. He'd lost about a stone in weight, and his hair, although still styled like a young Paul Weller's, was shorter. His skin was a little more aged, but bronzed as if he'd been away recently. He wore his green Harrington jacket, which made her heart melt, and she could see a black Doc Marten shoe at the side of the table. So some things on the outside were the same old Danny. On the inside, however. . .?

She drew level with him, taking a few deep breaths to calm her nerves.

He stood up, pulling out a chair for her. 'Hi.'

He went to kiss her on the cheek but she moved away.

His smile was goofy and nervous. The silence between them was filled by the noise in the room: a man tapping on his laptop on the next table, two mums and their children in pushchairs chattering away behind them and a couple sharing breakfast on the table in front. The steamer burst into life again.

'Can I get you a drink?' he asked.

'I'll have a cappuccino,' she said.

'Anything to eat?'

She shook her head and watched him walk away, knowing he was stalling for time. He hadn't changed really. Granted his hair was a little shorter, a little thinner in places, but he was the same old Danny. She wondered what she had been expecting. That he had fallen apart after being without her for two years? Who was she kidding? Danny had always been able to look after himself.

'How's Casey?' he asked once he was seated again.

'Growing up into a woman with the will of her mum. Teenage years – she's turning into me.'

Danny grinned. 'God help us all.'

Eden knew he was hoping to lighten the tension. But it lit anger inside her instead.

'Where have you been?' she blurted out.

'Staying with friends mostly.'

'Oh please! You've been sofa surfing for two years? I don't think so.'

She waited for him to explain further but he stayed quiet.

'Why did you do it?' she asked, taking a sip of her drink so that she could hide her pained expression behind the cup.

'It was too much to walk away from.'

'But not only did you ruin everything we'd worked so hard to do, you were willing for me to lose the thing I loved. My job. And then you walked away from us. Me I could understand, but *Casey?*' Tears brimmed in her eyes as she recalled the stunned look on her daughter's face when she'd told her that her father had walked out. 'I had to shoulder the burden of her pain, the hurt from rejection, her despair. How could you do that to her?'

'I had to go,' Danny insisted. 'It's better she doesn't know why. Unless you told her?'

Eden shook her head. 'I never said anything. Though it was to protect her, not you.'

'And to protect yourself?'

'How dare you say that, you bastard!' She whispered the last two words loudly through gritted teeth, thankful for the chatter of people and the clattering of cups on saucers around them.

'Sorry.' He had the sense to look sheepish, a slight blush appearing on his cheeks. 'Does she know you're meeting me?'

Eden shook her head.

He nodded in gratitude. 'Will you tell her?'

'That depends.'

He cocked his head in readiness for an answer.

'On whether or not this is a one-off. I won't build her hopes up that you'll be around to see her again. It isn't fair.'

'I guess not.' He hung his head for a moment, staring intently into his coffee. 'I haven't exactly been a role-model father.'

'You haven't been a father at all for the past two years.'

'Ouch. I guess I deserved that too.'

'I guess you did.' She put down her cup. 'What do you really want, Danny? There must be some reason you needed to see me. You said you wanted to talk.'

He wouldn't meet her eye at first but eventually he looked up at her. 'It's about Jed Jackson.'

Every vein in Eden's body turned ice cold. Jed Jackson was a loan shark from the Mitchell Estate. Recently out of prison, he was already causing trouble on his manor. Eden had helped put him in prison twice during her career but nothing stuck longer than a six-month stretch. Last year, he'd beaten up a lad who owed him money. It turned out Kyle Merchant owed him £1,000, but with interest over three months it had escalated to over £10,000. The lad hadn't seen him coming.

Jackson had left Merchant paralysed below the waist after pushing him down a fire escape. Although CCTV cameras had caught it all, Jackson had laid the blame on one of his cronies. Someone could clearly be seen kicking Merchant before he fell, but Jackson wouldn't admit to anything. He was sentenced to six months for a drug bust a few weeks later.

But it was when he went to prison that things started to get worse. He'd set up a group of people to look after his business. The police were still investigating who did what and to whom, but recently there had been some pretty horrific attacks on anyone who hadn't paid in time. It seemed Jackson hadn't learned his lesson. And neither had Danny.

'What about him?' she asked. 'I know he's recently got out of prison.'

'He's making threats, Eden, to you and. . . to Casey.'

'If. . .?'

'If I don't get him the money I owe.'

'And how much is that?'

Danny looked down into his coffee cup. 'Just short of twenty grand.'

'For fuck's sake, Dan,' she whispered.

'I was thinking you could sell the Lambretta. I know it's not worth that much but it would get him off my back for now and—'

Eden gasped. 'You came back for my money?' She stood up quickly, scraping the chair across the floor.

'No!' He placed his hand over hers.

Shocked as old feelings rushed through her, she lowered her eyes. How could she still be in love with him after what he'd done?

'Sit down again. Please,' he said. 'I have to tell you what I know.'

Ten minutes later, Eden's head was reeling. She couldn't believe what she'd just heard. She couldn't believe she was hearing it from Danny either.

'If you give in to him this time, he'll come after you again. Blackmailers always do.'

'If I don't get that money, I'm sure he'll kill me.'

'That's a bit dramatic,' Eden scoffed.

'Well at the very least, I'm in for some rough treatment, and I— I'm scared, Eden.'

Eden shuddered, trying not to cry at his words. Because he could very well be right, and she shouldn't care, but she did. Jed Jackson was a dangerous man when crossed.

'Please, Ede, can you help me out?' He threw her a nervous smile. 'For old times' sake?'

Her stomach overturned again when he called her the name that only he had ever used. But it was a mere moment.

'Old times' sake doesn't mean anything.' She pointed at him. '*You* walked out. *You* ignored me and Casey. I was under the impression when you contacted me, you. . .' Eden couldn't tell him she'd thought that he wanted to see her.

But he filled the gap anyway. Danny reached for her hand. 'I've missed you, more than you'll ever know, but I kept away because it was dangerous for me to be with you.'

'But it's okay for you to have my money?' she hissed. 'Which, incidentally, you took every penny of when you left. Why do you think I'd be willing to give you any more?'

'Because I'm desperate.'

Eden rolled her eyes and started to walk off. Then she turned back to him. Getting a five-pound note out of her pocket, she slammed it on the table. 'I always pay my own way,' she muttered before walking away again.

She left him in the café. Blackmail wouldn't work with her – especially the emotional kind.

CHAPTER THIRTY-THREE

Eden had a monthly Safer Streets Partnership meeting at 10 a.m. She tried to concentrate but after seeing Danny it was impossible. His confession was shocking, his cheek unbelievable. She wondered if she was thinking straight to even care about him. The man was a prick for doing what he did. But he was also the father of her child, and the man she had been married to – was still married to.

The meeting finished just before midday and, by then, she'd had enough of trying to figure things out alone. She needed to speak to someone who wasn't involved.

'Fancy grabbing a bite to eat with me,' she asked Amy. 'My treat?'

Amy looked up from her computer screen and beamed. Ten minutes later, they headed into town, updating each other on anything they had found out during their morning's work.

'Josie Mellor rang,' said Eden, as they waited to cross the road. 'Aiden Daniels isn't known to anyone in Housing.'

'Nor Scott Daniels?'

'No. I contacted him, though, and he isn't too happy about his brother using his references.'

'I can't say I blame him, but we have bigger fish to fry right now.'

Once they reached the sandwich shop, Eden studied the menu in silence.

Amy nudged her. 'What do you want?'

Eden looked at her in confusion and then back to the woman behind the counter, who was ready to take her order. 'Oh, cheese salad on brown please.' She paid for their sandwiches and they took a seat while they waited for them to be made.

'How are things with the wedding?' Eden asked.

Amy raised her eyebrows. 'I'm sure you don't want to hear about my latest disaster.'

'Oh?'

'The best man's wife wants to be a bridesmaid. She's forty-two!'

'And?'

'Well if she looked like you, I wouldn't mind so much.' Amy grinned. 'Really, my wedding isn't what you need to talk about, is it? What's wrong, Eden?'

Eden smiled. Amy had a caring attitude that wasn't pushy but gave you the impression that she was always there for you.

Sensing eyes on her, she felt the urge to look out of the shop window. The pavement was pedestrianised, most tables full of clientele during the lunch-hour rush in the summer but now practically deserted except for a few hardy smokers.

But something had caught her eye. Was someone watching her? She looked around but couldn't see anyone she recognised within the people walking by. Even so, she shuddered. Clearly the meeting with Danny had panicked her.

'Do you need an independent ear?' Amy urged, not realising the true reason for Eden's silence.

Eden looked back at her. 'I met with my ex, Danny, this morning,' she blurted out. 'Or rather, he would be my ex if we were divorced.'

Amy's eyes widened. 'I want to ask a million questions like *how, when, why* and *what for* but I guess that's what lunch is all about. How are you feeling?'

'Weird,' Eden admitted. 'The last time I saw him, I had no inclination he was leaving, and for two years I've heard nothing.

But he sent me a text message asking if we could talk. So I met with him this morning.'

'The meeting didn't go as you'd hoped?' Amy gave a faint smile. 'I've never seen you like this before.'

'I keep this part of me well hidden,' Eden admitted.

'Meaning there's more to it than him just walking out?'

Eden nodded.

'Was it another woman?'

'No.'

A pause.

'Was it a man?'

Eden couldn't help but laugh but it was short. 'Nothing like that. Danny wasn't unfaithful to me, but he did make me look a fool.'

Amy frowned as she waited for Eden to explain herself. Trouble was, she didn't really know if she could. Had she made a mistake coming here, telling someone what Danny had done – something no one but she knew?

But she had to talk it through with someone. A tear dripped down her face and she wiped it away.

'What is it, Eden?' asked Amy gently.

'Danny left me because he was in a lot of debt. His work had dried up and he'd started betting on the horses. I didn't know anything about it until after he'd gone. He'd cleared out our bank account, and what little savings we had – a few grand.'

'Didn't you know about the debt?'

'I had no idea. Call myself a copper – I didn't even have an inkling. He wasn't acting suspicious or anything. Well maybe for a few days before he left, but it was too quick for me to pick up on.'

'Is it a lot of money?'

Eden cleared her throat. It was still hard for her to say. 'Twenty thousand pounds.'

Amy's eyes widened again. 'Jeez.'

'That's not the worst of it. He borrowed money.'

'And put your name against it?' Amy shook her head. 'Please tell me that's not the case. He hasn't left you to carry the can. Those bloody bailiffs can be brutal when it comes to getting money back.'

Eden didn't interrupt her. She couldn't, because then she would have to tell her what she hadn't told anyone yet.

But Amy cottoned on. 'Who did he get the money from?'

'Jed Jackson.'

'Oh, Eden.'

'That's still not the worst of it.'

'If there's more, I don't know how you've slept at night.'

'He found details about a raid we were doing on Jackson's lock-up, plus we'd been looking into him in connection with a few cash machines being done over, and people being robbed as they were getting cash from the machine – cash and grabs. We also knew he was about to do a robbery at Cardman's Cash and Carry. I'd brought home the files with the details. They were in my car. I don't even know why Danny was snooping around. I didn't even know he knew Jed Jackson, but he stole information and gave it to him. The operation went tits up.'

Amy sat forward in her seat. 'Does anyone at work know this?'

'No – and I can't have them finding out either, or I'll probably be fired.'

'So what are you going to do?'

'Other than to watch my back, what can I do? I can't tell anyone about it.' Eden was teary eyed again. 'I can't lose my job, Amy. I have Casey to think about too. Not only does she have a liar for a father, now I have to protect her from the fact that someone might come after us to punish him as well.'

Amy shook her head in amazement. 'Does Danny think. . .' She stopped.

Eden nodded. It was as if what Amy was thinking was impossible, but it had to be true for Danny to make contact again.

'Danny thinks Jackson will hurt him and then come after me for the debt.'

'But you don't have that sort of money! Well you don't, do you?'

'No. Neither does Danny. He even suggested I sell my Lambretta!'

'What?' Amy shook her head in disapproval. 'You're not going to, are you?'

'There's no way I'd do that. But even so, that doesn't help my situation at all. He can't find the money, and I won't give him any either. So now I'll have to watch over my shoulder for Jed Jackson for the rest of my life. I am well and truly screwed.'

'Is there anything anyone else can do to help?'

Eden shook her head and gazed out of the window, feeling the dread that someone was watching her creep over her again. She turned back to Amy.

'I don't know,' she said, 'and if there is, how can I ask them without landing myself in trouble?'

With no easy answer, they sat in silence for a moment.

Their order was ready. Amy checked her watch as she got up to fetch the food from the counter. 'I think there's just time to squeeze in a vanilla slice before we go back to work.'

Eden gave a weak smile. 'It will certainly help, that's for sure.'

Eden's phone rang as she and Amy walked back to the station. It was Laura.

'Go ahead and I'll catch you up,' she told Amy and then answered the call. 'Hey, you.'

'What the hell is going on?' said Laura. 'After two years, you go to see Danny and you don't tell any of us?'

She groaned inwardly. 'How did you find out?'

'Jess saw you in Starbucks this morning.'

Eden hadn't spotted her niece in the coffee shop. She'd thought that Jess would have been long gone to school by then. Maybe she had been walking past. Then a thought struck her. She hoped it was only Jess who'd seen them and that Casey hadn't been with her. She wanted to tell her face-to-face that evening. It was only fair.

'Does Casey know?'

'Jess hadn't said anything to her so I told her not to. I think that's your job anyway.'

'It's not what you think,' Eden tried to explain. 'He contacted me yesterday and I said I'd see him on my own first.'

'And are you okay? You are, aren't you?'

'I think so. It was weird seeing him after so long.'

'Did he say why he left?'

'It wasn't for anyone else.'

'So what did he want? Did he tell you that much?'

'Can I call you back? I need to digest what he told me first.'

'You can't confide in your own sister?'

'No, wait, it's not like that! I'm at work.'

'Thanks a bunch.'

The call was terminated. Eden groaned loudly, causing a man across the street to turn and look at her. She looked in the opposite direction, as if she was trying to see where the noise had come from too. Then she kept her eyes straight ahead.

In the back of her mind, she'd hoped Danny had wanted to come back. If he had, then she would have sat down with her family: first with Casey to see how she felt about it and then with Laura. She had wondered if he'd want to take things slowly again, maybe see her a few times and then see Casey.

But he hadn't wanted to come back at all. And if Jess hadn't seen them together, then she would never have told anyone that she had met him. Now her sister had got involved. Being protective of Eden, Laura would want to know everything about Danny's time away. When he'd left, Laura had been convinced that he must have gone away with another woman and had been irate. The anger had died down a little over time, but the accusations still simmered in the background.

Eden gave a sigh. What a day so far.

CHAPTER THIRTY-FOUR

Standing in the doorway, he took a drag from his cigarette, folded his arms and crossed his legs at the ankles. To the casual observer, he blended into the crowd, as if he was waiting for someone. Which he was.

He'd seen her earlier that morning too. A smile crossed his face. She'd looked troubled. Perhaps she was using a coping mechanism. Something else to think about, concentrate on while she tried not to think of the inevitable. Even still, he admired the stance of her walk, as well as her shapely form, as she'd strode across the road.

She'd been in the building for twenty minutes now. He'd wait a few more and then he'd be on his way. He'd got what he'd come for, having seen what she was up to and where she was.

Five minutes later, his cigarette burned down, he flicked it to the floor and ground it out with the heel of his boot. A man tutted as he walked past and he glared at him. When he looked up, she was at the door again.

And then she came out. He stepped back a little as she crossed the road with another woman. He laughed as he watched her go. She didn't even sense him.

'Whatever you do,' he said quietly, 'don't look behind you.'

THIRTEEN YEARS AGO

I can still remember the time you first showed our child how cruel you were. It was Chloe's fifth birthday and she was having a party. We were still in Liverpool then. It was one of the rare occasions when you actually gave in and let her have her way, because she wanted a party at our house. We never entertained – we didn't have friends – so I'd gone out of the way to make it extra special for her.

There were eleven children invited, parents too. Chloe was beside herself as she waited for everyone to arrive. You didn't give me enough money for luxuries, so I'd saved a few pounds each week to get her something special. She looked lovely in a red checked dress and thick navy blue tights, with boots coming up to her knees. And, of course, red ribbon around her bunches.

It was an hour into the party and you hadn't shown. I had got fed up fielding comments from other mums about where you were and was becoming anxious that you'd even show up.

Chloe was running to me every few minutes.

'Have you heard from Daddy yet?' she asked.

'Not yet, darling,' I replied. 'Do you want to play pass the parcel while you wait?'

Chloe was too innocent then. She hadn't seen the dangerous man that only I ever saw.

When you hadn't shown up in another hour and guests had started to leave, Chloe had been distraught. She'd had a bath and was in bed by the time you finally came home. And, by that time, you said it was all my fault that I hadn't rung you to remind you. I had, lots of times, but you'd denied getting any calls. You see, by then I realised that you wanted me to suffer, no matter what.

But do you know what? I think she had a far better time without you there. You would have ruined her party. She was better off not knowing that you were too drunk to attend.

How could you miss your own daughter's birthday party?

Chloe never asked me about the damage to my face the next day. She just pressed her fingertips to it and said, 'That looks sore, Mummy.' Then she kissed it better.

I kept my tears in until she had gone into her bedroom to play with her new toys. What that child saw because of you – I hated you for that. You were the evil one, and I decided there and then to do everything in my power to get away from you. Seeing the hurt in my child's eyes while she waited for you to turn up was cruel, but seeing her scared face come round the corner of the door as you were laying into me? Well, I'll never forget that either.

CHAPTER THIRTY-FIVE

Eden left work just before six. There was nothing else that warranted her attention and she couldn't concentrate.

The traffic was busy, and as she pulled into the drive, she was glad to be home. Lights were on downstairs, which meant Casey was too. She sighed loudly, hoping that Jess hadn't said anything to her about Danny before she had chance to explain.

But she hadn't even pulled her key out of the lock and Casey was shouting at her.

'You've met with Dad and not told me?'

Eden stopped in the middle of the hallway as Casey came down the stairs and walked right past her. She followed her into the kitchen.

'Is this what you and Joe were talking about the other night?' Casey continued, folding her arms.

'No! I would never keep anything like this from you.'

'So when did he contact you? Is this the first time you've seen him? Or have you been meeting him on a regular basis without me?'

'Casey, slow down! He only got in touch with me yesterday. I thought it best that the two of us meet first.'

'Did you know last night?'

'Yes, he sent me a text message and I said I'd—'

'You should have told me! I'm sixteen, Mum. I'm a grown-up. I can handle it.'

Eden sighed. 'I didn't know what to expect when I met him, and I didn't want to drag you into that until I knew. He left two years ago and I wanted to know why before—'

'Did he ask about me?'

'Yes, of course he did.'

'Did he say why he hadn't contacted me? Not a phone call, or a card. Not even a text message on my birthday.'

Eden heard her daughter sob. 'Please don't be upset.' She stepped towards her.

Casey groaned and stormed out of the room. The bang of the kitchen door made Eden jump. She pinched the bridge of her nose and held in her tears.

Trust Jess to blab to everyone. All she'd wanted was to have a bit of time to get used to things herself before telling her family she had met with Danny. He'd walked away without a thought for anyone but himself, yet she was the one who got it in the neck.

What a mess. She'd upset the two women she cared for most because of one lousy text message she had replied to. She wished she hadn't bothered.

She grabbed a cushion and held it to her chest, lifting her feet up beside her on the settee. When did life get so complicated? She wondered: *what were the implications of Jed Jackson being involved with Danny?* If it ever got out that he had obtained information from her, information that he had gone on to use for his financial gain, she would lose her job. The file had been her responsibility. But she had brought home files for years, so that time wasn't any different.

She'd never talked about confidential work with Danny, but everyone in Stockleigh knew who Jed Jackson was, given how often they'd locked him up. He would have loved that Danny was her husband. She was surprised he hadn't used it against her yet, either to get her into trouble or to get her onside and do a bit of blackmailing of his own. She wouldn't be his bitch for anyone.

That could be his next move though. Either get to her through Casey or even through her with his fists as a warning. There were lots of things he could do.

'Bloody hell, Danny,' she muttered. 'You've really landed me in the shit.'

Her phone rang. It was Laura. Eden braced herself for another onslaught.

'I was just calling to see how you were.' Laura's voice was full of concern. It brought tears to her eyes.

'I'm all mixed up,' she admitted. 'I don't know what to think.'

'What did he say to you?'

Eden relayed as much of the conversation as she could. The rest of it, about Jed Jackson and the debt, she would keep to herself for now.

'I thought he wanted to come back,' she said quietly.

Laura gave a derisive snort. 'And you would have welcomed him with open arms?'

'No, but it would have been nice if he'd wanted to!' she snapped.

'Sorry, I didn't mean it that way. It just seems so maddening that he's come back to ask for money. I always thought he was a decent guy. Just goes to show how much you can be fooled.'

'Or how much someone can change,' said Eden. 'Was it Jess who told Casey?'

'Yes, sorry. I wondered if she'd keep it to herself.'

'It's not your fault.'

She chatted to Laura for a while and, once she'd ended that call, on impulse she rang Danny. Surprised when he answered, she took a deep breath.

'Why did you do it, Danny?' she asked again.

'I was desperate.'

'I don't mean the money. I mean, why did you leave me and Casey? We weren't in a loveless marriage. Okay, things might have been a bit complacent, but we got on well and I—I thought we were in it for the long haul.'

'I thought so too, but I couldn't keep it from you unless I left.'

'You didn't love me enough to stay.'

'No! Of course I loved you!'

Eden could almost picture him rubbing a hand over his chin the way he used to do. The worried look on his face, the angst he was feeling.

'Then why didn't you tell me?' she went on. 'Instead of leaving me wondering what I had done. I didn't know if you were dead or alive. You never even answered my text messages!'

'I couldn't. Believe me, it tore me apart not to.'

'Like I'll ever believe that.' She paused for a moment. 'Have you been following me?'

'No, whatever gave you that idea?'

Eden shuddered involuntarily. 'So this morning was the first time you've seen me?'

'Yes. I—'

'Where have you been all this time?'

'It doesn't matter. I—'

'It does to me!'

Silence.

'Look, things had started getting ugly with Jackson, Ede. When I took out the loan, I could pay him back at first. And then, when I couldn't, he threatened you and Casey if I didn't start working for him.'

'Wait a minute. Are you saying that you knew Jackson *way before* you stole that information?'

The line was quiet.

'Danny?'

'Yes.'

Eden groaned. All this was bound to come back on her one day. She didn't really want to know but she had to ask, to be prepared for it to be used against her. Jackson would have a bloody field day.

'What did you do for him?'

'I was the driver on a few jobs he did.'

'For God's sake!' Eden closed the door for a moment to stop her conversation from reaching Casey. 'Have you any idea how this will look on me when it gets out?'

'It won't get out! That's why I left – can't you see? He doesn't know I told you any of this.'

'You think he'll just sweep it under the carpet, never to be discussed? Come on, Danny, even you can't be that naive.'

Silence down the line again. Eden wasn't sure she wanted to hear any more. She went out into the hall and climbed the stairs.

'I'll tell you one thing for nothing, Dan. If he comes after me and he hurts our daughter, I won't be responsible for my actions when I get hold of you. I never had you down as a coward.'

'But you do still love me, don't you, Ede?'

'You think what you like, mate.' She knocked on Casey's door. 'There's someone here who would like to talk to you.'

She handed the phone to Casey and left the room. She wasn't going to let him get away with everything. He needed to know how much upset he had caused.

She stood on the landing while she waited for Casey to come off the phone, looking through the window on to the street below. All those people in Stockleigh having an ordinary evening together. Why couldn't she be one of them? Why was life so complicated all the time?

In Harold Street, Tanya stood at the window. She wondered if Vic was watching from the shadows. Taunting her, making her think she was safe when she was far from it.

She pulled her cardigan closer around her. That was the thing with Vic. He didn't love her, just the power he had over her. He just wanted to hit out if she didn't do as she was told. He enjoyed ruling the house.

She was his plaything. He said he loved her, but she knew she didn't mean anything to him, even though he was always saying if he couldn't have her, then no one else could either.

The room felt claustrophobic. She knew she wouldn't be able to stay here long. Maybe she needed to move from Stockleigh. But where would she go? She had no one outside the city who she could turn to for help. What a mess she had made of her life.

She wished she could turn back time. Even three weeks would do, and she could have disappeared before Vic came out of prison. Then she wouldn't have been dragged into his stupid plans.

In Granger Street, Carla stared out of her bedroom window. Was Ryan there in the shadows watching her? Waiting for her to slip up so that he could get to her? She knew he could be there. Even before she saw the man outside her house, she'd felt someone watching her for some time, both at home and at The Willows.

At work, the women were always talking about the fear of their partners catching up with them again and what they would do to them when they did. Maybe their anguish was rubbing off on her. She needed to stay strong. She'd done it for a few weeks now. She just had to stay on the right track.

But it wasn't a good feeling, especially after seeing someone in the garden. Again, she wondered if she should move on, just in case he caught up with her. Then she shook her head vehemently. No, she decided. She had to be sure it was him before she did anything else.

She got into bed but sleep didn't come easily. Every groan that the house made, every creak, made her alert.

She was listening for him.

She was waiting for him to come and get her.

She couldn't live her life like this.

She *wouldn't* live her life like this.

Outside, in the shadows, he stood watching her. He wondered if she sensed he was nearby. He hoped so. He wished she couldn't sleep, worried that he might turn up, wondering when he might strike. He wanted her to live in fear of when he would grab her and give her what was coming to her.

He couldn't believe he was so close, that he could reach out and squeeze his hands around her throat. But he had to bide his time. It wouldn't do to be seen hanging around.

He had to find the right time to strike. When she was on her own, at her most vulnerable. Or when she had let down her guard.

It would be soon. He couldn't wait much longer. There was nothing better than letting off steam with a good punch, a swift kick or slap. Especially to her. Her face came into his mind's eye and he smiled, licking his bottom lip in anticipation of the thrill.

The light went off and he imagined her getting into bed. Would her dreams be full of nightmares? He very much hoped so. He didn't want her to sleep.

He would get to her soon.

The day was drawing near.

CHAPTER THIRTY-SIX

Ramona Wilson closed the door on The Candy Club and checked the handle to make sure it was locked securely. It had been a quiet night, and there had been no trouble. The girls and their punters had all behaved themselves, enabling her to crack on with reading her book. She was really enjoying the latest Ian Rankin novel and couldn't wait to get home to read the next chapter.

'Come on, Ramona,' a voice shouted. 'I'm going past the chippy if you fancy something to eat.'

'I'm coming!' There was no way she could resist the lure of fish and chips at this time of night. She got into the car and turned to Angel with a smile. 'These are on me for the lift though.'

Twenty minutes later, Ramona popped the last chip into her mouth, screwed up the wrapping and tossed it in a bin on Davy Road. Angel had dropped her off and headed home. She only had a few minutes to walk and she'd be able to wash the grease from her mouth with a glass of something nice.

Bernard Place was quiet for once as she walked the last few metres, maybe due to how cold it was that night. Frost glistened on the ground under the light of a full moon, her shadow out in front. Her parents lived at the top of the cul-de-sac. It was an okay street to live on, but she much preferred where she had lived before in Christopher Avenue. There was more of a community spirit there. In Bernard Place, the benefit mentality was rife. It riled her how she worked for a living and most of the lazy sods asleep in their beds or still down the pub hadn't worked an honest day's job in their lives.

Despite what she did, she could hold her head high. She supported herself and her children. But it was still embarrassing that she was twenty-three, and her brother was coming up to twenty-nine, and yet they were both back home with their mum and dad.

Up above she could see a light on upstairs at her parents' house. She sighed loudly, hoping that none of the kids were playing up. That was the last thing she needed: earache off her dad because he'd been kept awake. Granny wouldn't mind what was going on. She loved having the kids under her roof, although she did feel sorry for her parents having Steve at home too. Ramona hoped he hadn't come home drunk and woken everyone up. Her brother really was a pain in the arse at times, giving no thought to anyone but himself.

As she walked past the entry to the garage plot, she thought she heard footsteps behind her. She turned sharply, listened, but there was no one there. She quickened her step. Nearly home.

An arm came from behind, and a hand pressed across her mouth. Ramona felt her whole body jump. She tried to scream as she was dragged backwards and into the entrance that would take her to the garage plot. Down by the side of the first garage, she was thrown to the ground. As she tried to catch enough breath to scramble away, she saw a man behind her.

'Please, no,' she whispered. Desperately she fought him as he straddled her. He forced her arms over her head, holding both her hands with one of his.

Coming to her senses, she screamed.

He silenced her with a punch to the side of the face. Dazed and disorientated, it took a moment before she realised he was pushing up her skirt, ripping away her knickers. She tried to shove him away again but gave up when he punched her in the face several times in quick succession.

The pain was worse than childbirth as he almost tore her apart. She had never known rage like this before and dared not move, deciding to stay quiet and close her ears to the noises he was making. She could see the outline of her parents' house from where she had been forced to the ground. A tear dripped from the corner of her eye. She hated herself when she realised there was nothing she could do but wait for it to be over. Ramona had a feeling that if she started to fight again, she might not come away with her life. And she wanted to see her children in the morning.

CHAPTER THIRTY-SEVEN

Despite a restless night's sleep, Eden was in work for 8.30 a.m. Casey had been up when she'd left but she'd been quiet. Despite Eden asking, Casey hadn't said much about what she and Danny had discussed on the phone the night before. Eden didn't even know if she was upset because of that conversation or because Eden hadn't told her she was meeting with him.

When she'd gone to bed she'd heard Casey sniffing and knew she was crying. But when she'd knocked on her bedroom door, Casey had said she was fine and didn't want to talk. Maybe she'd come round this evening. If not, she'd try to get Laura to have a word with her. It had been a shock for them all and it was going to take time to adjust.

Jordan had gone to Manchester to speak to some of his colleagues in connection with Aiden Daniels. After he'd been spending a lot of time on the phone, it seemed the easiest option to send him there for a few hours. Amy was across from her, already hard at work. Phil had just arrived and was adjusting the height of his chair.

Eden checked her messages from the previous night as she enjoyed her first coffee of the day, gasping when she read up on Ramona Wilson's attack the night before.

'Problems?' said Amy, popping half a Jaffa cake into her mouth.

'Another woman has been attacked. Someone I know.'

Amy's eyes widened.

'Ramona Wilson is the manager of The Candy Club. Her attack makes it five in less than a month across the city.'

'How badly hurt is she?'

'She was raped.'

Amy grimaced. 'Where did it happen?'

'On the garage plot off Bernard Place. She's pretty roughed up.' Eden scrolled down the screen, reading more details. 'She has the usual, plus bruises to the face and defence marks on her arms.'

'Does she live near there?'

'No, Christopher Avenue, on the same estate, I think.' Eden clicked on a few more links. 'Yes, I thought as much. Her brother is Steve Wilson. He lives in Bernard Place with their parents. I wonder if she was staying there overnight or if she's moved back to her parents' house with the kids. Her fella is a loser too. Rob something-or-other, can't recall his surname.' She clicked a few more links before continuing. 'I can't imagine for a minute that would be an ideal situation for any of them. Although, I must admit, I'm surprised Steve has been out of prison this long.'

Amy cocked her head to one side. 'I thought he was just a drunken idiot, Sarge?'

'He is, mostly. But he also thinks he can do and say what he wants when he's sober and that gets him into more trouble, believe me.'

Eden was referring to an incident that had happened the year before. Steve Wilson had flatly denied breaking into the working men's club on the Hopwood Estate. CCTV hadn't been in operation that night, and he had actually gone in wearing gloves. But the silly idiot had left his wallet behind. Uniform had nabbed him, and he was awaiting a court date for the theft of a couple of grand's worth of liquor.

'He's definitely not a full bag of shopping,' she added. 'Shame for Ramona, though. I like her. She's only young but she's a spunky chick. Word is, she has a temper if anyone says anything she doesn't like or if anyone touches one of the girls. I hope she can get over this attack. It would be a shame for her to lose that.' She reached for her mobile from the desk. 'Come on, Amy. Let's go see if we can link it to the ongoing case, or see if it's a one-off and she knows who attacked her.'

'Shall I see if there's a pool car available?'

Eden shook her head. 'We'll take The Mooch.'

Thirty minutes later, Eden parked her Mini outside a block of offices in the south of the city. The second floor housed the rape suite. She'd rung to see if Ramona was still there before heading out.

'I really hope we can nail this creep soon,' she said to Amy as they walked up the stairs. 'I wish we could find evidence that would link them all. Despite thinking that Daniels is involved, we have nothing to back it up, and I'm concerned that he'll soon make a mistake and go too far.'

Amy shuddered. 'I hope we can stop him long before that happens.'

At the end of a corridor, Eden knocked on a door. It was opened by PC Sharon Felix, a dedicated sexual assault officer. Eden had worked with her on many cases in the Domestic Violence Team.

Sharon held the door open for them. In the room, Ramona sat in an armchair. A small television was on but she didn't seem to be watching it. She was staring out of the window. A bunch of artificial flowers stood in a small vase on a bookcase.

Ramona had a mane of red hair, a large frame and ample bosom, but she looked like a tiny young woman as she sat in shock after the assault.

'Ramona,' Eden said, perching on the settee as close to the armchair as she could without the possibility of invading the woman's personal space.

Ramona looked up at them. Eden tried not to gasp at the state of her. Her face was a riot of bruising around the nose and side of her cheek. The swelling had risen to its fullest, she imagined. A little bit was clearly visible on her top lip and nose. Eden realised she wouldn't be able to keep her talking long without causing her too much discomfort, but it was imperative they got as much information as possible to try to catch the man before he struck again.

'Are you okay to talk about last night?' She reached for Ramona's hand as Amy took out her notepad.

'He won't break me.' Ramona's voice was soft but determined. 'I'll need a bit of time to recover. The staff here have been brilliant, but now I'm left feeling battered and bruised, and really angry.' She rubbed her hands together before they clenched into fists again. 'I just want to hit out at someone.'

'Were you staying over at Bernard Place?' asked Eden.

'Yes. Me and Rob have split up. I've been there with the kids for two weeks.'

'I'm sorry to hear that.' Eden was nothing of the sort and hoped she sounded convincing.

'It's for the best,' said Ramona. 'Although it's a little cramped.'

Eden recalled Ramona's home in Christopher Avenue. She'd been there a few times, trying to find Steve Wilson. The children – two boys and a girl – had a lot of space to play in. Whereas, in Bernard Place, she imagined all four of them were in the same room. It just didn't seem possible that so many people could live in a house that size. But people put up with things deemed out of their control whenever necessary.

'I can't begin to imagine how you feel,' Eden said truthfully. 'Are you able to walk me through what happened?'

'I finished work at twelve and locked up.'

'You're still managing The Candy Club?'

Ramona nodded. 'Yes. I had a lift home off one of the girls. She dropped me off in Davy Road.'

'Name?' asked Eden.

'Angel Baker,' said Ramona.

'Do you always get a lift home from Angel?'

'No, sometimes one of the other girls will offer, and sometimes I get a taxi.'

'Any particular firm?'

She shook her head before continuing. 'I was walking down the street minding my own business, and as I passed the garage plot, he grabbed me from behind. I couldn't scream because he covered my mouth with his hand. The other was across my chest, and before I knew it, he'd pulled me backwards and into the entrance. He pushed me to the ground, and it was then that I began to gather my senses and I screamed. That was the first punch.'

Eden hadn't wanted her to go through it in so much detail but it was all said in one breath, as if Ramona wanted to get it off her chest so that she wouldn't have to say it again.

'He just got on top of me,' Ramona continued. 'He held on to my arms and then, well, I'm not going to go through all that. I'm sure you can imagine.' Tears dripped down her face as she looked up at Eden. 'I think I just went inside myself, you know? I did try to scream once more but he hit me again, and after that I kept quiet. I was so scared he'd— he'd kill me.'

'You mentioned something about a bite?' Eden queried.

Ramona pulled back the neck of her jumper to reveal an angry red-purple bruise, as large as the face on a wristwatch. There were marks where the attacker had dug in his teeth.

'At least *that* will fade in time,' she said, before bursting into tears. 'But the memories won't. The images of him trying to get inside my clothes, I'll see that every time I leave my parents' house. I'll see it every time I come back to the house. I'll see *him*.'

Eden closed her eyes momentarily. What the hell did he get out of marking her in that way?

'Can you remember anything about him?' Amy asked. 'Did he speak in a local accent?'

Ramona turned to her. 'He didn't say a word.'

'Can you recall what he was wearing?'

Ramona shook her head. 'It all happened so fast.' She closed her eyes, as if it was too painful to think about.

'And what did he do when it was over?' Eden knew it sounded callous to dismiss the attack as if it was nothing, but it was better to be matter-of-fact about things.

'He just got up and walked away, as if nothing had happened. As if he was putting his car away in one of the garages and had just come home.'

'Did you see where he went?'

'No.'

'And, obviously, there was no one else around?'

Ramona shook her head again. 'Luckily, I didn't have too far to go home. In my state, I wasn't fit to walk far. I'm so sore.'

Eden pressed her hand to Ramona's arm. She clearly wasn't ready to say any more.

'Thank you for talking to us,' she said. 'Going over it all again must be hell so I want you to know how much we appreciate it. We'll do our best to catch the man who assaulted you.'

Eden and Amy left the building in silence, both saddened and angered by Ramona's plight. Eden tried not to shudder. Being attacked like Ramona was one of her worst nightmares. Yet, even though it hadn't happened to her, she'd had to live through other women's attacks for years. Working in the Domestic Violence Team, some of the things Eden had heard had been sickening. One particular attack, where a husband had tried to drown his wife in the bath because he thought she was going to leave him, had made her vomit. There wasn't much that shocked her nowadays, but it still hurt to watch victims suffering or shouting out in pain.

Eden made a mental note to run the team through all the attacks at their next team brief, to check again for similarities. This assault was far worse than the last one. They needed to catch this man, and soon, before he went further than he had done already. If things continued, it could be a matter of life or death.

CHAPTER THIRTY-EIGHT

After leaving the rape suite, Eden drove to the Mitchell Estate to have a look at the area where the assault took place. She was interested in the access to it, how the attacker could have got in there.

'Bernard Place is a cul-de-sac, isn't it, Sarge?' said Amy, sitting beside her. 'No one in their right mind would follow someone home without any escape route if something went wrong.'

'Alice Clough was attacked right outside her house,' Eden reminded her. 'He wasn't bothered who saw him then.'

'But he didn't rape her.'

'I wonder if he intended to. Maybe he got off on her being so close to home but then was wary of being heard when he attacked her.'

The garage plot was a block of twelve purpose-built garages, in two rows of six, that nearby residents could rent out from the local authority. Eden parked up on Davy Road and walked across to Bernard Place. Crime scene tape flickered in the wind, a uniformed officer with a clipboard standing at the entrance to the site. Eden could see crime scene officers combing the area behind him.

Both she and Amy covered up before they were allowed behind the tape.

'Don't mind us.' Eden held up a latex-gloved hand as she reached the officers: one stooping down examining the grass and another taking photographs of the scene.

'This is off radar for CCTV,' said Amy as she glanced around and up. 'I can't see any cameras on this site either, so we have no footage.'

'Ramona said the gates are usually locked.' Eden pointed at the lock. 'This has been vandalised. We need to find out if it's recent or if our attacker forced it open.'

As people worked all around her, Eden walked to the back of the site to see if there was any way of getting in from there.

'Where did you come from?' she said quietly to no one in particular.

'Do you think he was lying in wait for Ramona?' asked Amy, coming up beside her.

'Possibly, but if so, why? What's the link to the other women?'

'They might not be linked,' said Amy. 'But it doesn't feel like a random attack, does it?'

'I don't think so.' A disturbing thought crossed Eden's mind. 'So it might be someone who knows that Ramona works late most nights.'

There was no other entrance at the back of the garage plot but there was a hedge around the perimeter. Spotting a gap, Eden went to investigate. Being careful where she trod, she pressed herself through to the other side and came out on to a walkway. Looking both ways, she saw it was littered with crisp packets and chocolate wrappers, suggesting a cut-through to the local high school.

She walked to Davy Road, counting twenty-five steps before she was on the pavement. There was a lamp post at the head of the walkway and one at the other end. She looked back to where she had come from. How dark would that be after midnight?

'Anyone in their right mind would either walk around the long way to avoid that walkway in the dark or do a Usain Bolt and run like the clappers,' she told Amy as she rejoined her. 'It leads to Davy Road so our attacker could have got into the garage plot through either the front or the back. I'll check with uniform later once the house-to-house has been done, see if we can't nail one or two witnesses for a chat. This must be our man.'

Amy nodded then hugged herself. 'Just the thought of that happening to you. . . it's frightening.'

Eden pointed behind her. 'There are fresh footprints by that hedge, with a weird marking on the sole. A possible letter P as well, I think. I had to press down when I squeezed through to the other side. I'll get SOCO to check them out, and then let's see if we can cross-reference anything back at the station. We need to look at the evidence from the other victims too. Bacon butties on the way?'

Amy grinned. 'Need you even ask?'

It sounded callous to switch off, but in their line of work, there would be too much trauma and stress to relive and take home with them if they didn't.

'One thing we'll have to keep an eye out for is Steve Wilson,' Eden said as they were removing their suits, gloves and shoe covers. 'He's handy with his fists when he's had a drink, and no doubt he'll blame anyone he knows for the attack on Ramona.'

Eden recalled her threats to Colin Stanton. If she was a bent officer, she would have a word in Wilson's ear and somehow make out Stanton was involved. But that was bullying, tempting as it was to give him his comeuppance.

'You mean he actually cares for someone other than himself?' Amy ribbed.

'Family is important to most people.' Eden thought back to the trouble with her niece. 'Last year, I would have ripped one of Jess's kidnapper's testicles off if I'd found out he'd touched Jess in any way.'

Her eye caught something and she looked up. A woman in an upstairs flat was waving at them. Eden switched off the engine and removed her seat belt.

'Looks like someone might have spotted something after all.'

Amy looked in the direction Eden was pointing. 'Want me to come with you, or do you want me to bang on some doors?'

Eden smiled, knowing how much of a pain that would be. Most of the residents of Bernard Place wouldn't take kindly to being woken up by the police. 'Doors would be great, thanks.'

CHAPTER THIRTY-NINE

While Amy went in the opposite direction, Eden walked to the flat where she'd seen the woman at the window. An elderly man answered the door. He stared at her before opening it wider when she showed him her warrant card.

'Morning, sir. I'm Detective Sergeant Berrisford and I'm investigating an incident that happened last night. I saw someone waving from a window in your flat.'

'That will be my wife, Elsie,' he said.

'May I come in and speak to her?'

'What about?'

Eden wondered if he was hard of hearing and hadn't heard all she'd said. She repeated her earlier sentence a little louder.

'I'm not deaf,' he muttered. 'What do you want to have a word with her about?'

Eden put on a smile. 'Might I come in please?'

Reluctantly, he opened the door more to let her pass.

She stepped into a hallway brimming with photos and nick-nacks that she hadn't been expecting. On first impressions, if she hadn't seen the woman, she'd assume the neighbour was a loner, a bit of a Victor Meldrew. But she could see he had a big family. There was a portrait of him with a woman and five children: two girls and three boys. It had been taken many years ago, and she wondered if they were all as close now that the decades had passed.

'Have you lived in Bernard Place long, Mr. . .?' Eden questioned as she waited for him to close the door after her.

'It's Mr Booth,' he replied, 'and we've lived here too long if you ask me. We moved from a house when it got too much for us. But now the stairs are getting to us too.' He shuffled past her and she followed him up. 'Mrs Booth is in the back room. You can go into her if you like. No doubt she'll enjoy your company.'

Eden smiled, not quite understanding until she spotted a box full of bandages, vitamin drinks and prescription medicines crammed into the space on the landing.

'The police are here,' Mr Booth told his wife. 'Though I don't know what they want with us. We never heard or saw anything, did we?'

A woman batted him away with a hand and looked up at Eden. 'Don't take any notice of him,' she said. 'He can't see anything without his glasses.' She pulled her dressing gown around her chest a little. 'I can tell you what you need to know. Come, sit. Roy, make us a cuppa, would you, there's a love.'

Before Eden could speak, Roy had shuffled out again.

Mrs Booth was in one of two single beds crammed in the room. It had been made to look as homely as possible with a television and comfy armchair.

'I have late-stage cancer,' she told Eden. 'Not long to go now, but I'll be damned if I'm going without a fight.'

Eden warmed to her instantly. 'I admire your spirit, Mrs Booth,' she told her.

'Call me Elsie.' She beckoned her over to the bed. 'Please, sit here.'

Once Eden was sitting down, notebook poised, Elsie could hardly contain herself.

'I'm sorry, Detective, but as much as I like Ramona, this is the most excitement I've had in my life for some time.' She sighed. 'Being confined to this room is very similar to having a prison sentence, I can tell you. I've been unable to make the stairs for some time now, but I can walk a little. I pace the length of the room and back again. I'm on the waiting list for a stair lift. The housing association wants us to move, but I'm not doing that again.'

'You waved to catch our attention. Can you tell me anything about last night, Elsie?' Eden asked, desperate to move things on.

'Yes, I was still up when I heard a commotion. Roy must have been asleep on the sofa in the living room, as try as I might, I couldn't get his attention. I shouted but he didn't hear me above the sound of the television. He wasn't even watching it, silly man.'

'Are you talking about me again, Elsie?' Roy came into the room with a tray, two cups and saucers and a plate of digestive biscuits.

Elsie smiled at him. 'Yes, how did you know?'

'Tea, Sergeant?'

'Not for me thanks.' Eden smiled at him too.

'He'd shut me in here,' said Elsie. 'He often does that, you know.'

'It's only because you say that I have the TV on too loud,' he said as he walked out of the room.

'Fibber. I should report you to social services for cruelty.' Elsie's eyes twinkled.

Eden sat up straighter. 'Go on,' she urged.

'Well, it might be something or nothing as I often hear shouting and screaming at night time. There are some noisy buggers in this street, I can tell you. I was sitting in my chair, knitting, when I heard a scream. It took me a while to get to the window, and when I opened it, it was all quiet again. I thought nothing more about it until I heard that poor Ramona had been attacked.'

'Did you hear anything else?'

Elsie shook her head. 'I did see someone running down the walkway though.'

'What time would this be?' Eden asked, thinking back to the footprints she'd spotted by the hedge.

'Around half past twelve.'

Eden stood up and went to look out of the window. She had a clear view of the garages and the walkway that she'd walked along earlier.

'It takes you back to Davy Road,' Elsie told her.

'Yes, I—' Eden glanced at the old woman. 'I don't mean to be disrespectful, Elsie, but that road is a good twenty metres away, and it was dark.'

Elsie smiled and pointed at the window. 'Look behind that curtain.'

Eden pulled it aside to see a pair of binoculars.

'Don't tell anyone, will you,' said Elsie, 'but I have to find something to do when I'm stuck in this room all day and night.'

'But it was dark.'

'Now, my dear, look across to the square again and tell me what you see.'

Eden looked but could see nothing.

'Look up,' Elsie encouraged.

It was then she saw what she needed to. 'Floodlights.'

'It's the community centre. Everyone has been complaining about them for months because they're so bright, and keeping them awake at night, but not me. They give me a bird's-eye view all the time.'

'What did you see?' Eden turned back to her.

'I think it was a man. He ran to the end of the entry and got into a taxi. Then he drove off.'

'He had a taxi waiting for him?' Eden's brow furrowed. This could be another link if the man had used EveryDay Taxis. It was certainly a first for her where an attacker had used such a vehicle for a getaway. Then her eyes widened as she clicked. 'Are you saying he was the driver?'

Elsie nodded.

'Can you recall which firm it was?'

'Warbury Cars.'

Eden knew the firm well. They were in the north side of the city and weren't known to rip off their clients, so there were no shouts or bust-ups after someone had been dropped off and then didn't want to pay their fare. They had a good reputation for driving lone females in safety to their destinations. Eden hadn't had any trouble with them really. A frisson of excitement bubbled up inside of her at the realisation that they might have another lead.

'Elsie, you've been most helpful.' Eden handed her a card. 'If you remember anything else, please don't hesitate to call.'

Roy knocked on the door and came into the room. 'You done yet?' he asked. 'Only, Elsie's carer is due.'

'Yes, thanks.' Eden smiled at him.

'I've been telling this nice young lady what I saw last night,' Elsie told him.

'I bet it wasn't worth knowing. You see, Sergeant, Elsie loves to chat but never really says anything useful.'

Elsie looked outraged but Eden caught him winking at her and saw Elsie's demeanour soften. Biting the inside of her lip, she stopped herself from breaking out into a smile. She loved nothing more than seeing couples who had been together for years bickering with each other but equally still so much in love with each other. She questioned if she'd ever feel like that, given her current predicament.

'On the contrary,' Eden decided to play along, 'I think Elsie has given us a great lead to be going on with.'

'Good for something then,' Elsie said, beaming, 'even in this sorry state.'

Once outside, Eden texted Amy to say she would be half an hour. There would a press conference soon, and she wanted to be back as soon as possible to see what that yielded, but first she was going to pay a visit to Warbury Cars.

CHAPTER FORTY

Warbury Cars was in a new-build office block and was a much better set-up than EveryDay Taxis. Eden introduced herself at reception and was shown into a large, airy office. A young man with short, spiky hair and waxed eyebrows sat in front of her. His skin was tanned, showing sparkling white teeth when he smiled, but there didn't seem a hint of poser about him other than the fact that he looked after himself. He didn't seem much older than Jordan, yet Eden noticed his suit was retro sixties and his cup had *all mod cons* written on it. She liked him immediately.

'I'm the owner, Matt Turner.' He proffered a manicured hand. 'What can I do for you?'

'Do you have a driver working here named Scott Daniels, or Aiden Daniels?'

'Scott Daniels.'

Eden showed him the photocopied image she'd got from EveryDay Taxis. 'Is this him?'

Matt took the paper from her and nodded. 'Yes, he started last night on a trial.'

'Do you have his DBS?'

'Yes. Why? Is something wrong?'

'We're looking into an incident,' said Eden. 'Did he come with any references?'

Matt wheeled his chair across the office while he sat in it and opened a small metal filing cabinet. He rifled through until he found what he wanted. Another brown paper file.

'So he was working for you last night?' Eden asked as he looked at it in more detail.

'Yes.'

'Times?'

'Four thirty until 2 a.m.'

'And are you aware that he's working for EveryDay Taxis too?'

Matt shook his head. 'I wasn't, no.'

'Do you provide your drivers with a cab?'

Matt nodded this time. 'We have a few pool cars. Business is taking off now so we're looking to hire more drivers on a permanent basis. They'll lease the vehicles from us then.'

'Do you have a list of fares he took?'

'I can print them off for you.'

'And GPS? Or a taxi app? You have that too?'

'Yes. GPS.' He pressed a few buttons on the keyboard and a printer whirred behind them, spewing out the necessary document seconds later.

'Can you tell me where he was between midnight and 12.45 a.m., please?' Eden asked.

'He was parked up in Davy Road, on the Mitchell Estate.'

The hair on Eden's neck rose and she sat forward.

'He was due a break at midnight, but I'm not sure why he didn't move again for forty-five minutes. I was going to have a word with him about it today.'

Eden fumed inwardly as she took the papers from him.

'Is there anything I should know?' he asked. 'I don't want anyone to put my clients in danger.' He paled. 'This isn't anything to do with the guy in the news who's attacking women, is it?'

'We can't be certain but it is a possibility. The man you employed isn't named Scott Daniels. We think he's Aiden Daniels.'

Matt paled, seemingly shrinking in his chair. 'So the DBS is a fake?'

'No, it belongs to his brother, Scott. We've found out he's been using his identity.'

'Well I won't be using him again,' he said.

Eden left the building and went to collect Amy from doing house-to-house in Bernard Place. She was going to blow a gasket if she didn't get back to the station soon.

CHAPTER FORTY-ONE

Eden could hardly contain her temper as she drove back with Amy once she'd collected her from Bernard Place. She banged her hand on the steering wheel as she pulled up at traffic lights.

'That bloody useless idiot,' she seethed. 'I gave him a simple job to do.'

'He has been off sick, Sarge,' Amy appeased.

'Not an excuse in my eyes. Not when a woman has been raped.'

'Oh, I don't mean—'

Eden threw her an icy stare.

'Uniform must have missed it too,' Amy added.

'Uniform shouldn't have missed it either. That's why we go out and check these things. We could just sit at our desks and email folk or ring them on the phone to tick off the boxes, but that's why we visit. So that cock-ups like this don't happen.'

At the station, Eden updated Sean and then asked to speak to Phil in the conference room.

The atmosphere was tense as Eden marched off, Phil close behind her. It took all of her strength not to slam the door shut after them. But she didn't wait for Phil to sit down, nor did she invite him to.

'The couple you interviewed last week after Christina Spencer was raped – Mr and Mrs Reynolds. They told you our suspect got into a taxi.'

'Yes, that's right,' said Phil.

'What did they tell you about him?'

'That he was tall and small. They didn't agree on anything, to be honest.'

'Which door did he use?'

'Sorry?'

'The suspect! Which seat did they say he got into in the taxi?'

'I don't know.' He shrugged. 'I can't see its relevance.'

'That's because your mind was probably on the next bloody horse race,' Eden seethed. 'So you never checked whether he got in the cab as a passenger or if he was the bloody driver?'

Phil flushed.

'Well?'

'No, I assumed he got in as a passenger.'

'Well I suggest you get straight on to the phone to Mr and Mrs Reynolds and check. Because if it is our man, we didn't pick him up quickly enough.'

'I don't see—'

'I've just been to visit Warbury Cars. Aiden Daniels was doing a trial for them last night, working as Scott Daniels. His cab was stopped for forty-five minutes in Davy Road, the next street to where Ramona Wilson was raped. The times match. If you had realised it was the driver, then we could have questioned him more in relation to Christina Spencer. The CCTV footage wouldn't have taken so much time to look at, and we could have searched his car. As it is, a number of drivers will have used it since, so any evidence will be contaminated. Why didn't you think to ask?' Eden stepped closer to him and stabbed a finger in his shoulder. 'Because of you, Ramona Wilson was raped. We might have caught him before he attacked again.' Eden couldn't even take pleasure in watching him squirm. 'I've just spoken to a witness who saw a man running away after Ramona was attacked. Now, if a member of the public can give me the information that he got into the driver's seat, why the hell can't you?'

'Sorry, Sarge.' Phil's eyes darted around the room before landing back on hers. 'They were always swapping and changing what they said. They told me Christina was in the back of the car and then the front.'

'She was!'

Phil hung his head. There were wet patches beginning to form under his armpits, the sweat sinking into his white shirt.

'Sorry doesn't cut it, Phil,' Eden snapped. 'Now go and ring Mr and Mrs Reynolds. And after that, you can source the CCTV footage of the night in question and look at it again. Because you've missed that too, haven't you? No one was picked up on the street, but you should have spotted the taxi.'

'I—'

'I gave you two jobs to do – two – and you fucked them both up.' Eden left him in the room and went back to her desk.

Amy pointed at her screen. 'That's the taxi, driving away at 8.20 p.m., just after Christina Spencer was attacked. Daniels never picked anyone up. I can't see the driver clearly enough to be certain it was him though as he's wearing a baseball cap and keeping his face hidden. Shall I get the image enhanced?'

'Thanks, Amy.' She felt someone standing near her and turned to look. 'What?'

Phil stood at her side, his chin almost touching the floor. 'I've just spoken to Mr Reynolds and our suspect was the driver.'

'You idiot,' muttered Amy.

Eden couldn't trust herself to say anything to him. 'Amy, can you check in with Jordan, see what he's found out in Manchester? See if any of the girls from there had a lift home or caught a taxi, not long before they were assaulted. Here too. And cross-reference with what was found on Market Street. Also, can you check through the CCTV footage to see where that taxi goes and mark down the times etc., please? Phil,' she glanced at the clock on the wall, 'time for you to finish today, don't you think?'

'I'll stay over, if you don't mind.'

Eden slammed a hand on her desk. 'Yeah, I do mind.'

People around her stopped what they were doing. She opened her mouth to speak and then closed it again. The man was older than her and he was looking sheepish. No matter how angry she was, enough was enough.

'If you want to do something useful, you can help with the details for Ramona's attack. The press conference brought in a deluge of calls. There are logs to check from EveryDay Taxis. There's lots of stuff that needs cross-referencing, actioning and checking over.'

'Yes, boss.' Phil nodded and scuttled off to his desk.

Eden returned to the CCTV footage. Now was not the time to get into another slanging match. They had work to do. She went to have a word with Sean. They needed to bring Daniels in for questioning.

TWELVE YEARS AGO

I never managed to escape Ryan's clutches and continued to live in a relationship that was hot and cold. One minute everything would be fine – the next, chaos would rule.

I did try to leave once. He came round to my parents' home, nice as pie, saying he was sorry. He'd been so convincing that my father wondered if I'd imagined what had been happening, that I'd somehow ramped it up for added effect.

My mum had been outraged at his suggestion and had sent him to the shops so that she could cool down and talk to me about it. No one had seen the bruises until then. Once I had shown my mum what was hidden under my clothes, she must have had a word with Dad, as he never mentioned it again but hung his head in shame when he next saw me and gave me a hug. It was hard for me to trust him, but I think he just didn't want to believe what had been happening. He'd rather have been in denial.

It was my worst fear when I found out I was pregnant again. Chloe was six at the time and was in school during the day so Ryan felt better about leaving me in the house alone during school hours. He'd managed to get a temporary labouring job and had started to stop off at the local pub on his way home, which I didn't mind because it meant I spent less time with him too. And when he did finally come home, Chloe would be in bed and wouldn't see him taking out his mood on me.

When it came to the crunch, I couldn't tell him about the pregnancy. I knew what he would say. I was sure he wouldn't want another child after how possessive he had become over Chloe. First he'd probably shout at me, saying it was all my fault that I got caught in the first place. The truth was, I had been very careful. I'm not entirely sure how it happened, but the doctor said that my recent bout of stomach flu could have caused my contraceptive to fail. And when Ryan wanted sex, he got it, whether or not I wanted to oblige.

I wasn't sure what he would do. Would he try and make me get rid of the baby?

It was then that I started to plot my escape for the second time. I could take Chloe and stay with my parents until I found my feet again. I wanted to have this child, even though it was another part of me that would be a part of him. I just couldn't abort it. I knew it was wrong to bring a child up in my world, but I couldn't kill it either. It wasn't the child's fault that I had such a lousy life.

I was only four weeks pregnant when I found out and so I planned to take a couple of weeks to plan everything in readiness. I couldn't just walk back into my parents' home. They would need notice. I knew they'd welcome us but that in itself presented a whole load of problems. They lived in a two-bedroom house, so there would barely be room for us.

In the end, I didn't tell Ryan that I was pregnant. My body let me down. Morning sickness came on me like a ton of bricks. That particular morning, I raced out of bed and into the en suite, getting to the toilet just in time to throw up. As I pulled my head back and wiped at my mouth, I could sense him behind me. Feeling vulnerable sitting on the floor, I put my hands on each side of the seat and went to heave myself up. But he pressed a hand on my shoulder.

'This isn't the first time you've been sick in the morning, is it?' He spoke quietly, his voice calm yet dark.

I shook my head. 'I think I must have caught food poisoning or something. Maybe that chicken was dodgy the night before last.'

He leaned over me. 'This has nothing to do with food, has it?'

I pushed myself up to standing again.

'You're pregnant, aren't you?' he said.

'No, I— I don't think so.' I turned to him slightly, keeping my stomach well hidden. 'I just feel unwell, that's all.'

He held out his hand. 'Best you get back to bed then.'

I nodded slightly and took his hand. 'Let me wipe my mouth first,' I said, stalling for time. The look in the bathroom mirror of an ashen woman with sunken eyes and sick down the side of her face startled me.

He stood in the doorway as I wiped myself down. Then he took my hand again and led me to the bed. Before I could get in, he pushed me in the back and knocked me to the floor.

'You're sure you're not pregnant?' he said, his face next to mine again. 'Because I don't actually believe you.'

'No, no! I swear, I'm not.'

'Well, if you are, you soon won't be.' He drew back his foot and aimed it below my ribs. The pain was intense as the toe of his boot drove into me.

I coughed and retched, holding up my hand as I cried out. 'Please, don't!'

He aimed his foot at me again as I curled up into a ball. 'Having another baby is out of the question. You can't even look after me and Chloe. If you have another child, who will look after us?'

His fists came at me then, and I curled up tighter to stop the onslaught. He knew there was nothing I could do to stop him destroying the life I had tried so hard to preserve. And I had lied to him and told him that it didn't exist. What kind of a mother was I to do that?

While Chloe slept in her room, I fought off his blows. The last one, his foot connecting with my chin, sent me sprawling back into the corner of the room. It was then he stood over me, saw the fear in my eyes.

'You are not having another baby, do you hear me?'

I just about had the strength to nod. His eyes bore into mine, searching out my lies, my deceit, my pain. Then he drove his fist into my stomach several times in quick succession.

'That's just to make sure,' he said.

I could hardly move with the pain and didn't dare get up anyway. But it didn't matter. He'd done what he'd set out to do. About an hour later, I felt blood trickling down between my legs. The baby was gone.

CHAPTER FORTY-TWO

Before she went home for the night, Eden drove over to Bernard Place to visit Ramona Wilson. Amy had been sent out to see the other victims. Eden wanted to see their reaction to the photo image she had of Aiden Daniels posing as his brother. It was a long shot, and even if they couldn't identify him, she hoped they would all recover enough to get on with their lives again.

Eden couldn't begin to understand what these women had been through, but she always prayed that they could be stronger because of it. Though she knew some would go into their shell, never trust a man again; never leave the house for fear of attack.

Did each day that passed make it easier to bear? she wondered. Or did that depend on how strong a person they were before it happened? Each woman she had seen had acted differently.

'How are you feeling?' Eden asked Ramona as she sat down across from Eden in her parents' small kitchen.

'Like I don't want to go out ever again.' Ramona spoke in a low voice. 'I know I said I wouldn't let him break me but what if he's waiting for me? Waiting to do it again?'

Eden said nothing. There were no words of comfort she could offer. She smiled faintly at her.

'You didn't see his face but I wondered. . . Women say they never forget their attacker's eyes. I know you said that too. I have a photo that I'd like you to look at, if you're up to it?'

Ramona shook her head vehemently. Then as a tear fell down her cheek, she nodded. 'I have to do this,' she said.

Eden got out the paper with the photocopied headshot of Daniels. They'd Tippexed out his name and details.

'Is this him?' she asked, holding out the paper to her.

Ramona took it from her, her hand shaking as she stared at it. Then she looked at Eden with a shake of her head.

'I can't be sure,' she said through her tears.

Eden touched her arm gently. 'It was a really long shot.'

'Have you caught him?'

Eden shook her head. 'But we're exploring every possibility. The evidence we're processing from you and the crime scene might link us to him too. I know it's awful to say this but it's early days. We're waiting on lots of forensics.'

Ramona looked at her with so much pain in her eyes that Eden's began to well up too.

'Please stop him from ruining anyone else's life,' Ramona said quietly.

Eden nodded. 'And please use the counselling and support available at the rape suite. There will always be someone there to listen to you.'

When Eden left the house, she was more determined than ever to nail Daniels for the pain he had caused. It irked her that he was still attacking women, and yet they weren't far enough along in their investigation to charge a suspect. But she knew her team would come up with the vital piece of information that would soon lead to an arrest.

CHAPTER FORTY-THREE

At home that evening, Carla watched two episodes of a rerun of *Happy Valley*. It was one of her favourite programmes, and it still gave her a thrill that she could watch what she wanted, when she wanted. Already she had painted her nails and read a magazine from front to back.

Ryan would never have let her sit on the settee for two hours. He would say she had time on her hands and make her clean a room in the house, even though everywhere would have been spotless.

She'd relished the nights during their first few years of marriage when he'd stayed away overnight with his work. It became her time to relax and just enjoy the quiet and calm. But when Ryan had lost his job, his obsession to see what she was doing every minute of the day had increased. Still, that was all over and done with now. She would never have to do that again.

It was 9.30 p.m. She wondered whether to squeeze in another episode before bedtime or if, as usual, she would fall asleep halfway through it. Maybe a mug of hot chocolate was in order either way.

She took a plate she'd used through to the kitchen and flicked on the kettle. The roller blind was up, and it was dark. Damn, she should have closed it as soon as she'd come in from work. After what had happened the other night, she didn't want anything to frighten her. Reaching for the cord, she pulled it down quickly, trying not to panic at the thought of someone outside.

She wondered if she'd ever be rid of the sense that she was being watched, being followed – never alone. Sometimes she made herself look through windows, out into the unknown, just for the sake of it. She couldn't stay scared forever.

Deciding to go to bed and read, she went back into the living room and picked up Thomas, who had been with her all evening.

'Come on, you,' she told him as he tried to resist her embrace. 'Time for bed for me, and time for you to go out and do what you do.'

Quickly she opened the kitchen door and popped him outside. Then she slid the bolt across and switched off the light. At the bottom of the stairs, as she turned to go up, something caught her eye and she looked over the bannister and back into the kitchen.

There was a shadow of a person standing outside the door. A face pressed up to the glass at the top half.

Carla covered her mouth with her hand, not wanting to scream. It had to be the same person that she'd seen the other night, which meant that it couldn't have been an opportunist thief.

It was a man, she was sure. She could see the outline of his face but not his features because of the pattern in the glass obscuring them. But it wasn't Ryan.

She stood motionless on the stairs, unable to move as the man stared at her. He clearly wanted her to know that he had seen her, that he was watching her, that he could hurt her at any time.

After a few seconds, he turned and walked away.

Carla dashed around the house, checking all the doors and windows were secure and then she called the police. Twice was definitely not a coincidence.

CHAPTER FORTY-FOUR

Eden found a message on her voicemail from Carla asking to see her when she was free. She sounded distressed so she tried to call her back, but she wasn't picking up her mobile so she sent a text message to say she would call that morning on her way to the station. But first she needed petrol.

'Casey, I'm off now, if you want a lift to school?' she shouted up the stairs.

'I'm fine, Mum. I'm meeting Jake at the shops.'

Eden smiled to herself. Jake was a name that seemed to be cropping up on a regular basis. She hadn't met him yet, and Casey would only say they were friends, but it was obvious to Eden that there might be more to the relationship. She tried to switch off the anxious-mum vibe about a man on the prowl, but it was hard enough not to worry about Casey having a boyfriend.

'Okay, well, I'll see you tonight then,' she said. 'And don't walk home alone after school while we have this man on the loose.'

'I won't.'

'Just—' Eden didn't want to frighten her but she needed to reiterate her point. 'Just be careful.'

At the garage, she filled up the tank, absent-mindedly running through the things she needed to do that day. First on her list was to drop everything once Aiden Daniels had been brought in. They'd called at his address twice yesterday, but he hadn't been home. They'd go again this morning. He was out there – they would find him soon. In the meantime, they would keep on collecting evidence.

Eden was looking forward to and dreading interviewing him in equal measure. Once more people heard about the press conference, even though the rape happened around midnight, she was hoping a witness or two might come forward. Perhaps someone had seen the taxi driver getting out of his cab and walking towards Bernard Place. Maybe someone had seen the driver sitting in his cab before he attacked Ramona. Just to see his cab stopped there wasn't enough.

As she stared into the distance, a familiar figure came into view. Danny. He'd sent her a few messages since their last phone call but she hadn't replied. She groaned, pulled out the nozzle and went to pay for her fuel.

She stood in the queue, wondering why he was watching her. When he was still there when she came back out on to the forecourt, she moved her car from the petrol pumps and parked up at the side.

'Are you following me?' she demanded as he jogged across to her.

'In a sense, I suppose I must be.' He grinned sheepishly, burying his hands in his pockets. 'I wanted to see you and you're ignoring my texts.'

'Sounds familiar,' she muttered.

'Look, I'm sorry. I know I've been a bastard, but I need to know.'

'Need to know what?' A look of confusion crossed her face. As far as she was concerned, she'd said all she wanted to when they had last spoken on the phone.

'If you've given any thought to helping me out.'

'Money!' Eden rolled her eyes. 'You have the audacity to ask again?'

'I'm desperate!'

'Tough!'

Eden turned on her heel, but he reached for her arm.

'You don't know what he's like when he loses his temper.'

She pulled her arm away sharply. 'I remember exactly what Jed Jackson is like. I saw what he did to Kyle Merchant, even if we weren't able to prove it was him.'

'Exactly! Don't you care that he might do that to me?'

'Why should I? You got yourself into this mess.'

'He'll come after you once he's done with me.'

'Don't threaten me!'

'I'm not.'

Eden dropped her eyes as a group of schoolchildren walked past them. As soon as they were gone, she prodded him in the chest.

'It stops right now, do you hear? I said you weren't getting any money from me, and I meant it.'

'But. . . Eden!'

She got into her car and drove off. As she pulled into the traffic, she saw Danny sitting on the wall, looking forlorn. On impulse, she gave him the finger. Then once she was past him, her tears fell. By rights, he should be in prison for stealing that information, and yet all he was interested in was covering his own back. Sure, he might be scared but he was putting both her and Casey at risk because of his stupidity.

But much worse, how could he think so little of her after all she had done for him?

By the time she got to the refuge, Eden's watery eyes had settled, along with her temper, and she put on a smiley face before going inside.

'Do us a cappuccino, would you?' She rubbed her hands together in anticipation once she was with Carla. 'It's bloody freezing out there. At least I don't look out of place with my Docs on. I love this time of year for that.'

'You hardly ever take your Docs off anyway,' Carla teased. She pointed to a chair. 'Come, sit.'

'I'm not sitting in that chair.' Eden shook her head. 'It's the confessional seat. I've seen you in action. I don't want to be interrogated and tell you all my darkest secrets. You wouldn't want to know me afterwards.'

'Really?' Carla probed. 'What's dark about you?'

'You'd be surprised.' Eden stared at her, thinking back to her earlier confrontation with Danny. Then she broke into laughter to lighten the mood again. 'No, you wouldn't.'

'Good!'

'So what did you want to see me for?' Eden came straight to the point once she'd wrapped her fingers round the cup of coffee. 'You've been chatting and joking with me. I know the signs. What's going on?'

Carla puffed out her cheeks and blew out her breath. She told Eden what had happened over the past few nights.

Eden's mouth dropped when she mentioned the figures at the window. 'Did you report them?'

'I did last night but not the first time.'

'Why ever not?'

'I know it sounds stupid but I just thought it wasn't worth bothering with. I get scared by so many things that I wonder sometimes if I've imagined them.'

'But you didn't!'

'No.'

'And how are you feeling now?'

'Spooked,' Carla admitted.

'Do you think it was Ryan?'

'No.' When Eden frowned, she continued. 'His face was contorted because of the glass, but I could tell it wasn't him.'

'How long has he been out of prison now?'

'A month.'

'That's good, that he hasn't come after you then.'

'I guess.'

'You're not convinced he'll stay away?'

Carla shook her head, tears threatening to spill from her eyes. 'I— I haven't been honest with you. When you asked if I'd seen Ryan since he'd come out and I said no? Well, I have seen him.'

Carla told Eden of her visit to the cemetery on Chloe's eighteenth birthday.

'I had to be there,' she explained, a defiant look on her face. 'I hadn't dared to go since Ryan's release because I didn't want him to find me. But Chloe would have been eighteen. I couldn't stay away on that birthday.'

Eden sat back in her chair. 'And he was there?'

Carla nodded. 'I wondered if it was him who put the brick through the window here last week.'

Eden thought about that for a moment. 'It's possible, I suppose. Although I can't rule out Vic White trying to scare Tanya. It happened as soon as she arrived.'

Carla's tears overflowed. 'If it was Ryan, I didn't mean to bring harm to anyone. I just had to see Chloe. But I hate the fact that I now feel like I'm being watched.'

'All the women in here think that.' Eden tried to make light of the situation, to appease Carla without her thinking she was patronising her. 'Even I've been feeling as if someone is watching me lately. I think it comes with the territory.'

'Perhaps so.' Carla shuddered. 'It's not a nice feeling though. I know it probably won't be possible to stay, but I do like it here in Stockleigh. I was hoping to be here longer. He'll come after me eventually. Him not being around unnerves me too. He could be trying to lure me into a false sense of security. I'm always on the lookout for him. Everywhere I go.'

'Do you want me to help facilitate a move?'

Carla gnawed at her bottom lip.

'I don't think you have any choice in the matter,' Eden stressed. 'I don't want to find you injured – or, worse, dead, Carla. It's my job to keep you as safe as I can. Can you move into the refuge for a while?'

Carla shook her head. 'I can't put a burden on this place too.'

Eden groaned. 'You're never a burden!'

'But if I move in here, I might bring the trouble with me. I'd rather have it at my home than unsettle the other women.'

'But—'

'I can't cause them any more pain – or put them in danger,' she cried. 'It wouldn't be fair. And you don't know Ryan like I do.' Carla told Eden about Ryan's threats to bury her in a quarry.

'That bastard!' Eden wanted to kick out at something but refrained. 'All the more reason for you to stay over for a couple of nights.'

'He won't leave me alone.'

'I know, but I'd feel better if you were out of the equation for now.'

'I can't move again.'

Eden sighed. It must be a terrible way to live your life, always watching over your shoulder, always scared. A thought struck her as she realised this could be her future if Danny didn't sort out his business with Jed Jackson.

'Look, you were right to let me know,' she said. 'If you want to wait a little longer to be certain then that's fine by me. I don't like it, but I can't make you move either. Just please be careful. Try not to be anywhere that he could get to you when you're alone. And if at any time when you're at home you feel like you're in danger, you know you only need to press the call button and someone will contact the police for you. You're a priority response for us.'

Carla nodded. 'Thanks.'

'And if that isn't enough, I'll come after the bastard myself,' Eden growled, hoping to bring a smile to Carla's face. 'I can be a tiger when necessary.'

Carla laughed.

'That's better.' Eden reached for her hand. 'Right, do you have any chocolate biscuits?'

Eden's phone went. It was a message from Jordan.

You might like to see what we have.

CHAPTER FORTY-FIVE

'What's come in?' asked Eden as she joined her team in the office, determined to push her private life to the back of her mind where it belonged. She looked at Jordan. 'Your text sounded like good news, I hope?'

'A bit of both, as usual.' Jordan pointed to his computer screen. 'Some forensics are in for Ramona Wilson. There doesn't seem to be anything to link any of the other attacks in Stockleigh.'

'Oh, for—'

Jordan held up his hand. 'Ever heard of Declan Parry?'

Eden shook her head. 'Should I have?'

'Not even the Parry boot?' He sniggered. 'I thought you were a connoisseur of boots.'

'Docs, maybe.' She sat down and shook off her parka, hanging it over the back of her seat. 'Is it a match to our footprint?'

'The very same.'

Eden punched the air. 'Well done, Jordan!'

'I found it actually,' said Phil. 'It took a bit of digging but I sourced them last night at home.'

Eden almost raised her eyebrows in surprise but stopped herself in time when she saw Phil searching through papers on his desk. 'Ah, here it is.'

Amy frowned. 'I'd never heard of that make until now.'

'It's some designer brand that hasn't been out long,' Phil added. 'The letter P on the sole of the boot was where I started. I researched online, found the pattern, found the brand. They're only stocked in Manchester and there aren't too many pairs sold at the moment.' Phil passed the paper print off to Eden. 'They also give out email receipts so I'm waiting on a list of who's bought them recently. The tread on the sole is almost new.'

Eden glanced at him and a smile spread over her face. 'Well done, Phil.'

Eden joined her team, who were waiting in the small interview room for a briefing.

Sean came dashing in, taking a mug of tea as quickly as his seat. 'Let's look at what we have so far. Eden, do you want to go through everything?'

Eden stood up and went over to the whiteboard. There were five names written in black ink with arrows linking down from them. She pointed to the first one. 'Our attacker seems to be of medium build, tall or short if you go by three of the descriptions. He was wearing a dark hat and scarf for each attack so we don't know what he looks like, and he never spoke to any of the victims. He disappears as quickly as he appears.

'We've checked out some CCTV but nothing is good, not even the enhanced shots. We can't see him anywhere before he's covered up. We can't make him out anywhere either. Our main suspect is Aiden Daniels. Turns out he's been posing as his brother, Scott, who we know used to work as a taxi driver and he's been using his clean record and references.

'We have GPS on a taxi that Aiden Daniels was working in as Scott that places him near to the scene of one of the rapes, and a witness who saw the car. We don't know for certain that it's him, or even if it's definitely the same person in all attacks. And, whoever it was used a condom for each rape and wore gloves throughout.

'So far, we've spoken to Daniels twice. He seems to have lost his memory about where he was or wasn't on some of the nights in question. However, EveryDay Taxis say the taxi which he was driving that night didn't pick up a fare, as he told us.'

'Run me through these boots,' said Sean.

'We were waiting on forensics for some footprints with distinctive markings that were found at the site of Ramona Wilson's assault, but Phil has managed to source them for us. So we have a size ten Parry Boot. They're a designer boot – well, more of a trainer really – and they're not too expensive but the designer is new so there haven't been many pairs sold.' She smiled at Phil before continuing. 'The firm in Manchester gives optional email receipts out. They emailed us a list of purchasers through this morning but there is no Aiden or Scott Daniels.' She turned to the board again, tapping on Aiden Daniels' photo. 'If it is him, he's certainly done his homework in places.' She pointed to the next photo of a pretty girl with short blonde hair.

'Ella Brown. Eighteen years old – attacked and raped as she was returning home from Sparks nightclub. We also spoke to Becky Fielding, twenty-two years old, who fought off an attacker two weeks before Ella was attacked. I'm not sure if that's linked yet, but my instinct says so.' She pointed at the next photo. 'Alice Clough, twenty-one, had been to London for the day. She was attacked in her front garden when a man dragged her to the ground. No sexual assault but brutally beaten.'

Eden pointed to the next name. 'Christina Spencer. Twenty-four. She was coming home from work in the city centre when she was attacked in the multi-storey car park on Market Street. The suspect took her keys and forced her into the back seat of the car, a white Ford Fiesta.' She pointed to a registration number. 'Again, our man was disturbed, so we found no forensic evidence.'

'Was he trying to get it right or just trying whoever took his fancy?' Sean asked. 'I'm not sure he was really thinking about this one, and maybe the first couple were opportunities too rather than, dare I say, researched? Who's next?' He grimaced. 'Sorry, I made that sound like I was waiting in line to place an order for fish and chips.'

They all smiled. Sometimes making light of a situation worked wonders when they were discussing things of this nature.

'Finally, Ramona Wilson, twenty-three. Attacked on her way home from work as she was walking along Bernard Place, where she has been staying. It was less than a five-minute walk to her front door. She was the next woman to be raped.'

'So no positive identification for Daniels?' asked Sean.

Eden shook her head.

'Did you find anything solid in Manchester, Jordan?'

'Nothing on Daniels but two women were sexually assaulted last month and one three months ago.'

'Before Daniels came back to Stockleigh?'

Jordan nodded. 'I'm cross-referencing those cases with ours at the moment. Neither of those victims had caught a taxi recently, so I can't link him to Manchester yet. I'm also still checking with taxi firms to see if anyone hired Scott or Aiden Daniels, but it will be a long job.'

'I'm still going through the taxi logs too,' added Phil. 'All the women assaulted used EveryDay Taxis during the last three months.'

'Can we link that to Daniels?'

'It's possible, but I've asked for more information as the drivers share the cars.'

'It's looking likely that the evidence will come back to say all the cases are linked,' said Sean. 'If so, I think we need to move this to Major Crimes. I'll have a word with the DCI and see. But in the meantime, while we're dealing with this murder case, can you continue with things? Thanks for your work so far. There's been some great intelligence gathering. And keep at Aiden Daniels if you think it's him. Do any of the women have a link?'

'Apart from all being in their early twenties and being on their way home?' Eden shook her head. 'None of them work together or are friends with each other. None of the victims knows any of the others. There isn't even a link to their surnames or schools even. They're all from different corners of the city.' She ran a hand through her hair. 'Nothing – and we can't nail Daniels properly unless we have evidence. It's so frustrating.'

'What makes someone attack so many women in such a short space of time? It doesn't sound feasible,' said Jordan. 'Although I know there's no real answer to that.'

'What makes a man rape a woman in the first place?' said Amy. 'That's beyond me.'

'Nothing surprises me any more,' said Eden. 'Let's just make sure we get the bastard before he can strike again.'

There was a knock on the door. It was the duty sergeant.

'Uniform have arrested Aiden Daniels,' he said. 'He's in cell two.'

CHAPTER FORTY-SIX

Eden paused for a moment and took a deep breath before entering interview room one with Jordan. It would take all her professionalism to stand back and not lurch across the table and punch the man sitting across from her full in the face; to put a hand under the table, grab his balls and cause as much pain as possible. Seeing what had happened to Ramona Wilson made her blood boil, but professionally she pushed it to the back of her mind. She needed to put it in a box and not let it cloud her judgement.

While they were conducting their interview, Amy and Phil had been sent to visit EveryDay Taxis and Warbury Cars to see if they could find the boots. They didn't have enough evidence to charge Daniels with anything related to the assaults yet, but she and her team were building it up bit by bit. She prayed they would sort it before another woman became a victim.

Aiden sat hunched forward over his drink, a plastic cup full of tea. Martin Dinnen, the duty solicitor, sat by his side. Eden had left Aiden there for several minutes to observe his reactions as she stood in the corridor watching him via the camera. He seemed cool, calm, collected, not as if he was about to get a grilling over the attacks on several women.

Finally she turned to Jordan. 'You ready?' she asked.

'Yes, boss.'

They went into the room and sat across the table from the two men. Daniels wore a look of contempt. Dinnen wore a navy suit with a white pinstripe, showing a flash of his trademark red socks as he crossed one leg over the other.

Eden read Daniels his rights after pressing the record button on the machine. Jordan took notes while she led the interview.

'Scott Daniels,' she started, 'or is it Aiden Daniels?'

Daniels shifted uncomfortably in his chair. 'It's Aiden Daniels.'

'Why did you lie about who you were?'

'I needed to make some cash. I knew my brother had been checked to drive a taxi so I just borrowed his stuff.'

'Hmm, we'll come back to that. Can you tell me where you were on the night of Friday 7 January between the hours of 1 a.m. and 2 a.m. please?'

'I was working.'

'Work being where?'

'EveryDay Taxis, as you know.'

'Were you working on Saturday morning on 21 January between the hours of 1 a.m and 2 a.m.?'

'Yes.'

'And on the night of Thursday 26 January between the hours of 11 p.m. and midnight?'

'Yes.'

'And this Saturday just gone, the twenty-eighth? Were you working between the hours of 8 p.m. and 9 p.m.?'

'Yes, but you already know all of this.'

'I do.' Eden smiled. 'But when I questioned you previously about the twenty-eighth, firstly you said that you picked up a fare at 8.20 p.m. that evening, a lone male, and dropped him off outside The Snooker Club in the high street a few minutes later. Then you said that you'd got your times wrong and you hadn't picked up anyone outside the multi-storey car park. Can you tell me which of these is correct please?'

'The second version.'

'But the call logged by EveryDay Taxis said that you did pick someone up from outside the multi-storey car park. Are you now saying that you made up the fare?'

'Yes, I was trying to make a bit of cash in hand.'

'Knowing that is illegal?' Eden paused. 'I have you on camera at 8.20 p.m. coming out of the multi-storey car park driving a taxi.'

'Are you sure about that?'

Eden said nothing. The truth was they weren't certain, as the image from CCTV hadn't shown the attacker's face clearly enough. But it was the same registration number of the taxi he had been using that night.

'I'm trying to establish facts – and a timeline, Mr Daniels,' said Eden. 'You're saying one thing, and the proprietor of EveryDay Taxis is saying another. I need to know which one of you is telling the truth. So you say you didn't collect a fare from outside the multi-storey car park in Market Street at 8.20 p.m. on Saturday 28 January?'

'No, I had a cab ride out to Warbury. It was a good fare so I pocketed it, I'm ashamed to say.'

Eden nodded slightly.

'So you lied to me about picking someone up and dropping them off in the high street?'

'Yes.'

'Why? Because you wanted to make some money cash in hand, off the record?'

'Yes.' He hung his head. 'Sorry, but I'm a bit short. What with moving back from Manchester and—'

'Why did you leave Stockleigh so quickly five years ago?' she interrupted.

Eden watched him for signs of nervousness but there was nothing. No beads of sweat appearing on his forehead, no shaking of his leg, no wringing of his hands. But she could see a twitch in his left eye.

'I've already told you. I took a contract working on a building site for five years. It's finished now, so I'm back.'

'Does Sylvia Latimer's family know?'

His face darkened.

'You have a record of violence, don't you, Scott? Sorry – Aiden.'

'It's all in the past.'

'Yet you tell us you pick up a man who we believe sexually assaulted a woman in the multi-storey car park, take him from the scene of the crime and don't record the details through the cab firm you work for. And then you say you didn't. You made it up so that you could collect another fare, and take them to where in Warbury?'

'I can't remember now without looking at my notebook.'

'Is the notebook in your cab?'

Aiden shook his head. 'The cab isn't mine so I keep it with me.'

'So it's at your brother's house in Sudbury Avenue?'

'I think so.' He shrugged slightly. 'Can't remember where I last saw it, to be honest.'

'Oh dear, you don't have a very good memory, do you?' Eden tried to keep the sarcasm from her voice. 'So to clarify: you were working during all the times I've mentioned, but you were pretending to be your brother?'

'I wasn't pretending to be my brother. I was just using his stuff. But yes, I was working.'

'For EveryDay Taxis?'

He nodded. 'I'd have to check my notebook to be certain though.'

'Which you think you might have mislaid?'

'What is it with you?' Aiden's tone suddenly changed. 'Why are you asking me the same things over and over when I keep telling you what happened?'

Martin Dinnen put a hand on Aiden's arm and shook his head. Aiden shrugged his hand away and sat back in his chair. He folded his arms.

'Look, I lost a notebook, that's all,' he said.

'Do you work for anyone else?' asked Eden.

'No.'

'Not even for a few hours for Warbury Cars?'

Eden watched him shuffle in his seat before she continued her questioning. She raised her eyebrows, hoping he wouldn't clam up now.

'Where were you on Thursday 2 February at approximately fifteen minutes past midnight?' she asked.

'I was out on a job.'

'Yes, I checked with the owners. According to GPS, you were parked up outside the community centre on Davy Road at the time Ramona Wilson was raped.'

'I didn't attack her! I was on a break.'

'It was a long break, according to Warbury Cars.'

'I fell asleep, all right! I got a call from base asking where I was. It was my first time on nights.'

'So what time did they ring you?'

'I can't remember.'

Eden sighed dramatically.

'It's really not going to wash with me that you can't remember anything, Mr Daniels.'

'Do you have any evidence to suggest that I was involved?'

'We're working on that right now.'

'Well if anything happens to another woman while I'm in here, that'll be your fault.'

'And why would that be?'

'Because you're not questioning the right man yet.'

Eden stayed quiet. *Oh, I think I am.*

'Look, this is all circumstantial evidence,' Dinnen said. 'If you haven't got anything else to lay on the table then I expect you to release my client until you come up with it. We've been here—'

Eden interrupted him. 'What size shoes do you take, Mr Daniels?'

Aiden paused, looking from her to Jordan and then back again. 'I'm a ten.'

Eden nodded at Jordan and he pulled out a photo from his file. 'Do you have a pair of boots like these?'

Aiden glanced at them. 'No.'

'You're sure?' Eden slid the image closer to him. 'Here, take another look.'

Aiden sat forward and made a show of looking again. Then he pushed the image away. 'I'm positive.'

'Would you mind if we took a look in your brother's house to make sure?'

'Be my guest. You won't find any because I don't own any.'

As Jordan left the room to arrange a search of the property, the words of Ramona Wilson came to Eden's mind. At this moment in time, she wanted nothing more than to cause Daniels the maximum amount of pain, but she knew they didn't have enough to hold him. Sure, there would be enough for any detective TV show, but for the courts, nothing circumstantial would stick. They needed to dig deeper to find more.

Eden went back upstairs. Her phone went. It was Amy.

'Nothing so far,' Amy said. 'We've checked his lockers at both sites and some of the cars he's used.'

'We're going to search his property.' Eden raised a hand in thanks as someone held the door open for her to go through. 'Bloody Martin Dinnen, with his smarmy suit and his silly red socks, says we have to let him go if we can't find anything. Daniels attacked these women just because he could, and that's sick. We need those boots or he'll be out on bail.'

CHAPTER FORTY-SEVEN

With trepidation, Tanya walked up the path to her front door. After seeing Vic earlier in the week, she knew she shouldn't be going home yet, but she needed to see familiar things around her for a while.

She knocked on the front door to see if he was in. If he was, then she would have time to leg it down the street and hopefully get out of sight before he caught up with her. She'd already texted him to ask where he was. He'd replied to say he was in town, which is why she'd got here pretty sharpish. She hoped to be in and out before he was back.

She knocked twice more and, when no one came to the door, she got out her key and went inside. The hallway was always dark, and she almost put her keys into the small bowl on the hall table: force of habit. Now she pocketed them and moved further into the house.

She wasn't really sure what she'd come home for, except that she missed the place. It felt insane that she couldn't be here. She went into the kitchen and looked through the window into the garden. No one there either. She shuddered. It felt like she was trespassing in her own property. If she got caught coming back, Vic would have something to say, but she had something to say too. Maybe she could talk to him. She'd done what she'd had to – surely two weeks was long enough?

'What the fuck are you doing here?'

She jumped at the sound of a voice behind her. He was standing at the back door, and she knew by his face that he wasn't in a welcoming mood. She ran to the front door, hoping to get past him, but he was too quick. He seized her by the waist and dragged her into the living room. She cried out as he threw her down on to the settee.

'I told you to stay there for four weeks.'

'But I hate it,' she whined.

'I don't think you understand why you've been sent there. Do as you're told.'

'I don't have to do what you tell me to do at all.'

Tanya regretted the words as soon as his hand swiped across her face. Wiping her mouth, she tasted blood. Her lip had split. As she looked up, his fist was clenched and coming at her.

'No!' She shielded her face with her arms as he raised it in the air. It hit her arm, stinging so much that she screamed.

He grabbed a fistful of her hair and pulled her back up on her feet. 'You shouldn't have come here. Now I have to teach you a lesson to make sure that you won't come back again.'

'I won't! I promise.' Her breath came in fits.

'Damn right you won't.' He slammed her up against the wall and brought his forehead down on hers.

Tanya saw lights before her eyes, and she groaned. Dizziness washed over her as he moved his head back, and she thought he was going to do it again. Dark eyes glared at her. She tried to escape them by looking at the floor, but he squeezed her chin hard.

'You will go back to the refuge, and not a word of this. Tell them you were attacked. There's a man on the loose grabbing women. You were walking home and someone hit you, but you managed to escape.'

'They won't believe me.' Tanya winced as the pain in her head intensified.

'I don't care. All I want is you back in there. Do you understand?'

Tanya nodded as best she could. Although she didn't want to be part of this any more, she was in too deep. It wasn't right what she was doing, anyway. She was a despicable person, putting other people's lives in danger.

Maybe she should come clean to someone at the refuge. But looking at him now, standing in front of her, she knew if she didn't do as he said, he would carry out his threats.

'Now get back there and finish what we started.'

He grabbed her arm tightly and marched her to the front door. Opening it, he pushed her out. She managed to stay on her feet, but she couldn't see where she was going. Already her eyes were beginning to swell from the force of the blow to the bridge of her nose.

How could he do that to her? He was an evil bastard.

As soon as she was able, she was leaving Stockleigh. Leaving for good and never coming back. She wasn't going to stay loyal to anyone any more. Look where it got her.

Tanya staggered to the front gate and out on to the pavement. She'd have to go back to the refuge first. Yes, that's what she would do. And while she was being looked after, she could still do what she had come to do.

Because as much as she didn't want to play by his rules, by breaking them, she'd put herself in more danger.

CHAPTER FORTY-EIGHT

At the refuge, Tanya ran sobbing into the hallway. Lisa was in the kitchen and came rushing out to her before she could get up the stairs to her room.

'Tanya! What's happened?' she cried.

'Vic attacked me again.' Tanya looked down at the floor. She couldn't say it was the man who was on the loose because it would lead to too many questions and she was bound to slip up.

'When was this?'

'I was over by the shops,' she lied, 'and he ran over to me. He made me go home with him, and then he did this. But I managed to get away. I'm so scared. What am I going to do?'

'We need to call the police,' said Lisa, reaching for her mobile phone. 'He can't keep getting away with this.'

'No!' Tanya cried. 'You can't, or else he'll come after me again.'

'He'll come after you regardless unless you do something to stop him!'

'No, please.' Tanya began to sob. 'Let me sort it out.'

'Let's sit you down in the kitchen,' Lisa urged her. 'At least I can tend to your injuries. You're covered in blood.'

Carla had come through from the living room. 'Oh no. Did Vic do that to you?'

'Yes,' Tanya muttered before sitting down at the kitchen table.

'But going back with him after what he did to you on Monday?' queried Lisa as she took a clean cloth from the drawer and ran it under the tap.

'I didn't have a choice.' Tanya looked up at them. 'I don't feel safe here either.'

'If the refuge isn't safe for you, we can try to find another one that is,' said Carla. 'You'd have to move from Stockleigh, but I think your safety is far more important.'

Tanya shook her head. 'I'm not leaving.'

'But think about what he's capable of doing. If he does this now,' Carla pointed to the bruising around Tanya's face, 'think what he might do if he completely loses control.'

'He doesn't mean to harm me.'

Lisa sat down beside her and took Tanya's hands in her own. 'Don't back down to him again,' she said. 'Please, let us help.'

Tanya nodded and then lowered her eyes.

Lisa couldn't be sure Tanya was telling the truth, but she didn't want to push her. The woman had been through enough trauma.

'I have to stay here in Harold Street, don't I?' Tanya said.

'I think it's for the best,' said Lisa.

Tanya nodded. 'I think I'll go to my room now.'

'Will she be okay?' Carla asked once Tanya had left, a worried look on her face.

Lisa shook her head. 'I don't know. I have a feeling there's something she isn't telling us.' She shrugged. 'We all have secrets. Perhaps she'll speak to you at your next session.'

CHAPTER FORTY-NINE

Having found no boots at the house where Daniels was staying, they'd had to release him on bail while they waited on further forensics to come back. They hadn't even found his notebook, if there was one at all. It was frustrating being so close but equally if the evidence didn't stack up, there was no case to answer.

So, it was bittersweet when Eden received a phone call later that evening. She almost fell off her chair in her rush to speak to Sean.

'I've just had a call from Doreen, the receptionist at EveryDay Taxis,' she said, stopping in front of his desk, a little breathless with excitement. 'Although there was nothing found in Daniels' locker, or in the immediate vicinity, they kept looking around. She's found a pair of boots wrapped in a black bag and shoved behind some old piping in the store room.'

'Get uniform to pick them up and send them off for soil analysis,' said Sean. 'Great work, Eden.'

He looked up as she came out of the building. He dipped his head as she glanced his way before getting into her car, even though he was sure she wouldn't notice him from where he stood.

He heard the click of the remote control – watched as she opened the door and got in. His final glance before he could look no more saw her checking herself out in the rear-view mirror, moving stray hair from her face, before starting the engine. He knew she would be driving away, so he moved out of view.

As she drove off in the opposite direction, he was tempted to follow her, but he knew better. It was a sure-fire way of her seeing him. Best to stay inconspicuous for as long as possible.

But he was finding it harder and harder to stay away from her.

CHAPTER FIFTY

Carla was rushing around the house in search of her car keys. It was nearly 8.30 a.m. and she was going to be late for her morning session at work if she didn't get a move on. Where were they? Spotting them underneath a mailshot leaflet advertising two pizzas for ten pounds, she grabbed for them, plus her jacket, and finally she was on her way.

She marched down the path, glancing upwards to see a bright blue sky, not a cloud in sight. It had been unseasonably warm for the beginning of February, with clear skies and no frost for the past three days.

As she drew level with her car, she stopped in her tracks. An envelope had been slid underneath one of the windscreen wipers. It was large and padded and had her name written in black capital letters. There was nothing else on it. She looked up and down the street but there was no one near. Workmen sat in a van outside a property several houses down. An old man stood on the doorstep. A young woman across from her waved as she popped her baby into its pushchair.

Carla waved back as she walked slowly to her car. She removed the envelope and, with another quick glance up and down the street, got into her car with it and locked the door. She turned it over and over in her hands, beads of sweat forming on her forehead. There was no return address and no postage. The postman hadn't dropped it. Someone had left it there deliberately. Someone had been outside her house again while she slept.

It could just be one of the neighbours, she supposed. She'd been asked to join the neighbourhood watch lately. Perhaps it was a handful of leaflets.

Then she realised how stupid that idea was. Who in their right mind would leave them on her car?

Her hands shook, making it hard for her to tear the envelope open. She wasn't sure if she wanted to look inside, but she had to know what was in it.

She put a hand inside, gasping as it fell on material, silky to the touch. She pulled the contents out and, with a shudder of revulsion, threw them on to the passenger seat.

It was a lacy red bra and knickers. Their significance wasn't wasted on her. Ryan had found her, and he wanted her to know.

Images of him pushing her face to the wall and banging it over and over came rushing to her mind. Fists thumping, feet kicking, hands grabbing hair. She fought back tears as she squeezed her eyes tightly shut.

Overcome by nausea, she opened the car door and vomited into the gutter. Just the thought of him knowing, again, where she was proved too much. She had anticipated he would find her but still it shocked her. She didn't want to leave Stockleigh.

Quickly, she locked up her car and went back inside. Rushing around the house, she checked all the doors and windows were secure. She rang Lisa and told her she'd be late for work as she was sick. She wasn't lying, as she raced to the toilet to vomit again.

Upstairs, she grabbed the rounders bat and sat on the bed with her back to the wall. She had to be prepared for him coming after her, although she wasn't sure she would ever be ready. What would it be like to see him close up again, after nine years, and feel his anger as he squeezed the life out of her?

She closed her eyes, trying to rid herself of the images that kept on surfacing.

Then she jumped off the bed. Until her nerves had calmed, she'd feel safer with people at the refuge.

CHAPTER FIFTY-ONE

At the school gates, Melody Dixon bent down and gave the little boy standing in front of her a hug.

'Don't forget what I said to you this morning, Reece,' she said, wiping a hand across his forehead. 'If nasty Dale Worthington says anything rude to you again, you must tell Miss Armstrong. You mustn't repeat what he's said to anyone else, do you hear?'

Reece Dixon nodded his head vehemently. Melody kissed him on the cheek before standing up again. The morning bell went and she watched him run into the throng of children going into the school building. Melody sighed. A bit of peace and quiet was what she needed to get her head round things.

As she started the ten-minute walk back home, she thought of what she was going to do. She'd seen an advert in the window over at Shop&Save for women to help with Stockleigh Women Achieving Potential. Despite her young years and her terrible choice in men, she was a good mum, so she'd decided to look into helping out with young children. It was a huge step, but she was willing to take it. She was bored at home and she had a few hours a day she could spare. Volunteering would look good on a CV for when Reece was in junior school alongside Nathaniel, and she could perhaps get a decent job.

Her thoughts turned to what she'd have to do next as she let herself into the house. Going through into the kitchen, she sat her phone down on the worktop, flicked on the kettle and opened the post that had been on her doormat. Really? Her Visa bill was due to be paid again? With dread, she opened the envelope and sighed heavily. How could she have run up that much debt in just under four weeks? She'd have to cut up her card.

Her head turned as a flash of light caught her eye. There was glass on the floor. She moved towards the glass and the utility room at the back of the house. A shiver ran down her spine.

The small window had been broken. The larger window was open wide – and large enough for someone to climb through. She walked backwards slowly, grabbing her phone.

She heard another noise. It came from upstairs. There was someone in the house. She rushed to the front door, phone to her ear.

'Hi, Dad, only me. I've had a break-in, and I think there might be someone in the—'

Her hand touched the door handle. Steps thundered behind her and she was pulled back by her hair. She screamed as she was dragged upwards, her feet grappling to keep her upright.

At the top of the stairs she held on to the bannister, but the grip around her waist intensified as she was pulled backwards. She tried to look behind her to see who it was, but all she saw was black.

She screamed again as a fist pummelled at her fingers until she released them. The door to her bedroom was kicked open, and she was thrown on to the bed. Her attacker had olive skin and deep blue eyes, dark hair curling from underneath a black woollen hat.

'No!' she cried. Scrambling up the bed, she tried to get away. But his hands were on her. He grabbed her around the waist again and turned her round. In seconds he was straddling her, pulling at her clothes. She slapped at him, squirming under his touch.

The first punch dazed her. He had her shirt up and hands on her before she realised what was happening. She tried to fight him off again.

The second punch hurt really badly, but she wasn't going to go down without a fight. Her hand reached out, desperate to find something to hit him with. As he ripped at her clothes, her fingers clasped her alarm clock. It was small, but in her fist was more of a weapon. If she could just lift it up.

She smacked him across the side of the head, but his hat buffered the force.

He sat still for a moment. She could hear him catching his breath, see his eyes turn darker. Trying to memorise everything about his face, again she tried to push him off, her flailing hands catching him a few times.

But he was too strong. Several punches one after the other rendered her useless to do anything.

CHAPTER FIFTY-TWO

Eden and Amy were in Sudbury Avenue. They were going house-to-house, trying to see if anyone knew the whereabouts of Daniels as he wasn't at home. They stopped when they heard a shout coming through.

'All units in the vicinity of Warbury. Intruder alert at fifteen Sidney Place. Member of public says his daughter has been beaten, and he's not sure if she's breathing. Ambulance en route. Anyone able to respond, over.'

Eden pressed the button on her radio. 'D429 to control room. We're a few streets away, show us responding.'

'Received, D429. Victim's father isn't sure if she is unconscious or if it's a fatality.'

Eden and Amy ran to the car. They were only two minutes away, so they would be first on the scene.

'Do you think it could be Daniels?' asked Amy, as they left Sudbury Avenue.

Eden glanced at her as she took a sharp corner. 'I don't want to jump to conclusions as it could be a domestic. But it does seem too much of a coincidence.'

'He's going to kill someone soon if it is him, isn't he?'

'Not on our watch he isn't.'

She turned in to Sidney Place. Outside number fifteen, a man stood waving his arms at them as they approached.

'She's in her bedroom.' He pointed up, his hands covered in blood. 'I— I think she's dead.'

'Is there anyone else inside the property that you know of?' Eden pressed.

The man shook his head. 'She rang me this morning saying something about a break-in, then the line went dead. I came as quickly as I could. But I think I'm too late.'

'Which room is she in?'

'The front bedroom. Second door on the left.'

'And you're her father?' asked Amy, taking the man's arm.

'Yes. Malcolm Dixon.'

'And your daughter's name?' asked Eden.

'Melody. She's only twenty-three. Please, you have to help her.'

Eden left the man with Amy as she flicked out her baton. She stepped inside the property. Ahead of her were stairs, the bannister covered in patches of blood. She suspected Mr Dixon had steadied himself to get down quickly to go for help. She doubted the attacker hadn't been wearing gloves.

'D429 to control room, receiving.'

'Go ahead, D429.'

'We're at the property now. The victim appears to be a female in her early twenties. The property seems to be secure so I'm going upstairs to check on her.'

'Received, D429. Waiting for further.'

With no immediate threat that there was anyone else in the property, Eden took the stairs three at a time. Getting out her pepper spray just in case, she rushed into the room at the front of the house with it high in the air. Her arms sunk to her sides as what she was greeted with took her breath away.

Melody Dixon was lying on her back in a state that Eden knew would haunt her father for years to come. She had been beaten severely, her eyes glazed over. Someone had pulled the duvet over her nakedness, destroying forensics. She assumed it must have been her father. Eden could understand his concern about ensuring her dignity, even though the forensic team wouldn't be happy. She would have done the same if it was her daughter.

In the distance she heard sirens. She took gloves out from her pocket and flicked them on as she moved to the side of the bed. If this was Daniels, he was escalating quickly and violently. Melody had obviously put up a struggle.

She pressed a hand to the girl's neck, sighing with relief when she felt a pulse. It was weak, but it was there.

'D429 to control room. Victim is alive but unconscious. Request ETA for ambulance.'

'ETA two minutes.'

Knowing she could do nothing, Eden raced downstairs. Two uniformed officers had already arrived, and there was another car pulling up. It was a first responder paramedic.

'Seal the road off as soon as the ambulance arrives,' she shouted her orders, waving to the paramedic to come quickly.

Amy arrived by her side.

'She's alive,' said Eden. 'Well, at the moment she is.'

'Is it Daniels?'

Eden shrugged. 'I can't be sure. He's left her in such a state that I can't even see beyond the blood. But he must have left forensic evidence now. We'll need to get it fast-tracked.'

As more paramedics rushed past her, she went back to Mr Dixon.

'She's alive, but her pulse is weak,' she told him. Seeing his face whiten, she caught his arm just as he was about to collapse on the pavement. She helped him sit down on the step. 'Put your head between your legs for a moment.'

Leaving him with Amy once more, Eden popped shoe covers over her Docs and went back inside the house. She knew she'd be ushered off the scene as soon as the crime scene officers were there, but she wanted to take a look downstairs too. In the kitchen, she saw the broken glass and the open window. Nothing else was out of place. It didn't look as if Melody had disturbed a burglar and he'd flipped.

But as she glanced through the window, she could see the door to the shed had been forced open. She wondered if the attacker had lain there in wait or even stayed there overnight. She shivered at the thought.

As the paramedics worked upstairs, Melody's battered face kept popping into her mind. She shuddered, vowing to get the man who had done this once and for all. He couldn't keep doing this.

Outside again, she tried to calm her nerves, feeling so angry for the victim that she wanted to lash out. She kicked at the wall and then sat down on it, taking a deep breath and trying to steady herself so she could think. The street was starting to come alive with people on their doorsteps or standing talking at their gates. Response vehicles were blocking off the road, officers going about their duties. A routine they had done so many times, yet to the residents in this street it could be something new. She glanced up and down. Someone must have seen something. If she had to work all day and night, she was going to find out who had attacked Melody.

Sean arrived and came straight over to her. He rested a hand on her shoulder and bent down to her level. 'Are you okay?'

'Yes, I'm fine,' she said. 'She's alive, but we're failing these women not catching that bastard.'

'We'll fish him out.' Sean looked up and down the street.

'Surely he can't get too far covered in blood?'

'This needs to go to Major Crimes now, Eden,' said Sean. 'We're on a full-scale manhunt if this is Daniels too.'

CHAPTER FIFTY-THREE

At the refuge, Carla tried to act normal. She needed to figure out what it was best to do next before she involved anyone else. But she felt safer here than at her home.

'Morning, Carla,' said Lisa as she came up behind her. 'How are you feeling?'

'Oh, not too bad now, thanks.'

'Have you heard the breaking news? It looks like another woman has been attacked this morning.'

'How awful!'

'The police aren't saying if it's that bloke they're looking for. But it's got to be him, hasn't it? I hope they catch him soon.'

'I hope so too.' She shuddered before going to set up.

Of all the sessions she did, Carla enjoyed this one the most. It was a casual sit-back-and-chat session. Nothing formal, just a group of women talking about their problems. Often it was harrowing listening to their tales – what they'd been through. Sometimes it was inspiring too. Some of the women had been through so much but got out in time. Just like her, luckily. And at least it took her mind off her own problems for a while.

Carla never shared her background with anyone. As far as they were concerned, this was just a job to her. To them, she had never been a victim of domestic violence. Yet every time one of them shared a story, she cringed inwardly because it had happened to her too. Painful memories always came flooding back. She felt their pain just as much as them because she had been there: too scared to make a move – run down, put down; made to feel worthless because someone wanted to take his own pain out on her. It was all a form of control.

It was a horrible situation to be in and that's why she admired every one of the women she got to see. Because she hadn't been able to leave at all. It wasn't until her life was threatened that she'd got away from Ryan. She wasn't brave like these women were. After the parcel delivery earlier, she was plain scared.

There were three women in the session when she went to join them at 11.30 a.m. There was no sign of Tanya, which was a shame because Carla really wanted to catch up with her. She wondered if she was deliberately keeping away after her attack.

But a few minutes into the session, Carla was surprised when she came in to join them. Even without the prominent bruising to her face, she seemed more flustered than usual. Her eyes flitted around the room before landing on Carla.

'Come and sit down, Tanya,' she said. 'We were just discussing that there's been another attack this morning.'

Tanya brushed the remark to one side. 'People will talk about it for a day and then it will be old news. No one listens to us.'

'We'll listen,' said Marsha, the woman sitting next to Carla.

Tanya took the seat furthest away and sat down. Carla noticed that she kept looking out of the window as if she was waiting for someone, and it put her on edge.

The three women in the group continued to chat, talking about the fear of someone getting to them while they were here, finishing what they'd started. So all the pain of leaving would have been for nothing.

'And as long as she doesn't invite that fella of hers here again, we'll be fine,' said Andrea, her head nodding in Tanya's direction.

Tanya must have felt them staring at her as she turned and glared at them all in turn.

'I have a right to be here as much as any of you,' she said.

'*You* do, but not him.'

'Leave her be, Andrea,' said Maggie. 'We've all been that scared at one time or another when our man has threatened us.' She smiled at Tanya. 'It might help you to talk, you know. Share your pain.'

Tanya looked away for a moment and then, folding her arms, looked at the women again.

'I remember one time when Vic locked me in the bathroom. He'd put a bolt on the outside when I'd been to the doctors, and when I got back he pushed me inside. I screamed for ages but he wouldn't let me out. He left me there overnight.'

'How awful.' Marsha leaned over and gave her hand a squeeze.

Carla froze. She couldn't be sure but was Tanya looking at her in particular when she'd spoken those last few words? Because that had happened to her too. Ryan had locked her in the bathroom overnight after a particularly bad drinking binge. He'd convinced himself that she'd been having an affair with the man two houses along, who had just moved in with his family.

The en suite had no window, just an extractor fan. She'd banged on the door but he hadn't come to her. She'd sat and cried to no avail, wondering if she would die in there with no food. The incident had left her with a fear of enclosed spaces.

'He let me out the next day,' said Tanya, still looking at Carla. 'Said he was sorry and bought me a present to make up for it.'

Andrea snorted. 'Typical behaviour.'

'It was some underwear. Red with black ribbon.'

Carla dropped her coffee mug, the remains of her drink spilling over the laminate flooring. She tried to stay composed as she wiped it with a tissue while Maggie went off to get a cloth.

Tanya never once took her eyes from Carla. Luckily, the women in the group didn't notice.

Carla tried to keep her composure for the rest of the session, but it was as if Tanya was goading her. She thought back to what had happened over the past few weeks – the brick through the window here, the figure coming past her window at home and standing by the door, the parcel left on her car. Then there had been the teddy bear memento, and now this story about being locked in the bathroom too? Was Tanya somehow involved with Ryan? Surely not.

As soon as the session came to an end, she called to Tanya as she was about to leave the room.

'Could I have a word with you please?'

'I'm busy,' snapped Tanya. 'Places to go, people to see.'

'It won't take a moment.' She pointed to a chair. 'Please.'

Tanya huffed but sat down, folding her arms again like a sullen teenager. 'What do you want?'

'What you said, about being locked in the bathroom – is that true?' she asked.

'Are you calling me a liar?'

'No, not at all. I was just asking. It must have been horrific to go through.'

'It was, but you wouldn't know, would you, because you've never taken a punch in your life. Or is *that* a lie?'

Carla opened her mouth to defend herself, but she stopped at the last minute. How could she tell Tanya that she had experienced a similar situation without giving the game away?

'Yes, it happened,' Tanya went on, 'and exactly how I told you. Vic can be an evil bastard at times. But then, you know all about cruel men, don't you?'

'I don't know Vic.' Carla ignored the question.

'You know more than you're letting on. People don't work in places like this unless they know the pain and the torment suffered by the women who find refuge here.' She pointed around the room. 'Look at this place. Would you stay here unless you absolutely had to? It smacks of unloved people, and I wouldn't be here if I didn't have to be.'

'No matter how horrible it is, it's still a safe place for you.'

'I have to go.' Tanya stood up to leave.

'Don't go,' said Carla. 'I— I—'

'What?'

'Just make sure you stay safe, okay? He might hurt you more than you think.'

Tanya stared at Carla. 'You don't know what I've been through, so stop pretending. It will only make things worse.'

'What do you mean by that?' Carla frowned.

Tanya lowered her eyes, a blush forming on her cheeks, and she played with her ponytail. 'It doesn't matter. But you need to look after yourself as much as I do. You need to stay safe too, don't you?'

Once she'd left the room, Carla sat and thought about what she'd said. Was Tanya goading her – or warning her off? She wasn't quite sure, but something didn't ring true. She wished she had someone to confide in. Maybe it was time to call Eden.

SEVEN YEARS AGO

Once Ryan had been sentenced to nine years, I went home. I sat and cried for hours. The tears surprised me, but I was soon laughing through them. I was safe, for a while at least.

For the first week, I went around the house making a mess, scrunching up towels, leaving cups out, moving tins round in the cupboard. I left the bed unmade. I ate what I wanted, when I wanted. Junk food, chocolate, whatever I fancied. I didn't have to cook a full dinner every evening. I could watch what I chose on the television. And as I could wear what I felt like, I went on a small shopping spree online.

After two weeks, I left the house. I got a part-time job at a local bakery, serving on the counter. I wasn't qualified to do much more, but I loved being with people, being out in the community again.

I had a lot of time to think about what I would do with my life. I read up on rehabilitation and realised that most people didn't change. I read up on domestic violence and counselling. I joined a gym and got myself into shape, took a few basic self-defence classes. I found a bit of confidence and made some new friends, female and male. But I never went on any more than a few dates. I couldn't trust myself not to give in again. I didn't want anyone to control me. I didn't want to be run down, trodden on, insulted, hit, abused – ever again. I wouldn't allow it to happen. If it meant shutting myself away, then so be it.

I left the house and rented a flat. Every day, life improved. And every day I prayed he wouldn't find me. Despite him being sent down for nine years, I couldn't settle anywhere. I gave my address to as few people as possible. One of the first houses I rented was a tiny terraced house near to Birmingham. It was beautiful, and for two years I set up home, tried to forget my past and got on with my life. Of course, there was the niggle in my mind that one day he would be out, but until then I could be happy. I could sleep in my bed.

Until the day I had a knock on the door.

I never rushed to open doors. I always see who's there first. But I knew I couldn't always live my life thinking about Ryan, and I had to trust people. So a man with a white van was one of the people I trusted.

He handed me a large envelope and asked me to sign. I took the pen from him and waited for him to pass me something to sign.

When he gave me a piece of paper, it was blank.

I looked up at him, and he sneered. He seemed to be in his early thirties with a lived-in face that spoke of troubled times. His clothes were clean but scruffy, dated. He wore a jacket as if it was a uniform, mud on his shoes.

'He wants your autograph,' he said.

I frowned, my hand poised to receive something from him. 'I'm sorry?'

'Ryan. He wants your autograph so he can look at it on his cell wall.'

Everything went into slow motion, and I couldn't speak.

'I've just been released and he asked me to give you a message.' The man bumped the toe of his boot against the step. 'He says he's known for a while that you're here, and he wants me to tell you that no matter where you go, he *will* find you.'

I shut the door before he'd finished speaking. Drew over the three locks and double-locked the handle. It was then I realised I still had the envelope in my hand. With trepidation, but a need to know, I opened it up. I pulled out a red bra and knickers to match. It was delicate lace, with soft padding and black ribbon detail.

It was similar to a set that Ryan had bought me for the anniversary of our first year together.

Dropping to the floor with my back against the wall, I wrapped my arms around my legs and sat, tears pouring down my face, as I began to shake violently.

He'd found me.

Would I ever have my freedom? The sense that I didn't have to look over my shoulder forever more. A sense of not being someone's property. A sense of not being there for someone to beat to death once they found out where I am.

I sat there for over half an hour, not daring to move. Then, as if a switch had been clicked, I ran around like a lunatic, packing a bag, tears pouring down my face. He had me where he wanted me, running away with fear, worried that he would get to me. If he could get that close with one of his friends, anyone could come back and harm me. Kill me even – finish off the job that he'd started.

How gullible was I to think that it would all be over?

I have no idea how he found me, but everyone can be traced, can't they? It's laughable when people say you can go into hiding and never be found. I can't change my looks, can I? I can change the colour of my hair, the style even, but underneath it's still me. I can change my name, but I'm sure he'd still find me.

I can't go to ground. I have to work so I have to register. I have to use gas, electricity, a phone.

I can't keep on running either.

But I do. Because I know what he'll do when he finds me.

CHAPTER FIFTY-FOUR

Tanya lay on her bed, curled up on her side. Tears spilled down her face as she realised how much trouble she was in – and just how much danger too. She hadn't thought things through properly when she'd agreed to the plan with Vic. She was worried that she'd gone too far.

Last night, Vic had contacted her several times to get her to continue with everything. She reread the last text message that he'd sent.

If you don't go through with our plan, I'll be for it too.

Had she said too much about the underwear? She had hoped to tease Carla, but she would know now that she had something to do with it.

Even that nosy cow, Sergeant Berrisford, would go mad if she found out what she'd been doing – she would lose her support too. The police might always give her grief, but she knew they would be there if she needed them, if she had to move somewhere else quickly.

Maybe she should confide in someone. Maybe Lisa? But she might kick her out of the refuge. Would anyone believe her if she told them what she had been forced to be a part of?

Eden Berrisford thought she was a troublemaker, crying wolf because she kept on going back to Vic. But it wasn't like that this time. She was doing this for both of them. The money would come in handy.

She just needed to bide her time and keep her mouth shut. Then she could leave this place behind, never to come again. These women were nothing like her. They were the weak ones. She was strong. She could stick up for herself if she wanted to.

But she had made a fool of herself. Crying wolf all the time meant that people didn't trust her. What if Carla didn't believe her when she told her she had nothing to do with it? She couldn't believe she had been drawn into it, as she had begun to like Carla and tricking her wasn't nice. She was always trying to help her, and the look on Carla's face today when she had gone too far in the counselling session was ingrained on her mind. She was a nice person. Tanya was a horrid one.

Lonely and upset, she sent Vic a text message.

I can't do this any more. I miss you, and I want to come home.

A message came back a few minutes later.

One more thing and it's all over. Then you can come home. Promise.

Tanya shivered and sat down on the bed. Another day, and she would feel lonely, guilty and miserable. Another day she had no friends, no one to trust.

She didn't want to do what Vic said, but she had no choice. And she hated herself for it.

CHAPTER FIFTY-FIVE

Now that the case had been passed to Major Crimes, Eden and her team were working alongside a large team of officers. Sean had briefed them all and a press release had gone out at lunchtime – Daniels' photo had been all over the television and local newspapers. A uniformed officer had been made available to help check known areas for homeless sleepers, as well as one being stationed outside the house in Sudbury Avenue. Daniels would be covered in blood. It would be hard for him to stay invisible after this attack.

The local journalists were out in force when Eden got to the entrance of the city hospital at 3 p.m. She pushed through them, giving no comment, and went to find ward 106. Melody Dixon had, thankfully, been found in time to make her twenty-fourth birthday next month. Eden couldn't help but wince as she caught sight of her. She looked like she'd been in a car crash. Her face was now one mass of swelling, and there was a cut under her left eye. She could barely see through the other one. Her right arm was in a cast. But she was alive, though what her mental state might be was another matter.

Melody had been assigned a sexual assault officer, but Eden thought she'd see if she was fit to answer a few more questions.

'Hi, Melody.' Eden pulled the curtain around the bed. 'I'm Detective Sergeant Eden Berrisford. I'm here to ask you about this morning, if you don't mind. I'm certainly not going to ask you how you're feeling.' She smiled to encourage a connection.

A tear slipped down Melody's face, and she wiped at it with the back of her good hand.

Eden held up a carrier bag. 'I was grabbing a bar of chocolate from the hospital shop so I picked up a couple of magazines for you.' She put them on the bedside cabinet, noticing a large vase of flowers. 'Have your family been to see you?' she asked.

'Yes.' Melody's voice came out croaky as she fought to speak. 'The flowers are from my dad.'

'That's nice. I expect you'll need his support when you go home.' Eden was never one to beat about the bush. 'Are you able to go through what happened with me? You can take your time. The more you can tell me the better, as I very much intend to catch the bastard who did this to you.'

Eden pulled up a chair and sat nearer to her, taking out her notebook. Melody went through her attack again. Eden hated that she had to ask, had to inflict pain on her once more as she relived the memory, but she had to listen to it from her point of view.

'Is it him?' Melody asked afterwards, looking at her with so much fear in her eyes. 'The man who's been attacking all those women? Because I heeded the warnings. I didn't go out alone. He attacked me in my own home.'

Eden gave her time to compose herself as she cried. As much as she wanted to know every detail, her information gathering needed to be as sensitive as possible. She reached for Melody's hand and gave it an encouraging squeeze.

'Do you have a partner to look after you?'

Melody shook her head. 'There's just me and the boys now. I got pregnant with Nathaniel when I was sixteen, and Reece is five. Their dad is still around, and he sees them regularly. We were just too young to stay together.' She burst into tears. 'I only moved into the house three months ago. My dad said I could stay with him forever but I wanted my own independence. I should have listened to him. I know he blames himself for letting me go. It wasn't his fault. It was mine.'

'It wasn't anyone's fault,' Eden stressed. 'This man is dangerous. The description that you gave matches one of the victim's. You mentioned that he wasn't wearing anything on his face. Can I show you a photo I have?'

Melody looked away for a moment and then nodded.

Eden wasn't sure how the woman was going to react, but she needed to know. She held up the photocopied sheet of paper with Daniels' photo on it.

'Is this the man who attacked you?'

Melody gasped. A tear dripped down the side of her face. It took a moment before she nodded. 'Do you know who he is?'

'Yes, he's wanted in connection to other assaults too. Thank you, Melody. You've been so brave. It can't be very nice looking at the image, but it could stop him doing this again if we can charge him with your assault. This is the first time he showed his face.'

'I hope he rots in a cell,' she said.

Eden could understand her anger. Right now, she thought the same. She hoped they could catch him soon. There were a lot of women who would sleep better in their beds if they could.

'You need to catch him before he does it again. Before he kills someone next time. That's what he was doing with me, wasn't it? He thought he'd killed me. And if he thought that, it's only a matter of time before he tries again.'

Melody was a smart kid. She had almost taken the words right out of Eden's mouth.

'When we get him, I'm going to come back and let you know,' Eden told her. 'If that's okay with you?'

Melody nodded. 'Please don't take too long about it. I don't want anyone else to go through what I did. The man is an animal.'

Eden left the room shortly afterwards. Along the corridor, she spotted the ladies' loos and bolted into them. In a cubicle, she put down the toilet lid and sat for a moment in the quiet. Tears poured down her face.

They would get him.

She would get him.

An hour later, back at the station, the investigation was still going strong in the hunt for Daniels. Every available hand was answering calls after the recent press conference.

'I've had a call from EveryDay Taxis, Sarge,' Amy told her after putting the phone down. 'They have a taxi missing.'

'Missing?' Eden cried. 'How can a bloody car go missing?'

'One of the drivers left the engine running in the yard to warm it up before he started his shift, and when he went outside, it was gone. It was called in this morning, but it wasn't linked to our case. Doreen has just phoned to let me know and to say that someone mentioned seeing Daniels hanging around.'

'Get a vehicle check on it.'

'Already on it.'

'Sarge.' Jordan held up his hand after he put his phone down too. 'That was a call from Manchester. Forensics on one of their victims who was bitten has come up with a match to the saliva found on Ramona Wilson.'

Eden punched the air as Jordan's phone rang again. 'Let's hope he hasn't taken that taxi out of the city.'

'Or worse,' said Amy. 'He could have hidden himself in full view of us. If he's got a number plate covering it, he could attack again.'

'Where would he have got a number plate at such short notice?'

'They do get cloned all the time.'

'Unless you're dodgy, you need a log book to have one made, and he isn't going to have that, is he? And I don't think he's likely to have connections here that would do one that quick for him. No, he's still here somewhere. He'll be spotted soon.'

'I hope he isn't watching someone now.'

'He doesn't have the time.'

'It would make sense in the case of Melody Dixon, as he knew she was out,' said Amy.

Eden shook her head. 'Not necessarily. He could have broken into the property and found it empty.'

'But if he wants to attack a woman, he needs to be pretty certain there's one living there. And certain that she'll be coming back soon?'

'I guess.' Eden paused. 'Or maybe he's picking out the victims in terms of age or area.'

Jordan put the phone down. 'That was the control room. A couple have returned from work to find someone has broken in, raided their fridge and taken a shower. Apparently, their bathroom is covered with diluted blood and a few handprints. The scene is being processed but time won't be on our side.'

'It looks like our man is cracking up.' Eden ran a hand through her hair, a worried look on her face. 'Which makes him all the more dangerous.'

CHAPTER FIFTY-SIX

Carla got out of her car and hurried down the path to her front door. She heard footsteps behind her as she put the key into the lock, and then a hand on her shoulder.

'Carla.'

She turned to see Tanya. 'You almost scared me half to death,' she cried. 'What are you doing here? And how did you find out my address?'

'I've known for ages where you've been living.' Tanya held a hand up for her to stop talking. 'Listen to me. You're in danger. Things have got out of hand, and I need to tell you what's been going on.'

Carla looked puzzled. 'What do you mean?'

Tanya pushed her into the house and slammed the door shut behind them.

'What the hell do you think you're doing?' Carla said.

'I need to talk to you. You're in so much trouble.'

As Tanya ran past her, Carla followed, hot on her heels. Tanya opened the door to her living room and let it bang against the wall so that she could see all of the room from where she stood. 'You need to check the house is secure.'

'For who? Is Vic here?'

'Ryan! He knows where you are.' Tanya ran her fingers through her hair and bunched her hands into fists, pulling hard. 'He's been staying at our house. He's been watching me all the time. He's been standing outside the window, looking to see if I was doing what he'd told me to do. If I stepped out of line, he would hit me. It wasn't Vic I was afraid of in the end. It was Ryan.'

'What?' Carla went cold.

'I'm sorry, but I had no choice. Vic came out of prison with this plan. Someone had given him money to scare a woman. Vic got it into his head while he was inside that he would help him. I had to pretend that he had beat me up so I could turn up at the refuge again.'

Carla didn't like where this was heading. Her feet were glued to the floor, her eyes never leaving Tanya's.

'Was Vic getting in and attacking you part of the plan?' she asked.

Tanya nodded, tears running down her face now. 'I'm sorry – I was so scared. He threatened to kill me if I didn't help him.'

'But you know Eden was looking out for you after Vic—'

'Not Vic – Ryan! He beat me up because I didn't like what he was doing. And then Vic hit me because I wasn't doing what I should. Vic left the underwear on your car and kept sending me texts saying that I had to scare you. He told me about how Ryan had locked you in the bathroom, and about the teddy bear with the collar, and said I had to tell you that those things happened to me too. I didn't like what they were doing but two grand is a lot of cash. We couldn't turn it down.'

'Wait a minute.' Carla held up a hand. 'Ryan paid you £2,000 to pose as a victim at the refuge.'

'Yes! To get at you!'

'But I don't live there.'

'He thought you did until I went to stay there. Then he said, as he'd just got out of prison, he wanted to scare you at work as well as at home.'

'The things happening here at this house, they were Ryan?'

'No, they were Vic.' Tanya shook her head. 'Ryan paid him to scare you here so that you wouldn't feel safe anywhere.'

'Have you any idea what you've done!' Carla yelled. 'He's a very dangerous man.'

'I didn't have any choice. If I didn't do what they said, they'd both beat me up! I was stuck. And anyway, Ryan told me what happened to Chloe – what you did.'

Carla felt all the air being sucked out of her. At the mention of her daughter's name, all the pain came flooding back.

'It was him. He – he killed Chloe!'

'What?' Tanya's shoulders fell even further. 'He said that he left her in your care, and she fell, and he came home to an ambulance. He told us it was your fault, and he was coming after you to get even.'

'Even?' Carla gasped. 'Ryan doesn't get even. He wants to kill me. I had years of violence at his hands.'

'I'm sorry,' whispered Tanya. 'You need to get away.'

Carla nodded. 'We'd better call the police.' With shaking hands, she took out her phone. 'But first you need to tell me how this plan of yours is supposed to end.'

Tanya stared at Carla. Another tear dropped from her eye and rolled down her cheek. She wiped it away quickly.

A voice came from the hallway. 'I think you know exactly how this ends.'

Every hair on Carla's body stood to attention, her skin crawling as she turned to the doorway. Ryan was standing there, and he was blocking their only way out.

CHAPTER FIFTY-SEVEN

Eden wasn't easily shocked but when she walked into the bathroom at Lydia and Michael Sheldon's home, she drew in her breath. It resembled a horror film: dried blood on the sink and taps, a towel striped with red on the floor and diluted blood in the bottom of the shower tray.

'The bastard took a shower?' She gagged at the thought. She had seen Melody lying close to death on her bed and to think this could be her blood. . . It would be a while before it was confirmed but they all knew it would be hers.

'There's food missing too,' said the forensic officer who was taking samples. 'He's some weirdo to do this.'

'He's going off the rails, isn't he?' Jordan said, glancing at Eden. 'He doesn't care about being found.'

'I wonder what tipped him over the edge?' Eden didn't for a minute think it would be down to anything they had done, except perhaps getting closer to catching him. Serial killers and attackers were mostly methodical. This was way off target.

She went downstairs to speak to the owners.

'So you came home to find it like this – at what time?' she asked.

'Five thirty. I got in from work first and noticed the kitchen door had been forced. Then when I went upstairs. . .' Mrs Sheldon covered her mouth, tears glistening in her eyes. 'My house doesn't feel like my own anymore.'

Her husband came up beside her, pale and shocked. 'It isn't him, is it?' he asked. 'The man who attacked that girl in her house this morning?'

'Please, no.' The woman began to shake.

'We can't be certain,' Eden said truthfully, not wanting to alarm her.

Eden left the scene shortly after with Jordan.

'It's horrendous, isn't it?' she said, as she walked down the driveway towards the patrol car. 'I can't believe how anyone can be so barbaric.' Just as she was about to get in the driver's seat, a movement caught her eye. There was a taxi at the end of the road. The engine started up and as it drew away from the kerb, the logo of EveryDay Taxis came into view.

Eden looked at Jordan. 'Did you just—'

'The bastard is watching us!'

They got into the car. Jordan contacted the control room while Eden raced away.

'All units. Suspect wanted for the attempted murder of Melody Dixon – taxi has been spotted driving out of Princess Drive and on to Stockleigh Way. We're in pursuit.'

'Why is he goading us?' Eden banged her hand on the steering wheel as she waited for a car to get out of their way.

'He's not going to stop, is he, Sarge?' Jordan replied, hanging on to the door handle.

'Possibly not, but he'd better not take anyone else down with him.' Eden put her foot down a little more, easing the car as quickly as she could through the traffic.

'Suspect has turned in to Stanton Street,' Jordan continued his running commentary to the control room.

A sharp left and the taxi was in front of them. A few minutes later, it veered off into the Horse and Hound car park and they pulled in behind it. Eden got out of the car, leaving the door open, and followed after Jordan who was already in pursuit.

'Stop! Police!' she cried.

Jordan grabbed Daniels' foot as he was about to jump over the fence but lost his grip when Daniels kicked out. He reached for him again, crying out when the heel of Daniels' boot connected with his shoulder and he disappeared over the fence. Jordan went after him.

Eden raced back to the car. She unlocked the boot and searched for what she needed. She found pepper spray, her baton and a torch, slammed the boot shut and ran after Jordan. She pulled herself up the fence and hurled herself over. There was a field at the back so she landed on grass, her hands breaking her fall. It was pitch black where she was, lights far away in the distance, but she knew the area well. There was a path up ahead that was used by dog walkers that took you straight through the heart of the city for over five miles. She switched on her torch and ran towards it.

She could hear more sirens as she ran along the path, waving her torch around.

'Jordan?' she shouted but there was no answer.

Daniels could have gone in any direction, and it would be like looking for a needle in a haystack in the dark. At least if a helicopter could be scrambled, they could locate him by body heat. She pressed on regardless.

After a minute of running, she stopped. She couldn't see a thing that wasn't lit up by the beam of torchlight. Slowly she turned around in a full circle, relief washing over her when she saw emergency lights flashing, heard doors slamming shut and footsteps.

A shadow crossed in front of her. Before she could react, she felt pain erupt in her jaw as a fist connected with her face. Eden dropped the torch and baton in surprise when she was grabbed around the neck.

'Your turn now, bitch,' Daniels whispered in her ear.

Eden thought back to all the times she had wondered why women would freeze in these situations, why some wouldn't fight back. She had never condemned anyone for not fighting. But that wasn't in her nature. She balled her hand up into a fist and smashed it against the arm that was around her torso. Again and again. She could hear him breathing in her ear, but he had the advantage as he pulled her backwards.

He pushed her to the ground and sat astride her. 'I haven't got time to do what I want to you, but I do have time to do this.' Aiden punched her in the face. 'You never give up, do you?'

Eden groaned, struggling to push him off as pain engulfed her. His hands were around her neck, squeezing hard. She gasped, trying to drag in air as he shut off her airway, and her arms flailed, trying to push him away. But he was too strong for her to gain any ground. Her only hope was that her colleagues would arrive quickly enough.

But then, as she choked, she remembered she wasn't unarmed, and her hand went to her pocket, searching... and landed on the pepper spray. Thinking of all the women he'd attacked, she let her anger take over, pulling it up and squirting it in his eyes.

He let go of her immediately, and she gasped for air. They both rolled around on the ground. Torchlights bobbed up and down as someone ran towards them.

Daniels was screaming obscenities. She could just about make out his form in the dark, how he was rubbing his eyes. Seeing her opportunity, she sat up and scrambled over to him. Then she punched him in the stomach. As he doubled over, she followed it with an uppercut.

'Eden!' Jordan pulled her away, dragging her to her feet. 'It's me. Stop. It's all over.'

Daniels was pushed over on to his stomach and handcuffed by two uniformed officers. Jordan wrapped his arms around Eden and held her close until she felt safe enough to buckle.

They had him.

CHAPTER FIFTY-EIGHT

'Hello, darling,' Ryan said, the smile on his face anything but friendly. In two strides, he was across the room and in front of Carla.

He hadn't changed much since she'd last seen him. At the graveside, she had been able to see his physique but now it was even clearer that he'd kept himself fit. There were lines on his thin face and his hairline had receded a little, dark hair greying around the roots. But for his years, he still had that charm she had fallen for when she was nineteen, and the swagger that would trick a woman into trusting him.

His fist lashed out at her face, and she crumpled in a heap on the floor. Behind him, Tanya ran to the door but he took a step back and stopped her with a backhander. She stood in the corner of the room, holding her face.

'Leave me alone,' she cried. 'I've done enough for you.'

'On the contrary,' said Ryan. 'You haven't done enough, and I told you what would happen if you didn't do as you were told.'

Carla watched in horror as Ryan laid into Tanya. The sound of his boot as it crashed into her stomach, the noise of his fists pummelling her body, made her retch. In fear for Tanya's life, she hurled herself at him.

'Leave her alone!' she cried, grabbing his arm. But he shoved her with so much force that she stumbled backwards, falling and hitting her head on the wall. Dazed, she tried to get up again, alarm him, shake him out of his frenzy. Because, if she didn't, he would kill Tanya. She knew what he was capable of.

She pushed herself up with the help of the coffee table and reached for a glass bowl sitting on top. With all her strength, she threw it at the wall opposite. It smashed, sending pieces shattering with a bang.

Ryan stopped, foot in mid-air and turned to her.

'Ah, diversionary tactic.' He grinned, a manic look in his eyes that she recognised.

'You're going to kill her,' she said.

'You're right,' he replied. He kicked Tanya in the stomach again. 'That's my intention.'

Spent from his attack, Ryan stood catching his breath. Carla could see that Tanya was out cold. She hadn't meant for that to happen! Was she breathing? She wasn't moving at all.

Ryan sat down on the settee and took out a handkerchief. Carla scrambled to the corner of the room, fearing she would be next. But he sat still as he wiped Tanya's blood from his hands. The room was deathly quiet, the metallic tang of the attack in the air.

'Have you any idea what I've been through? Nine years of hell.'

'You killed Chloe,' she said, tasting blood in her mouth. She wiped at her lip with her hand.

'It was your fault! If you had just stayed in line, I wouldn't have had to punish you. You always made me so angry. I couldn't trust you to do anything right. You couldn't even look after our daughter properly.'

Carla wanted to scream at him, needed to say it was nothing to do with her. Wanted to say it was all his fault – that he was a lunatic and didn't see how he had done anything wrong. She wished she had the courage to call him a murdering bastard but she didn't.

'Why didn't you just come after me?' she sobbed, her lip beginning to swell where he'd hit her. 'You kept tabs on me. You knew where I was. Why involve Tanya?'

'I met Vic in prison and we hatched a plan, and we needed her. He got out a month after me. So while I waited for him, I kept an eye on you. I've been cooped up for years with a bunch of men, some of whom put the fear of God in me. It was your fault that I attacked her.' He pointed at Tanya. 'But I'm no psychopath. Look at me now, sitting here all nice and having a conversation with you.'

He was deluded. Carla knew that now. She had got away from him once. She had to do it again. But to do that she would have to play him at his own game.

'I came back because you told everyone that I killed Chloe,' he continued, 'and you know that isn't true. You lied! You just used anything to get rid of me. And now you have to pay for that.'

Carla watched a vein pulse in his temple and hoped she hadn't upset him too much, too early. Memories of the court case came flooding back to her. She'd had to tell the truth, and she wouldn't have done anything other than that. Even after the prosecution accused her of fabricating her story to get back at Ryan because this was the first time it had been mentioned, she still told the truth. It had been her time to have her say.

Tanya coughed.

Carla almost cried out. She was alive! For now at least. . .

Ryan lunged for Carla, grabbing her by the hair. 'You need to see something.'

Pain seared her scalp as he pulled her through the hall, opened the kitchen door and pushed her through. She fell to her knees. Lying next to her was a man. There was blood all over the floor, seeping through a wound in his stomach. A knife lay beside him, the blade bloody.

Carla screamed. It was the same man who had been in her garden, who had stared at her through the window in the kitchen door. Dead, on her kitchen floor.

'That's Vic, your friend Tanya's fella,' Ryan said. 'He got too big for his boots. The same thing will happen to you if you don't do as you're told and keep quiet.'

Ryan came towards her. She cowered as he gripped her arm, reached behind her and drew out a bucket.

'Here, you might need this.' He thrust it at her. 'There's two bottles of water inside. I wasn't expecting company.'

He pulled her out of the kitchen and back into the living room, where he pushed her forcefully on to the floor.

'Wait!' Carla turned to face him. 'What are you doing?'

'I'm holding *you* prisoner.' He pointed to the door. 'I'll be in the kitchen. If you make a noise, I will come at you. If you try to get out, I will beat you until you wished you hadn't. If you try to attack me, I will kill your friend.'

'No.' Her voice came out quieter than she had intended.

'Piss in the bucket or piss yourself. See how you like it.'

'But what about Tanya? She needs help!'

As quickly as she could, Carla scrambled to her feet. But Ryan had closed the door before she could follow him. She heard a bolt being drawn across and a sob escaped her. He hadn't even needed to tie their hands because he knew she wouldn't dare retaliate.

How long had he been planning this? He must have been watching her for some time, learning her work routine, and had come into the house to prepare it once she had left that morning. He could have scuppered his plans by sending the underwear, as she might have left there and then. Instead, she had gone to seek refuge with her friends. What a fool she'd been to come back to the house.

CHAPTER FIFTY-NINE

Carla ran to the door, pushed the handle down and pulled as hard as she could. There was no way she could get the door open but she had to try until she was convinced otherwise. Her arms ached as she pulled. Defeated, she banged the palm of her hand on the wood.

Tanya groaned, awake but groggy.

Carla dropped to her side and rested her hand on Tanya's chest. 'I'm so sorry,' she said. 'Are you okay?'

'I've been better.'

Carla almost laughed at her reply.

Tanya tried to sit up, wincing as she pressed a hand to her eye. 'Has he gone?'

Carla shook her head. 'He's in the kitchen.'

'Can we creep out?'

'I don't think so.' Carla shivered as she recalled his threatening words, the menace in his eyes. 'He's taken our phones.'

'So we're trapped?'

'For now. Let's look after you first and then see what we can do.'

A bang from outside the room made them jump. Tanya clung on to Carla. They sat with their backs to the walls.

'Where are you hurt?'

'Everywhere. I think he's broken my ribs. It's painful to breathe.'

As Tanya began to shake, Carla checked her over as best she could. Two fingers on her left hand seemed to be broken where he must have struck her with his boot. With her sleeve, she carefully wiped the blood from Tanya's nose and lips. There didn't seem to be anything more than bruising, although she couldn't be sure. But it was Tanya's breathing that was giving her the most concern, and the gurgling sound that was coming from her chest. She needed medical help as soon as possible.

She glanced around the room. Ryan had removed anything she could use as a weapon. There were locks on the uPVC windows and she knew the last time she had checked, they had been secure. And though she wanted to bang on the window to alert anyone passing, she didn't have the courage. She had Tanya to think about. Even if she was spotted, she'd have to make some noise and he would come in the room. After the state he had left them in, as well as Vic, she didn't doubt he would carry out his threat. She'd just have to bide her time.

'What happened between you and Ryan?' Tanya's voice came out raspy.

Carla still found it painful to talk about the night in question, but she needed to explain all of the lies Ryan had told.

'I'd had years of violence at his hands, but one night he lashed out at our daughter. She came to my defence when he was attacking me one night. He blamed me when she died. Stupidly, I stayed with him afterwards – well, you know how that is. And then he tried to kill me.'

'No.' Tanya's voice was raspy.

'He left me for dead. I survived, and he went to prison. And now he's punishing me for it.'

'I'm so sorry,' said Tanya, determined to speak even though Carla could see she was in pain. 'I didn't want anything to do with it, but Vic forced me. He said it was easy money. But then when I got to know you, I realised how nice you were and. . . I thought he might have been lying, but I was scared, and. . .'

'It's okay,' Carla said softly. 'It's going to be okay.'

Tanya tried to nod. 'My chest hurts so much.'

'We'll be out of here in no time,' Carla soothed, knowing she was lying. Ryan would be taking great pleasure in seeing them suffer. He'd string it out for as long as he could. Then what? She didn't want to think about what he had planned.

CHAPTER SIXTY

Eden's eye was throbbing where Daniels had punched her. She'd felt the swelling worsening during the hours that she'd stayed on after Daniels' arrest but she hadn't said anything, as she knew Sean would send her home. Daniels was in a cell and they were waiting for a solicitor to turn up before they could interview him.

By 8.30 p.m., it was too noticeable, and she'd been told someone would drive her home. But she was determined to get there by herself.

Jordan walked her down to the car park.

'Are you sure you'll be okay, Sarge?' he asked as he held the car door open for her.

Eden tried to smile but it hurt too much. 'Thanks, but I'll be fine.'

'You did take quite a blow there. If I—'

She put up a hand. She heard him sigh.

'Well, if you're sure. I'll ring you later, see how you are.'

Eden nodded, thankful that she didn't have to argue with him. She should stay off, but she wanted to be there to get everything wrapped up with Daniels.

She almost jumped at her own reflection in the hall mirror when she let herself into the house. Her eye was a mess; her lip too, with a split that she didn't dare touch. Although she'd seen off Daniels herself, she knew things could have turned very nasty if her colleagues hadn't arrived in time. A man obsessed with getting power and inflicting pain as much as Daniels had been wouldn't have been floored for long. But at least now he would be behind bars for a very long time.

A tear dripped down her face as she thought of how lucky she had been. She might have acted all hard once she was back at the station, but she was certain she would go to pieces soon. Luckily, Casey was staying at Laura's so at least she'd be able to have a good cry in the shower. But first, a large drink to calm her nerves.

She couldn't believe how much had happened today, but it was the same whenever they were working a case. It left a bitter taste in her mouth that they hadn't caught Daniels before he had attacked Melody Dixon, but at least he wasn't going to be hurting anyone else.

After she'd knocked back a whiskey, she went through to the kitchen and flicked on the kettle. While she waited for it to boil, she slipped into the garage. Over in the corner, her scooter sat covered in a protective sheet. She pulled it off and, once she had a coffee, she sat on it.

She often came to sit on the Lambretta when she had things on her mind. It was associated with happy times, memories, friends, and it always soothed her. But this time she was angry. How could Danny ever think she would sell it? How could he even ask her to do that? He knew how much it meant to her. She wouldn't part with it for anything.

Her thoughts turned to Joe then. She hadn't heard from him either; expecting him to call her as he'd said. But there hadn't even been a text message. She wondered if he was giving her space or if it was his way of dealing with the break-up – a complete break.

She sat quietly, hoping to calm down her thoughts enough to sleep. If she didn't, she would stay up, go in to work early and continue with the paperwork for the charges against Daniels. There would be plenty of them – that was a dead cert.

One thing she was happy about was that the women in Stockleigh were safe from one attacker this evening. She and her team had done a good job. She was proud of them.

But she had never felt more alone, more vulnerable, in her life.

CHAPTER SIXTY-ONE

Eden was up early the next morning, unable to sleep with pain and adrenaline whooshing through her. Yet she couldn't wait to get back to work. Her eye was sore but she was controlling the ache with painkillers. It looked worse than it was, and once she'd toned it down with a bit of foundation, she felt passable.

On the drive to the station, she decided to stop off to buy cakes for the team.

She tucked her scarf into her parka to stop it blowing in her face and pushed her hands inside her pockets, remembering her phone conversation with Casey half an hour earlier. Yet again she had mentioned meeting up with her father. Eden had snapped at her, saying it wasn't the right time to talk about it and had regretted it since.

She knew only too well that she needed to talk to Danny again. He'd sent her several texts, which she had ignored. If she didn't contact him soon, he'd find another way to see her.

She'd been distressed at first when Casey had said she wanted to meet him. What if it didn't work out and she felt rejected again? Eden didn't want Casey to see him, but Casey was old enough to make her own decisions – and mistakes – so she had to let her be.

She wondered if money could run to the two of them having a night away together soon. Maybe a girlie day shopping and a meal, if she couldn't afford a show, would be better than nothing. It could be good for them both to get away for a while. Maybe Laura and the girls might want to come too.

She came out of the shop, mobile phone in hand as she walked to her car. Scanning her emails, she put her shopping in the boot and closed the lid. Jed Jackson was standing right beside her.

'What do you want?' she asked, almost jumping in fright.

'To see you.' He came closer to her.

She took a step back. 'You'll have to contact me at the station if you want to talk to me.'

'No need if I can talk to you now.' His smile was all sweetness and light, but she knew it was fake. 'I was just passing and saw you. Nasty shiner you have there, and that's *before* I caught up with you.'

Eden still had her phone in her hand. As she looked down at it, Jed hit out. Her hand flew up into the air, and her mobile went skidding across the car park.

'You need to remember you'll be caught on camera and that, if you do anything to harm me, we'll have you up in court by tomorrow morning.' Eden's threat was meaningful, her words clear and concise, but inside she was shaking. She'd met a lot of creeps in her time but none as dangerous. 'Goodbye, Mr Jackson,' she said.

'I'm not done yet.'

'Oh, but I am. You don't intimidate me like you do Danny.'

Jed laughed. People milling about in the car park turned to look. To them, maybe it would seem they were old friends catching up.

Eden stayed quiet as cars passed them by. She looked at Jed from the corner of her eye. He was a bad boy, a charmer, but a downright thug when pushed. Yet to look at him, you wouldn't get that impression. His long coat was expensive, the suit under it tailored and his shoes designer. Groomed to perfection, he was slick, in every sense of the word. The shaved head suited him, and the scar underneath his right eye was faded compared to the blue of his irises.

'I know Danny's told you that he owes me. I also know he's told you that I'm coming after my debt. But what he hasn't told you,' he smiled at a young girl as she skipped past holding a woman's hand, 'is that his time is up for getting it back.'

'Danny and I are through. You already know that.'

'But you're family!'

'Not any more.'

'Okay, so if he's not family, then the force is. So either you get my money, or I'll tell your boss and your colleagues our little secret about where he got the information.'

Eden paled. Surely he wasn't thinking she would become his informant? She wouldn't do it. But she didn't have what he wanted.

'I don't have that kind of money,' she said.

Jed stepped closer to her. He looked her up and down, slowly. 'Then maybe there's another way to clear the debt.'

'Over my dead body.'

Jed laughed. 'Oh, I don't mean you and me getting jiggy with it.' His laugh stopped as quickly as it had started. 'I mean either you get me that money or I'll be coming in to see your boss.'

'And tell him what? You didn't go ahead with the robbery at Cardman's Cash & Carry so I kept you out of prison?'

Jed glared at her.

'You'll land yourself in it if you say anything and you know it.'

'Maybe, maybe not. But I will be seeing you around, you mark my words.'

Eden stared back at him. Would he hurt her, a serving police officer? Would he deem her as more of a challenge?

'Did you enjoy the vanilla slice that your friend bought you the other day?'

Eden froze. The only vanilla slice she'd had lately was when she'd gone out for lunch with Amy. She'd sensed someone watching her – surely not?

'She's a looker, the woman you work with, isn't she? I bet she'd like to know what—'

'What's your game, Jackson?' she cut in.

'Nothing. I just like keeping an eye on my favourite sergeant.'

She stepped towards him, pointing into his face. 'You stay away from me, and my family,' she demanded.

Jed raised his hands and smiled. 'I'll be seeing you, Sergeant Berrisford.'

Eden watched him walk away, get in his car and drive off before she moved. Her hands shook as she got into her car, and she sat for a few moments to catch her breath.

That bastard. How dare he threaten her! He was the crook. She would never bow down to his threats.

Despite her fear of what he might do to her, she'd just made it her mission to go after him. Before he came after her – or Casey.

CHAPTER SIXTY-TWO

Eden's office was buzzing as she walked in, and after telling everyone she was fine, she stopped by at Detective Sergeant Adam Ridley's desk to check what was happening with Daniels. Handing the case over to Major Crimes was a godsend in a way, because more hands had got the job done. But she still wanted to be there to follow through to completion, if she was allowed.

'Care to get me up to speed?' she asked him.

'Grab a pew, Twiggy,' he said.

Eden smiled. She liked working with Adam. He was in his early thirties, married with twin girls aged five and very well liked. A stickler for tidiness, with a bit of OCD thrown into the mix, he'd been known for pushing everything off an untidy desk in temper if he couldn't find what he wanted. Eden loved that he was feisty and passionate – two of her own qualities. And two qualities that most officers needed to get the job done. Adam had been in the Major Crimes Team for three years. Across from him sat Detective Constable Sam Croft and Detective Constable Tim Purcell. Their heads were down as they worked. Sam was on the phone, nodding as someone spoke to her. Tim was tapping away on his keyboard.

Eden wheeled over a chair and sat with them while Adam updated her on what had happened so far.

'We kept at him last night and we're just heading in to interview him again,' he said, once she was up to speed. 'Dinnen should be here in about half an hour. Your team did a terrific job of gathering evidence so we have enough to go at him. And with the sixth victim in Stockleigh identifying him from the image you showed her, not everything is sticking yet, but we'll get there. We're sure to nab him for one of the attacks in Manchester, at least.'

'I hope so.'

That afternoon, Eden was at her desk with her team when the door to the office opened and an almighty roar was heard. She looked up to see Adam walking towards them.

'We nailed him!' he cried. 'We twisted him round in knots until he eventually confessed to all six attacks here, and two in Salford. The job's a good 'un, Eden.' He held a hand in the air and she leaned up to high-five with him as a round of applause went around the room.

'Nice work.' Adam bumped fists with Jordan and Phil in turn. Then with outstretched arms, he turned to Amy. 'Hug it out?'

'In your dreams,' Amy huffed, then let herself be enveloped into his embrace for a moment.

Eden smiled as she laughed along with her team. There was no better feeling than the euphoria of solving a case.

CHAPTER SIXTY-THREE

Carla woke up with a start. By her side, Tanya was curled up, asleep for now. Her breathing was laboured, but she seemed to be stable. She listened but all she could hear was the drone of the television from the kitchen.

It was nearing 4 p.m. She and Tanya had been in the living room for near on twenty-four hours. Neither of them had been hungry at first but she could feel the first pangs starting. Tanya's breathing was still cause for concern and she'd pleaded with Ryan to get some help, but he'd just laughed at them. It was clear that he'd enjoyed saying no.

Instead, he had come in every two hours, waking them if they had dozed and yelling at them if they were awake. Already she dreaded the sound of the bolt being drawn. It seemed as if he was their prison guard.

Tears poured down her face as she fought with her resistance. If she tried to escape, he would harm Tanya. Images of Vic on her kitchen floor filled her mind. What had happened for Ryan to kill him? Vic was a big man. It would have taken some force to overpower him, unless Ryan took him by surprise with the knife.

Was Ryan's plan always to do away with Vic? And Tanya too, once she had fulfilled her need? Carla shivered. What was going to happen to them?

She couldn't understand why he would keep them both locked up for so long. What was his reasoning? Just to punish her? And then what? That was the part she was dreading.

She heard the ringtone on her phone. Ryan let it ring until it stopped. She wondered who was trying to get hold of her. Perhaps it was Lisa, as she hadn't turned up for work at lunchtime. Holding on to the thought that help would be with them soon, she checked on Tanya again.

Suddenly she heard the lock on the door pull across.

Ryan came into the room. Carla cowered as she saw the knife in his hand.

'Best get moving,' he said, urging her to her feet. 'Seems you have a friend on her way over to see you.'

Carla tried not to show her relief. If he was taking her somewhere, at least Tanya would get help.

He pulled her towards the front door. 'No funny business,' he warned as he pushed her through it. Outside, it was dusk, people were returning home from work. Unless Carla screamed, no one was going to come to her rescue. But she couldn't do that. It was too risky.

At the pavement, Ryan held her close, as if he was supporting her. They walked down the road together until he came to a car.

He pressed a key fob and opened a door. 'Get in, and don't even think of trying to escape.' He pushed her inside. 'You and I are going for a drive.'

She got into the car.

'Fasten your seat belt,' he said, getting into the driver's seat. 'Don't want you to jump out.'

She wanted to leave it undone, in case she saw the means to escape, but she knew the car would sound an alarm so she clicked the fastener into place.

'Did you enjoy being locked up for twenty-four hours?' he laughed snidely.

Carla didn't know what to say, so she shook her head.

'Now imagine it for nine years! Every day I spent in that prison cell, I thought of you and what I would do to you when I got out.' He started the engine and pulled away from the kerb. 'I've been watching you since I came out a few weeks back. I couldn't do anything until Vic the prick came out too, but once he did, I swung right into action. He was such a gullible fool.'

'Why – why did you kill him?'

'Collateral damage.' An ugly laugh came from him. 'He thought he could blackmail me into giving him more money. I had to finish him off.'

Carla kept quiet, trying not to antagonise him as he ranted regardless, pushing his foot down on the pedal. They drove for a few minutes, tears building up in her eyes as she watched families going home, people on the pavements walking to get shopping, some teenagers still hanging around after school. She thought about jumping out of the car, but it was too dangerous. Even through rush hour, he was driving too fast.

He glared at her, the car veering to the right as he fought with the control. 'I have something special planned for you.'

Carla tried not to cry out. They drove for a further fifteen minutes. And then the thing she feared most of all came into sight.

The sign came up on her right. Stanley Quarry was just ahead. Ryan was fulfilling his threat. Flashes of the night he almost killed her came crashing into her mind.

NINE YEARS AGO

I had gone to see my parents with a view to leaving him, but when I got home, he was incoherent and so angry that I had been out on my own. He grabbed me by the hair and threw me into the bathroom. My hip connected with the side of the sink and I groaned as I sank to the floor.

His boots came down on me, kicking me in the stomach and then in the back as I curled up into a ball. I heard my fingers crack as he stood on them, the excruciating pain taking my breath away. All I could think was that I was going to see Chloe soon. He was getting his wish. He was going to kill me. There was nothing I could do to stop him. Until he was spent, he would do his worst.

I wasn't sure if I would be around to see what damage he'd caused this time. His fists pummelled at my head. I was so weak I couldn't even put up my arms to defend myself. I can't remember how long he was hitting me because it all went black soon after as I slipped into unconsciousness.

When I opened my eyes, I didn't know if I was on my own until the memories came flooding back. Fearing for my life, I moved my arms slowly, then my legs, twisting my body a little. The pain was unbearable.

I was broken but not dead. I pushed myself up to my elbows, crawling along the floor to the bathroom door where I sat for a while until I had the strength to open it. I reached up to the handle and pulled myself up. The door opened but I flopped to the floor.

Sheer determination pushed me forward again and I crawled into the hall. I knew not to try the front door, as he would have deadlocked it. I could see the phone base at the end of the hall, but the phone wasn't there. Inch by painful inch, I made my way along the floor, hoping I wouldn't pass out before I got help. Blood was pouring from a wound on my head, and I was finding it hard to breathe.

Nausea washed over me but I pressed on. The door to the living room was closed. I managed to reach up and push down on the handle – falling on the floor with relief when it opened.

Where was the phone? Had he taken it with him on purpose?

I sat up, holding on to my chest as I coughed, tasting blood in my mouth. My right eye was swelling and the pain was thumping in my head, but I had to stretch it wide to see, which hurt like hell.

I had to get out of there before he came back to finish what he'd started.

There! The handset was on the coffee table. My breathing became laboured as I dragged myself along the carpet, leaving a trail of blood behind me.

My vision was starting to tunnel. I put out my hand and tried to grasp the phone, only to knock it out of my reach. But as it fell, it bounced back in my direction and I grasped it again.

Pressing three times, I sat back with relief.

'You're through to 999. What's your emergency?'

'Ambulance. Eighty-seven. . . Raferty Drive. Help. . . me. Can't breathe.'

I stayed on the line with the operator until help arrived. I have never been so pleased to see someone break a window. I tried to speak but there were no words as I fought for breath. Little did I know that he had ruptured my lung, and if I hadn't got help I would have died.

CHAPTER SIXTY-FOUR

Eden sighed. There was so much stuff to fill in – things to check, items to cross-reference. All were time-consuming but crucial to the pending court case and it helped keep Jed Jackson's threats at bay. She could worry later what would happen if Danny didn't sort himself out.

Her mobile rang and she grabbed for it, realising she'd missed a couple of calls. There was one from her sister and one from Lisa.

'Hello, Eden Berrisford.'

Every hair on her body stood to attention as she listened to the caller. She stood up. 'What time was this? I'm on my way.' She grabbed her parka from the back of her chair. 'The emergency alarm has gone off at Carla's house. Control room say all they can hear is groaning. They've asked us to respond.'

'I'll get a pool car and wait for you downstairs,' said Jordan.

'Are you sure you're fit to go?' Sean asked her as she went to alert him.

'Yes, I am,' she nodded fervently.

As Jordan rushed past them, Sean stopped him. 'Grab an Enforcer too, in case you can't get in.'

'Yes, sir.'

'Take Amy with you, too.' Sean turned back to Eden then. 'Let me know what's happening as soon as you find out anything.'

Eden checked her phone as she went outside to the car park. Laura had sent a text message saying she was just checking in with her to see if she was okay. Lisa had left a voicemail.

'Shit.' Eden ran her hands through her hair as she listened to it. 'I missed a call from Lisa. She's worried about Carla. She's been out all afternoon for a meeting, and it wasn't until she was back that she noticed she hasn't turned up for work today.'

'Do you think Ryan Gregory has got to her?' Jordan asked as he drove the car towards Granger Street.

'I don't know what he's capable of because I took my eye off the ball looking for Daniels.' Her fingers splayed out and she brought her hand down on the dashboard.

'You're not to blame, Sarge,' Amy said from the back seat.

'If he's hurt her, I'll never forgive myself. I used to work on the Domestic Violence Team and—'

'You helped to stop Daniels from attacking anyone else. You can't be in two places at once. Even you're not that good.'

Eden knew Amy was trying to appease her, but she was so frustrated with herself. She pushed back tears of anger as they drove along. She had let herself down. She had let Carla and Tanya down, and she had let down everyone at the refuge.

In Granger Street, they parked outside Carla's home. There were no lights on.

'Watch your back. He's a dangerous character,' Eden warned as they got out of the car. 'No heroics.'

'That's very polite of you, Sarge.' Jordan flicked out his baton. 'But it just might slip my mind that the asp is a last resort.'

'Police!' Eden knocked on the front door as Jordan peered through the window.

'There's no one in there, but something's been going on. I can see a bucket.'

Eden's blood ran cold. Surely they weren't too late – had someone been cleaning up? She bent down and lifted the letterbox. There was a woman on the floor.

'Jordan, use the Enforcer to break in,' she ordered. 'She's on the floor!'

Jordan brought back his arm and aimed the key at the wood around the lock. A sickening thud went through the air, and again and again until the frame gave way and they were in.

Eden kept her eyes and ears on alert. Keeping her back to the wall so that she could see anyone coming through the door from the hallway, she dropped to her knees. She gasped as she turned the woman to face them.

'It's not Carla. It's Tanya White.'

'I'll check upstairs, Sarge,' said Jordan, already halfway up.

'I'll check downstairs.' Amy had her handle on the kitchen door.

'Tanya?' Eden said, getting out a pair of latex gloves. 'It's Eden. Tanya, can you hear me?'

'Vic White is in the kitchen, Sarge,' Amy shouted through.

Eden reached for her radio. 'Is he alive?'

'I can't find a pulse.'

'I have one for Tanya,' she said, calling it in.

Suddenly Tanya's eyes flicked open. She coughed, her arms flailing around as she tried to comprehend what was happening. Eden grabbed for them.

'You're safe, Tanya. There's no one here that will harm you now.'

'Carla,' she whispered.

'Have you seen her?'

'Carla.' A little louder this time.

'Where is she? Has she been here?'

'Carla!' Tanya said again.

'Who did this to you, Tanya?' Eden came closer to her. 'Was it Vic?'

Tanya spluttered again. Eden held on to her hand.

'Control to D429, receiving.'

'Go ahead control,' said Eden.

'Ambulance en route. ETA three minutes.'

'He took her,' said Tanya. There was blood crusted at the corner of her mouth.

'Who did, Tanya?' said Eden. 'Who took Carla?'

Tanya's head went from side to side as she tried to sit up. Eden pushed her down gently.

'Ryan,' she said. 'Ryan took her.'

'Ryan!' Eden stood up as Jordan came down the stairs, wary of what she said in case Tanya overheard. 'We have an incident in the kitchen too. Sit with her until help arrives,' she told Jordan. 'I need to speak to Sean.'

'I think I know where they might be, sir,' she said to him over the phone. 'Carla told me once if he ever found her, he would take her to the nearest quarry. Do you know how far we are from Stanley Quarry?'

'Hang on.' The line went quiet. 'According to Google Maps it's fifteen miles from you. I'll send you through the location and scramble a chopper while I do the necessary here.'

Eden could hear sirens getting louder. She raced through the front door and down the path. At the sight of an ambulance, she waved an arm in the air to direct them.

'Leave Amy in Granger Street and take Jordan with you to the quarry,' Sean commanded. 'I'll get a team together to meet you there.'

CHAPTER SIXTY-FIVE

As Ryan stopped the car, Carla turned to him. Her face was a picture of fear mixed with emotion. Somewhere among everything that had gone wrong, she used to love this man. She needed to remember what it was like to have him worship her before he began to lose control and take it out on her. Before they were married and she didn't have an inkling of what he was capable of.

Before he killed their daughter.

Because she needed to keep her strength up, maybe try to talk to him about happier times. See if she could stall him, calm his anger. She knew he would more than likely kill her, but she had to give it a shot.

He removed his seat belt and turned to her, a dark glint in his eyes. 'I'm getting out of the car, and I'm going to come round to the passenger side and get you. Don't even think of trying to escape or I will find you again, and I will do more to you then. Just think of this as a walk for old times' sake.'

Carla nodded, her teeth chattering uncontrollably. She could almost feel her head shaking but she kept his eye for as long as necessary and then looked away.

Ryan got out of the car, leaving the door open. 'Can't have you putting down the central locking, can I?' His smile was manic and didn't reach his eyes.

As he walked round the car to the passenger door, Carla tried to face her fear head on so she wouldn't panic. Was she capable of doing what she needed to do?

But he was opening the door before she could steel herself any more, pulling her out by the arm and forcing her to walk with him.

'Please,' Carla said. 'Think of what you're about to do. If you do anything to me, you'll end up back in prison, and you said you hated it in there.'

'It will be worth every second if I know you're not around any more.' He tugged on her arm so hard that she ended up on his chest, almost causing them both to stumble. 'I want the pleasure of doing what I set out to do. You need to be taught a lesson.'

'For what?' Carla cried. 'I haven't done anything wrong.'

'You told the court a pack of lies and everyone thought that I had killed Chloe. That it was my fault she died. That she fell because I hit her. That gave me an extra couple of years.'

'You don't know that.'

'My brief said I'd get about three years tops for GBH but you,' he held a finger close to her face, 'you lied to them about Chloe.'

'I couldn't lie under oath.'

'I did!' he screamed. 'I fucking lied to everyone. I covered it up well. But you, you stupid bitch, spoiled it all. Why did everyone believe you over me? Why? WHY?'

Carla didn't want to say it was because Ryan had lost his temper under questioning and had shown everyone in the courtroom his true colours. She didn't want to antagonise him.

They were at a gate now, next to a lodge. Carla wondered how he would get in but he pressed a keypad four times and swiped a card. She frowned.

'Did you pay someone to give you that too?' she asked. 'Or did you beat it out of them?'

Ryan laughed. 'Funny – not. I got friendly with someone who works here, and I stole his pass. And surely you didn't think for a minute that I would pay that lowlife scumbag a penny?'

'What?'

'You know I don't have that kind of money. Vic was so gullible. His woman was too.'

Carla lost a little hope then. Ryan had planned this far better than she had imagined. Not only had he come out of prison having befriended Vic White to help him get to her, but he had also managed to get inside the one place where he said he would take her to kill her. It would be too late by the time anyone found him. And no one knew where she was.

She had last been seen leaving The Willows after her shift had ended the day before. No one knew that Tanya had followed her home and got into the house. No one knew that Vic had been murdered. No one knew that Ryan had been waiting there. No one would know that he had taken her against her will. Tanya might die if she didn't get medical help. It was up to her now to go through with her plan.

Inside the yard it was pitch black except for the odd night light. Ryan pushed her towards the back, leaving the noise of the traffic behind them. A smell like damp mud was all around her as they marched across the tarmac. In the distance she could see lights on in houses. People would be getting ready to eat, returning home to a loving family. Everything around her was normal while her life was in turmoil, in the hands of a killer. She wasn't sure if she was brave enough to do what she had set out to do.

When they came to another set of gates, while Ryan was swiping the card, she pulled her arm away from his and ran.

CHAPTER SIXTY-SIX

'Why do people feel the need to beat the shit out of their partners, Sarge?' Jordan asked as he negotiated the traffic. Despite the rush hour, the emergency lights were helping and vehicles were moving out of the way.

'It's all about control,' Eden replied. 'I have no idea what goes through people's heads.'

Finally the sign came up for Stanley Quarry and they pulled into the car park.

Eden's phone rang as she got out of the car. It was Sean.

'It's taken us twenty minutes to get here, sir. I'm wondering if they're already here. There's a car sitting on the road in front.' She gave him the registration number automatically. 'I'm going to take a look inside with Jordan.'

'We're ten minutes behind you at the most. I'll ring to get you access to the quarry.'

Eden and Jordan ran to the gate but it was locked. Eden pressed on the buzzer.

'Police!' She got out her warrant card and placed it over the camera.

'I'll come down to you,' a voice said.

'I don't have time. Just open the gate.'

'I need to check your ID first. I can't just let—'

'This isn't a game. Open the gate and give me access or someone is going to die.'

Jordan flashed his card up to the camera too. 'Open the gates!' he shouted.

There was a pause long enough for Eden to hold her breath and then the buzzer went as the gates slid open.

'Someone's just gone through. I'll make sure the second set are open by the time you get there.'

Sean's instructions must have reached the man in charge of the gates. Eden acknowledged him with a raised arm and darted through the first one. They ran to the next one. As they drew close, it opened and they raced through.

'That'll have given us a few minutes on Ryan,' said Eden, catching a breath.

CHAPTER SIXTY-SEVEN

Carla ran as fast as she could.

'Come back, you mad bitch!' she heard him shouting behind her, and it propelled her forward. She rounded the corner of a building. Knowing he was catching up on her, she squeezed herself in-between two metal bins. She watched him race past and then came out and ran back in the direction they'd come from. Maybe she could alert someone at the gates.

But her heels on the ground gave her away, and Ryan turned back. He ran towards her as she made for the gate but before she could reach it, he'd caught up with her, taking hold of her arm again.

'You never listened to me,' he raged. 'You were a useless wife. You were a useless mother. That's why I had to take control. Even though I was working and you stayed at home all day, you wouldn't even look after everything for me. I brought in the money and you just sat on your lazy arse all day, watching TV and stuffing your face.'

Carla let him ramble, but as he dragged her towards the edge of the quarry, she screamed.

'Please, no!'

But he wasn't listening. She could just about make out a wall in front of them, no higher than three feet. When they got to it, he tried to shove her over the side.

'No!' She resisted, pulling away from him, but he kept a firm grip on her. Pushing her forward again, she lost her footing and toppled over.

She was falling, falling but not in mid-air. The quarry was built of old marl tiles, rubbish accumulated, so she rolled down and down. Her body bumped against things as she went, and she tried to stop the momentum with her arms acting as a windmill. It didn't do anything but, eventually, she landed with a thump and it all stopped. Pain crashed through in so many places that it took her a moment to get her bearings.

She lifted her head and could see a large pool of water ahead. Rocks everywhere. She was at the bottom of the quarry.

The sound of footsteps made her turn the other way. Her neck ached and she cried out in pain. Ryan was jogging down to her.

'Thought that might slow you down a little,' he said. He took a handful of her hair and hauled her to her knees then leaned down so he could thrust his face in hers. 'Don't want you alerting anyone to the fact that we're here, now, do we? This is our little party.'

He pulled her upright, her body screaming out in pain. She groaned, trying not to give him the satisfaction of knowing he'd broken her. But he wasn't listening. Keeping a tight hold on her hair, he dragged her to the water's edge.

'Let's go for a swim.' He pointed up to the moon. 'It's a beautiful evening for it.'

Carla's legs were hurting and she could feel blood trickling down her right arm. She almost walked on her hands as he pulled her deeper into the water. Then he pushed her head under.

Even though she didn't have much strength left, she thought of Chloe as he held her there for a few seconds. Her arms flailed as she battled to gain control, but he was too strong.

Then, all of a sudden he let her up for air, standing by her side as she spluttered.

It was shallow enough that she could prop herself back up on her elbows. She managed to sit up, the water seeping into her clothes making her seem lethargic. She looked up at him with hatred in her eyes.

'Okay, get it over and done with,' she said as she gasped for air again. 'You want to kill me then do it. But. . . I want you to know that. . . I'm not frightened of you any more.' She took a big breath in. 'You might have scared me once. . . but you don't now. You overpower me. . . because you're bigger than me, but you won't get the better of me ever again. I—'

His hand lashed out at her face and she fell back in the water with the force. She scrambled to sitting again, knowing that if she stayed on her back too long, he could sit astride her. In his state of mind, he would probably drown her. She had to stand up.

'You're nothing,' he said, pointing into her face. 'With me you were useless. Without me you are powerless.'

'We could start again.' She'd said the first thing that came into her head.

His laughter was cruel. 'Don't give me none of that bullshit that you teach in your self-assertiveness classes. All that psychobabble is pathetic. *You* of all people teaching it is a laugh. You should know that it's useless. If I want to get to you, I will, and nothing you say to me will help or hinder. I might become angrier so it's over quicker but, then again, I'm going to relish this so much that I think I might want to take my time.'

'You won't have a lot of it,' she said, looking up. 'I can see lights.'

Ryan turned as he saw a torch being shone down on them. As he did, Carla saw her chance. She stood up quickly, and as he turned back to face her, she threw a punch. She'd learned the move in a self-defence class. Hit someone in the right place between the eyes and it momentarily blocks out all their senses. It disables an assailant, giving a victim enough time to get away.

Ryan went down into the water.

She gasped for breath while his face stayed covered with the murky liquid and watched for signs of movement. He went deathly still for a few seconds. Had she done enough?

But then Ryan began to move. Knowing that someone would be with her soon, she realised this was her last chance at freedom. She picked up a rock and held it high in the air.

'This is for Chloe, you heartless, cruel bastard,' she said. Then she brought it down on the side of his head.

TEN YEARS AGO

'If I ever catch you outside this house again, I will kill you, do you hear?'

I hadn't a clue what I'd done wrong this time. Next door's cat had gone missing. Charlotte, our neighbour, had come round to ask if I'd seen it.

But I'd left the house without his permission, and this was my punishment: being dragged down the stairs so that my back bumped on every step; being forced to stand as he yanked on my hair before he shoved me on to the living room floor. In an instant, he'd overpowered me and thumped me full in the face.

My nose burst, blood spurted out and I gagged as it ran into my mouth. For some reason, this time, I fought back, and I landed a punch to the side of his head. Enraged, he pummelled my hands and arms as I held them up to protect myself.

A scream came from behind us. 'Mummy!'

I turned my head to see Chloe standing in the doorway.

Ryan glared at me, panting, as he caught his breath. 'Now look what you've done!' he seethed. 'If she says anything about what's happened, you're dead, do you hear me?' He grabbed my chin and squeezed hard.

I gasped as the pain shot through my face. Trying to breathe, I put a hand to my nose to stop the flow of blood.

It was then that Chloe ran across the room and threw herself on to Ryan's back.

'Leave Mummy alone,' she screamed, pounding his back with her tiny fists. 'I hate you. I hate you. I hate you.'

Ryan tried to reach for her but she hung on like a leech and dug her nails into his cheek. He howled.

'You little bitch,' he cried, lashing out with his hand. 'You're just like your mother.'

The force threw Chloe across the room, her head connecting with the corner of the coffee table. She gave a short gasp and then her eyes closed.

'Chloe!' Finding strength I didn't know I possessed, I pushed Ryan off me and raced across the room to her side. Despite my nose bleeding, I took her in my arms.

'Chloe? Chloe, darling. It's Mummy. Chloe, can you hear me?'

I pressed my hand to her cheek but her eyes stayed closed. I slapped her face to rouse her but still nothing. Then her eyes opened before rolling back inside her head, and she began to spasm.

'What have I done?' Ryan was standing beside me, whispering over and over. 'What have I done?'

'Ring for an ambulance,' I told him.

'But they'll say it's my fault and I'll go to prison.'

'I don't care! She's going to die if you don't!' I screamed.

It was enough to make him react and he picked up the phone.

'Chloe.' I patted her cheek again. 'Chloe-bear, please wake up. Mummy's here. I want you to open your eyes. Can you do that for me? Chloe?'

I sat with her, soothing her while Ryan spoke to the operator. 'Mummy's here,' I said, over and over again.

'The ambulance is on its way,' Ryan said, coming to sit next to me again. 'The operator wants to talk to you. Is she going to be okay?'

I pushed the phone away, cutting off the operator. I couldn't talk to anyone. Then I spoke to him, finding courage from somewhere.

'I swear to God, Ryan, if you have harmed our child, I will kill you,' I said.

Ryan grabbed me by the hair again. 'Don't threaten me, you stupid bitch, or I will put all the blame at your feet and tell everyone it was you.'

'You'd lie about your own daughter?'

'You came home drunk, you carried on drinking and then you hit out at her because she wouldn't go to bed.'

'You're the alcoholic! I haven't had a drop. People will know!'

Ryan's grip lessened as he realised what I was saying.

'She tripped and fell, right?' His voice wasn't convincing. 'We had nothing to do with it. She was excited about school in the morning and was telling us about a project, and she tripped and fell.'

'Did I fall with her?' I laughed snidely. 'What about my bruises? They're not self-inflicted.'

'She pulled you down the stairs with her.' He pushed her away. 'You'll do as you're told or it'll be you next!'

Despite my earlier bravery, I began to cower at his raised voice. Would I ever get enough courage to walk away from this man?

The ambulance arrived, and he went through his planned speech. I didn't say anything. When the paramedic said I was in delayed shock, I went with that. I was shocked that my husband had killed my child. I had seen Chloe's eyes. If she wasn't dead now, she soon would be. There must be some damage to her brain from hitting the corner of the coffee table.

We went in the ambulance to the hospital. I was tended to as well, Ryan never leaving my side. Chloe was being taken straight to theatre with a brain bleed. I sat like a zombie as they attended to my face. The police arrived, and I knew they'd taken one look at me and realised that Ryan was lying.

'Did your husband hit her?' the female detective asked.

I paused for a moment before shaking my head. 'It was an accident.'

I couldn't say anything else because Ryan was coming up behind her. And it was best to keep the peace – then figure out what to do next.

It was touch and go that Chloe would survive. If she died, I would make him pay. I would make him suffer. I just didn't know how.

CHAPTER SIXTY-EIGHT

When Ryan didn't make a noise, Carla stood watching. His face was still in the water. She hoped he would drown before help arrived. She could always feign shock, like she had when he had hurt Chloe.

She'd known all along she'd been playing a dangerous game, but she'd needed to let him come closer. It was the only way – to let him think he was winning. If he killed her, then so be it, but she needed a shot at getting rid of the fear.

She'd been terrified over the past few weeks – the man in the garden and then at her door, the brick through the window at the refuge, the man loose in Stockleigh assaulting women – but she'd had to push it all aside and go about her life as normally as possible. If she didn't seem threatened, he would come to her. Just like he had. She hadn't intended anyone else to get hurt and for that she was truly sorry. But she needed closure, one way or another. She had spent ten lonely years without her daughter.

She looked down at him. Time stood still. It could have been thirty seconds or several minutes but she prayed it was enough. She wanted to be free. Then maybe she would be able to rest in her bed each night.

'Carla!'

Recognising Eden's voice, Carla looked up to see the silhouette of two figures making their way slowly down the side of the quarry.

With one last look at Ryan, she threw the brick as far as she could into the water.

CHAPTER SIXTY-NINE

At the bottom of the quarry at last, Eden came rushing past Carla, splashing into the water.

'Get him out, Jordan,' she shouted as she grabbed one of Ryan's arms.

Jordan reached for the other. A dead weight, they battled to drag him out and on to the embankment. It was hard to see where they were going in the dark.

Eden's foot slipped in the mud and she stumbled, holding a hand out to stop herself from falling. Jordan pulled Ryan up and the force launched her upright too.

Back on solid ground again, they laid him down. He was unconscious. She checked for a pulse but couldn't find one.

'Is he breathing?' asked Jordan, as she opened his mouth.

Eden shook her head. She began to pump on his chest, hoping to get some of the water out. Together they tried to resuscitate Ryan, blowing air into his mouth too, but after ten minutes, she stopped. She sat back on her haunches, putting a hand on Jordan's arm to make him ease off.

'He's gone,' she said, pointing upwards where people were congregating. The shadows of two people were almost upon them on their level. 'The paramedics are here now, though.'

She turned back to see Carla still standing in the water, shivering. She stood up, caught her breath for a moment and then went into the water to her.

'He's dead, isn't he?' whispered Carla, shaking uncontrollably.

'Yes, he's dead. Come on, let's get you out of there.' Eden wrapped an arm gently around her shoulder and guided her back to the embankment. 'It's over.'

EPILOGUE –
ONE WEEK LATER

Eden sat at the desk in her office. Jordan and Amy were laughing about something on Jordan's mobile phone, and Phil was making coffee – wonders would never cease. He'd really pulled through and worked hard to ensure that Daniels could be charged. Yes, he'd made an error, but he'd more than made up for it since. It had been refreshing to watch him change over the past fortnight as he'd gelled more and more with the team.

All around them officers were going about their duties. Sean was in his office, and everything was calm. It was 8.15 a.m. Things could change within an hour depending on what the residents of Stockleigh woke up to.

Phil brought a tray of drinks over to them then produced several packets of biscuits and put them in the middle of their desks. He handed a box of Jaffa cakes to Amy.

'Thought you might like a treat before I leave you,' he said, smiling sheepishly. 'I'm sure you can't wait to see the back of me.'

Amy grinned. 'Anyone who gives me a box of Jaffa Cakes is a friend for life.'

'Don't eat too many or you won't get in that wedding dress.'

'Mate!' Jordan cried. 'You said the "W" word.'

'I haven't mentioned anything to do with weddings in about three days, Jordan,' Amy retorted, trying to put on a stern face.

Phil smiled and looked over at Eden. 'Thanks for making me so welcome after I was such a knob.'

Eden laughed 'The more the merrier in this team. I shall be sad to see you go now.' She meant it too. You didn't get to pick your work colleagues and there were bound to be clashes of personalities once in a while.

'I just felt my age when I came back, and a little resentful for being placed in your team. But I really started to enjoy myself. You do such a great job. And, now I feel on form again, it's a shame I can't stay with you.'

'Not to worry,' Jordan joined in with the banter. 'At least you don't have to work for Twiggy anymore.'

'Oi!' Eden screwed up a piece of notepaper and threw it at him. 'Talking of work, Amy?' She waited for her to finish eating. 'How do you fancy running the drop-in session at The Willows? I think it would be great for you to build up a rapport with some of the key workers there.'

Amy smiled enthusiastically. 'That would be great, thanks. When shall I start?'

'Come with me to the next session. I'll introduce you to everyone and you can settle in. It's only an hour every fortnight.'

Amy beamed. 'Thanks!'

They settled back to work. Eden answered a few emails and read a few new ones. The results for the soil analysis on Daniels' boots had come back to a match with the crime scene for Ramona Wilson. After she skimmed through another email, she went to see Sean.

'The results are in from the post-mortem on Ryan Gregory,' she said, moving a file off a chair opposite him to sit down on the seat. 'Cause of death was drowning, due to being unconscious because of a knock to his head.'

'What kind of a knock?'

'He couldn't say for certain whether it would have happened as he fell down the quarry bank, or if he was hit while he was in the water. But the blow was enough to stun him and then he drowned.'

'So there's no funny business, you reckon?'

'I'm not sure we'll ever know that for certain,' she replied. 'But there's no evidence to suggest anything happened other than what Carla told us.'

'And Tanya White? How is she?'

'She's doing okay too. She's back at home now. I can't help but feel for her, as she loved Vic so much. In their own way, they were a couple, I guess, at least when he wasn't in prison. Tanya may have to go to court, but I'm hoping, in view of the circumstances, that the judge might be lenient.'

'It has to be done,' said Sean, pushing his glasses up his nose. 'She did commit a crime – aiding and abetting.'

Eden ran a hand through her hair. 'True, but under the threat of her life.'

'After seeing the state that Ryan left her in, I can well believe it.' Sean paused. 'Keep an eye on her for now. You never know if that mad bastard has paid someone else to finish things if he couldn't. Carla too, but I'm sure you don't need to be told that.'

She nodded.

'Maybe a visit is in order in light of those results?'

'Yes, sir.' Eden stood up and went back to her team. Yet again, she had failed to tell Sean what she needed to about Jed Jackson. Jackson's warning last week had shocked her, and she knew she would lose her job if anything came out about what Danny had done. But, to a certain point, she would protect her family, especially Casey. Just like Carla and Tanya had protected themselves, she needed to protect herself too. People would talk if what Danny had done came out, and she couldn't have that. It would hurt Casey too much, and she was Eden's main priority. She knew what she had to do now. She had to stop this before it went any further.

She needed to speak to Danny but, first, she had somewhere else to go.

Carla walked through the cemetery, head held high. The weather was overcast but at least it was a little warmer than of late. She'd picked up a bunch of pink carnations from the stall at the entrance. Chloe would have loved the colour choice, she was sure.

She had never felt so light as she turned towards her daughter's grave. The sense of being watched was gone, and she felt free to lift her head and embrace the world.

After a moment standing in silence, she placed the flowers on the grave.

'I'm not sorry for what I did, Chloe. It was only because of what he did to you. He should never have taken you away – and so young. There's not a day goes by that I don't think about you, how you were, what happened. But just lately, I've been imagining how you would be if you were alive, and it's such a comfort. Going through school and college, boys, friends. What you'd look like now.'

She paused for a moment, lifting her face to the sky. 'I can come and visit you any time I like now, Chloe-bear. I'm so sorry I had to stay away.'

She stood like that for a while, embracing the day. No one to scare her, to maim her, to hurt her. She was free to love again if she chose to. She was free to do anything she wanted.

Her freedom had come at a price, and what happened to Vic and Tanya White would be forever on her conscience. She should have been stronger and left Ryan before he had lashed out at

Chloe, and she would never forgive herself for that. But at least now she could move on with her life, safe in the knowledge that he would never get her again.

Later that afternoon, Eden knocked on Carla's door.

'I have the results of the post-mortem,' she said, once they were in the kitchen. 'Ryan drowned, but he took a blow to the head as well. That wasn't the cause of his death. He drowned because he fell unconscious into the water.'

Carla nodded slightly to show she had understood. A tear dripped down her face.

Eden paused for a moment. When Carla had been able to be interviewed after she had been seen in hospital and treated for shock, and her cuts and bruises tended to, she had spoken to Eden at great length about what had happened. She had told her that Ryan had dragged her to the edge of the quarry, and when he had pushed her over, she had clung on to him, and he had gone over with her – and must have knocked his head.

She had got up, and he'd come after her, and she'd had nowhere to run to but into the water. She said he must have tripped as the next thing she knew he was face down in the water and the police were running down the quarry side to help.

Eden looked at Carla, hoping that it was the truth, but deep down inside, she knew she was lying. If she had been in Carla's position, maybe she would have done the same thing, acting in self-defence. It didn't make it right but there was no proof and no witnesses to insinuate anything else.

'At least I can settle here now.' Carla smiled. 'I'm so pleased that I can finally have some roots again. I might even get in touch with my family.'

Eden frowned. 'You have family? I've never heard you talking about them.'

'My parents. I didn't dare go and visit them, as I didn't want them to know where I was. If Ryan had gone after them, he would have hurt them to get information on me. I couldn't have that on my conscience as well as him hurting my daughter.'

'How did you get through that?' asked Eden. 'I couldn't begin to imagine life without Casey.'

'I don't think I ever did get through it,' Carla said truthfully. 'A part of me will always be missing as I think about her, how she would have been now. She wanted to be a doctor when she grew up – live in a large house, get married, be happy. One day she hoped to have her own children. I'll miss out on all of that because of him.'

'Well it's not too late to start again,' said Eden, patting Carla's hand.

'It is for me.' Carla shook her head. 'I can't have any more children after Ryan left his mark on me.'

Eden reached forward and gave Carla a hug. Nothing else needed to be said.

Before going to see Melody Dixon, Eden called at the newsagent to get some comic books and some sweets. She knocked on the door.

Melody answered it.

'I'd said I'd come and see you when I caught the attacker. I'm sorry it's a bit later than planned, but I was working on two cases and, well, anyway. . .'

'Come in,' said Melody.

'How are you?' Eden asked as she sat down opposite her in the living room.

'I'm getting there,' said Melody. 'The bruising and the physical pain have gone, but I still have my mental issues. I'll deal with them over time though.'

Eden smiled. 'I hope so.'

'I want to thank you for getting him. I was told that he attacked you as well. Are you okay now?'

Eden pointed to her feet. 'He chose the wrong person. Anyone who messes with me gets the possibility of a Doc Marten in their groin.'

Melody smiled. It lit up her face, and Eden knew that even though she had gone through a traumatic experience that would floor some people, the young woman who sat before her was going to be okay.

The door opened and a small boy with a mop of blond curls popped his face around the door frame.

'Hiya, lady,' he said, his face lighting up with a smile as wide as his mum's.

'Hello! You must be Reece,' said Eden.

'How did you know that?' Reece's face was one of pure confusion.

'I know everything,' said Eden. 'I brought something with me that I thought you might like.' She looked across at Melody. 'Is he okay to have sweets now?'

Melody nodded. 'Just a few though.'

Reece came racing across and sat next to Eden. She gave him the comics and the bag of sweets she'd bought earlier. Seeing his face light up was enough to make her smile too.

'Off you pop, while we talk about grown-up stuff,' said Melody, patting him playfully on the leg.

'Will it go away?' she said softly to Eden.

Eden looked at her with questioning eyes.

'Looking over my shoulder; being scared of my own shadow; jumping every time I hear a noise. Am I always going to live with the fear of it happening again?'

'Now that is something I can't help you with. But I can put you in touch with an organisation, and lots of people who have shared a similar experience.'

They spoke for a bit longer before Eden said goodbye. Once in her Mini, she selected a track on The Jam CD in the stereo and turned up the sound. She still loved old-fashioned CDs over audio rips.

'Beat Surrender' burst into the car.

It warranted her pounding the palms of her hands on the steering wheel for a few minutes. She thought back to what Melody had said about the fear. Eden would never give in to the likes of Jed Jackson, but she had a feeling that she'd be looking over her own shoulder for the foreseeable future too.

Before starting the engine, she picked up her phone and typed out a message. It was time to sort things out once and for all.

Can we talk?

She was surprised when her phone began to ring almost immediately. She killed the sound, took a deep breath and answered the call.

'Hi, Joe.'

A LETTER FROM MEL

First of all, I want to say a huge thank you for choosing to read *Don't Look Behind You*. I have thoroughly enjoyed my second outing with Eden and her team and I hope you enjoyed spending time with them as much as I did.

If you did enjoy *Don't Look Behind You*, I would be forever grateful if you'd write a review. I'd love to hear what you think, and it can also help other readers discover one of my books for the first time. Or maybe you can recommend it to your friends and family…

Many thanks to everyone who has emailed me, messaged me or chatted to me on Facebook or Twitter and told me how much they have enjoyed reading my books. I've been genuinely blown away with all kinds of niceness and support from you all. A writer's job is often a lonely one but I feel I truly have friends everywhere.

You can sign up to receive an email whenever I have a new book out here: www.bookouture.com/mel-sherratt/

Keep in touch!

MelSherrattauthor

@writermels

ACKNOWLEDGMENTS

This book is a milestone for me as it is my tenth crime novel. I have had a blast working on each one of them. They are very much a labour of love and it's an amazing feeling to see how they have been received. Each one might have my name on the cover but there is an awful lot of teamwork happening in the background to make it happen. Thanks to my super agent Maddy Milburn, my super editor Keshini Naidoo and my publicity manager extraordinaire Kim Nash – three talented women I have the pleasure of working with. Thanks to everyone at Bookouture, Oliver, Natalie, Hannah, Noelle and the rest of the gang.

Thanks to Alison Niebieszczanski, Caroline Mitchell and Angela Marsons – a support and inspirational group second to none. Thanks to all the bloggers and reviewers who give up their time to help me. I can't mention every one by name as there are far too many and I would be afraid to miss one out, but each and every minute you spend reading my books and spreading the word about them means so much more than I can ever put in to words.

Thanks also must go to a certain group of cockblankets who make me smile every day, and also give me genuine support amongst the tears of laughter.

Finally, thanks to Chris. Fella, you still make the best tea, and it's always stirred with love…